R. J. Parker's creative career began as a TV script writer, editor and producer. It was this background that fed into a series of cinematic, high-concept thrillers that grabs the reader from the very first page and doesn't release them until the last. R. J. Parker now lives in Salisbury.

@Bookwalter
@RJParkerUK
richard-parker.com

Also by R.J. Parker

The Dinner Party

While You Slept

R. J. Parker

OneMoreChapter

One More Chapter
a division of HarperCollins*Publishers*
The News Building
1 London Bridge Street
London SE1 9GF

www.harpercollins.co.uk

This paperback edition 2020

First published in Great Britain in ebook format by
HarperCollins*Publishers* 2020

A catalogue record for this book
is available from the British Library

Ebook ISBN: 978-0-00-838278-0
Paperback ISBN: 978-0-00-838279-7

Set in Birka by Palimpsest Book Production Ltd, Falkirk
Stirlingshire

Printed and bound in Great Britain by
CPI Group (UK) Ltd, Croydon CR0 4YY

To the mighty Carr family – Dave, Eimear, Benjamin and Beibhinn – who know what it takes to build a home and fill it with love.

Chapter 1

An intruder was standing motionless in Lily Russell's back garden, and when she saw him, she stood from her swivel chair and released an incoherent exclamation.

It was a sunny September lunchtime and the man was stock-still in the middle of her small lawn as if waiting for her to see him there. He was wearing jeans and a dark-coloured sweat top with the hood pulled over his head.

But it wasn't his presence that alarmed her the most. It was his face. It was tilted up so she could get a good look.

He was wearing the smile of her daughter. A cut-out mask of her five-year-old's laughing features with holes cut out of her eyes for his to look through. Maisie's innocent countenance on his adult body resonated cold at Lily's core.

But Lily couldn't rush out into the garden. She wasn't at home. She was at work. The intruder and her lawn were over sixteen miles away. The motion detector in her garden had sent an alert to the app on her phone.

Lily glanced briefly up from the handset at her three colleagues who had reacted to her cry and turned from their desks in her direction. Most of the team had gone to the park for their break and it was the usual crowd who had stayed on to work through their lunch.

'What's up?' Martin Pickton asked, his wide-eyed reaction mirroring hers.

Lily's attention returned to the security app on her phone. 'Somebody's standing in my garden.'

Martin rose from his seat, but Julie Medlocke reached her first.

She squinted at the black and white image. 'Jesus. Is that?'

Lily nodded. 'It's Maisie's . . . face.' She felt goose flesh on the backs of her arms. 'Tell me this isn't any of you.' But, even if her colleagues did ever play practical jokes, she knew nobody could be capable of this. She didn't wait for a response but immediately hit the microphone button at the bottom of the display. 'Get out of there! I've called the police!'

The figure didn't move.

Was the mini speaker beside the kitchen window not working? She'd had some glitches with it since she'd had the system installed. She should be able to speak to anyone through the app who came to the front or back doors. Nobody could access the rear of the property. Lily had had the second speaker positioned there so she could shoo away the flock of pigeons that frequently congregated on the wall to use it as a toilet.

The figure angled their head further up and suddenly they were looking directly at her through the camera that was positioned above the kitchen window. He *had* heard her. His eyes fixed on her through the face of her daughter.

'They're coming now. The police are coming right now!' Lily yelled at her phone.

The intruder didn't seem perturbed by her threat. Didn't move.

'I'm calling them.' Bridget Holby was already dialling her phone.

'Take that off!' Lily shouted at the phone. 'Take that off and get out of there!'

The man looked theatrically around the garden with Maisie's happy face and then waved at the camera. A child's wave, palm open, four fingers rippling.

'Try and keep him there until the police arrive,' Martin said over her left shoulder.

'What's you address?' Bridget asked.

Lily couldn't think of what else to say to him. Or had the tiny wave made her think twice about shouting and swearing in the way she felt compelled to?

The man dropped his hand and continued staring at her through the camera.

'Lily, your address,' Bridget asked again.

'Number 8 Fallstaff Gardens.'

But before Bridget could relay the information the figure had turned and started leisurely walking away.

'He's leaving. Quick, Bridge!' Martin ordered.

But the figure jumped onto the back wall, scrambled over and disappeared out of sight.

Chapter 2

'Sit down and think a minute.' Julie put her hand on Lily's shoulder.

But Lily didn't want to. She ran her hand through her long red hair and paused her palm on top of her head. 'Are the police calling back on your number?'

'I just told you that,' Bridget reassured her. 'They're sending someone over to your address now.'

'I have to go home.' Lily was pushing past her three colleagues.

Martin was blocking her way with his considerable frame. He'd conceded the battle with his bachelor fast-food lifestyle but still sank into frequent depression about it. 'Wait. If their usual response time is anything to go by you might actually beat them there.'

'Let them make sure it's safe first.' Bridget Holby held her gaze with her wide green eyes. She was the new intern and in her early twenties. Compact, slim, with her fair hair shorn elegantly close to her head, her heart was in the right place, but she infuriated everyone by behaving like a world-wise den mother.

Lily tried to move past them.

Julie took hold of Lily's wrist. 'Where's Maisie?'

Lily halted.

Julie glanced at her watch. 'Another few hours till she gets out of school, right?'

Lily nodded, found the number for All Saints and dialled.

'I'm sure she's safe.' But Julie's face was as pensive as the others while Lily waited for a reply.

'All Saints.' An elderly female voice answered.

'Hello, I have a pupil with you, Maisie Russell.'

'Oh, hello, Mrs Russell.'

'Hi, Mrs Hooper.' Lily knew the starchy secretary from the school's orientation day. Maisie had been overcome by everything she had to remember and so had Lily. 'I'm sorry to bother you but can you put my mind at rest and tell me if Maisie is in class? I think she should be with Mr Dalton this afternoon.'

'Lunchtime has just finished. They should all be coming back to class now. Anything wrong?'

'I just need to know she's there.'

Mrs Hooper paused. 'Why would you have any reason to believe she—'

'Just tell me,' Lily said brusquely. 'Sorry, I just . . . can you tell me.'

Mrs Hooper inhaled. 'Very well. I'll just look out of the window. They're all standing in line to come back inside.'

Lily tried to restrain her panic. 'If you wouldn't mind.' She waited and listened to Mrs Hooper's breathing under hers.

'Yes. I can see her.'

Lily felt relief filter through her. 'You're sure?'

'Yes. Quite sure,' Mrs Hooper replied with a trace of irritation.

'What is she wearing?' She knew Mrs Hooper wore thick specs.

'An orange top.'

That was her. But Lily's shoulders remained tight. 'Thank you. Can you please let her know that I'm coming to pick her up?'

'Why? She still has classes.'

'It's an emergency.'

'Oh dear, what sort of emergency?'

'But please don't tell her that. Can you take her to your office? I should be over in half an hour.'

'Yes . . . all right. If you feel you have to.' Mrs Hooper didn't sound sure now.

'Half an hour, I'll meet you at your office.' Lily hung up before she could protest.

'OK?' Julie asked.

Lily nodded and gulped.

'OK, just try to calm down. Go and pick Maisie up and I'll cover for you here.'

'Thanks.' Lily had worked with Julie for three years. They were both single mums and always had each other's backs at work.

Julie flipped the fringe of her henna bob out of her face and fixed Lily with her sharp blue eyes. 'This isn't Ewan up to his usual?'

It had immediately occurred to Lily. It felt like her ex-husband's ugly circus had left town a long time ago, but it had only been just over a year since the divorce was finalised. 'That wasn't him in the garden.'

Martin was still hovering, breathing heavily. He didn't cope well with the heat and the ring of hair around his bald pate was plastered to his head. 'Can you take another look?'

He was right. Lily returned to the app and accessed the camera recording archive. She opened the most recent file and dragged the slider at the bottom of the black and white clip. The figure dropped back into her garden, walked backwards and turned around on the spot. She paused the recording.

She shivered inwardly as she caught the end of the wave to her via the camera. It wasn't Ewan. Ewan was a foot shorter and not as well-built.

'That's twisted.' Martin was at her shoulder and breathing onion against the side of her face.

'He must know you. How else could he have got the photo of Maisie?' Bridget observed.

Lily looked at the three framed photos of her fair-haired daughter on her desk then back to the smiling mask of her. Her front teeth were showing and there was no gap. The picture the intruder had used had to have been taken recently. Where was it from? Had he stolen it? Lily didn't use Facebook or post any photos of Maisie online. She didn't like sharing with anyone other than people she knew. Didn't like to think of strangers looking at images of her. Or Ewan having access to their life.

Bridget's phone rang and she answered. 'Yes. Thank you. I'm not the owner of the property so I'll just pass you over.' She held it out to Lily. 'The police. They're at the house.'

Chapter 3

A squat uniformed male officer opened the driver's door of his patrol car as soon as she got out of her Nissan. 'Mrs Russell?'

'Yes.' She wasn't Mrs Russell, but she hadn't reverted to her maiden name yet because she didn't want Maisie to experience any more confusion than she already had. Or was it because, despite everything that had happened between her and Ewan, a small part of her misguidedly hoped there was still the chance of a reconciliation?

'Police Constable Michaels. I'm sorry but I couldn't access the garden.' The straight fringe of his unkempt fair hair was dark with sweat. The officer closed his front door.

She closed hers. 'Couldn't you have climbed over the wall, like he did?' But she realised she'd snapped at the officer.

'I checked the passage behind it but I couldn't get a foot-hold,' he mitigated.

Lily estimated him to be at least in his mid-thirties. Wasn't he a little old to be a constable? Maybe that and his conspicuous paunch were why he hadn't been able to scale it.

Maisie knocked on the window of the back passenger door.

Lily nodded emphatically at her. 'Just stay there a moment. We'll go inside in a minute.'

The officer smiled encouragingly at Maisie and then held up his hands. 'I'm sure your intruder is long gone, but I'd rather go in and make sure everything's OK first.'

'I know it's clear. Look . . .' Lily showed him her phone with her security app open. She quickly flicked through the rooms of her house that were covered by the mini cameras. 'Empty. And so is the garden.' She jabbed her finger at the black and white image.

Officer Michaels seemed intrigued. 'And you spoke to him via this?'

'Yes. Told him to leave. Look.' She played him the clip of the intruder in the garden. 'That's my daughter's face.'

Officer Michaels studied the screen and frowned his faint eyebrows. Then he looked again to where Maisie had her face pressed against the window. 'That's . . . unsettling.' He shook his head. 'Not just an opportunist then.'

Lily wanted to scream no, but retained her composure for Maisie's benefit and shook her head.

Officer Michaels straightened, as if suddenly realising he hadn't been summoned to a routine break-in. 'Any ideas who might do something like this . . . a friend . . . maybe for a prank?'

'Would a friend really do something like this?'

Officer Michaels grimaced, as if chiding himself for asking the question. 'Nobody you could think of who has a grudge against you?'

'An ex. He's behaved erratically in the past . . .'

The officer narrowed his green eyes at her and nodded as if they'd found their explanation.

'But that's not him in the clip,' she added quickly. 'And I really don't think this is something he'd do.'

'When people are overtaxed . . . emotionally . . . particularly where children are involved, you'd be surprised what they're capable of.'

Lily wondered if he was talking from more than just his experience as a police officer.

'You should give me his details.'

'Of course. His name is Ewan Russell but I think it would be a waste of time. He's never tried to scare us. Not deliberately anyway.'

Officer Michaels regarded her with a trace of fatigue, as if she were making excuses for him. 'When was the last time you saw him?'

'Probably about eight months ago.' But she knew for certain it was eight months and three weeks.

'Under what circumstances?'

'He came to see Maisie before he went away. He lives in Dundee now. Working for his brother.'

'And how were things between you then?'

'Not good but civil. I won full custody of Maisie. He'd resigned himself to that and I thought leaving London was his way of responding. He's always run away. It's his default setting.' Lily felt like she was sharing too much.

'And you're sure he's not around?'

'No.' She had to be honest about that. But even though Ewan had lied to her in the past she still couldn't believe that he would be capable of what had happened in the garden. Even if he'd got someone else to do it for him.

Maisie knocked the window again.

Lily beckoned to her. 'OK. Come and say hi to the policeman.'

Maisie opened her car door.

Lily turned to him. 'Shall we take a look now then?'

Chapter 4

'Hello, missy,' Officer Michaels said to Maisie as she climbed out of the car.

Maisie reluctantly lifted her dark-blue eyes to him. They were almost as dark as Lily's. Then she focussed on the kerb as she stepped down to it.

'She's a little shy,' Lily explained. That was an understatement. She only spoke above a whisper at home and had yet to make any friends at school. She'd been there for a couple of weeks, and Lily had hoped the other kids would bring her back out of her shell. It appeared she was already being bullied though. Lily was positive the divorce and the events that had led up to it had made her so withdrawn. She'd been such an outgoing girl beforehand. Lily thought the ugliness at home had been insidious and hadn't realised how sensitive Maisie had been way before all the resentments had manifested themselves. Now she felt as though she'd lost a connection with her daughter and guilty that Maisie blamed her for not being able to see her father. Most telling was the fact that Maisie used to call her 'Mamma' but now didn't use any name for her. Treading the path between overcompensating for that and trying to bring her up with love and discipline was a daily trial. 'I've told her exactly why she had to come home so early from school.'

Officer Michaels's attention shifted from Maisie as he waited for Lily to elaborate.

'I said we're very lucky to have a policeman run a check on our house, to make sure we're a hundred per cent safe and that you wanted to speak to her personally to make sure she knew that.'

'Oh yes.' Officer Michaels immediately picked up the baton. 'I'll make sure everything's in order here.'

Maisie didn't look up at the officer, but hefted her empty pink tin lunchbox like a suitcase. She had her banana yellow rucksack on her back that only contained her pencil case. Maisie was obsessed by anything banana yellow. She'd had it for her fifth birthday, and it was still a bit big for her.

'I think we should get straight on with it,' Lily said.

'Absolutely.' The officer gestured them to the little gate that led to the tiny front garden of their home.

Lily locked the car and then opened the gate to the short path to the door, gazing briefly up at the window above. The navy curtains were closed.

Mr Sargeant lived above them. He'd taken early retirement in his mid-fifties and was always jetting off somewhere. He used the rooms as a base but was rarely there. She was sure he was still in Dubrovnik.

Lily gestured Maisie to follow, and Officer Michaels waited for her to reach Lily before joining them on the doorstep.

Lily slid her key into the door and, as she opened up, it

hissed against the usual fast-food menus that had been posted through the letterbox.

Maisie methodically gathered them off the polished porchway floor, and Lily waited. She'd appointed her the job and knew she wouldn't be rushed.

'Good quality lock on the front door,' Officer Michaels observed for Maisie's benefit.

Maisie took off her green jelly shoes and carried the junk mail through the second door and along the black and orange carpet tiles in the hallway to the kitchen door.

'Just a minute.' Lily opened the lounge, bathroom and two bedroom doors on the way there so the officer could take a look inside. Although Lily knew none of the rooms had been broken into, she still felt relieved as he nodded at her.

'OK.' Lily unlocked the kitchen door. She always secured it because it meant that if anyone did break in through the back, they still wouldn't be able to access the rest of their home. She scanned it. Everything was in place. Mr Gingerbread, their overweight ginger tom, was at his bowl in the corner. Then her eyes shifted to the window above the sink. The oatmeal hessian blind, her sister had made her, was pulled down.

'Go and put the TV on and I'll bring you in some milk,' she told Maisie.

Maisie seemed glad to be released and darted into the lounge without a word.

Lily held her breath and lifted the blind. She exhaled as her little walled garden was revealed. Nothing out of place there: tiny patio with her wicker chair on it; Maisie's yellow plastic one was on the edge of the small square of lawn, which was bordered by flowerbeds on three sides. She'd planted pink and white geraniums in all of them, but they were just starting to shrivel. When Lily and Ewan had rented the property, the garden had been the key selling point. Maisie had been a baby and they both thought it was a contained and safe garden for her. At least that was what she'd thought until today.

'Can you let me out?' Officer Michaels asked unnecessarily.

Lily was already fumbling the key from her bunch and her hand shook as she slid it into the lock and turned.

A plane buzzed noisily overhead as they walked onto the patio. Lily hung back, and the officer carefully made his way onto the lawn as if he were stepping through a minefield. He kept going until he reached the red brick wall at the back and surveyed the pigeon droppings that crusted the top.

Lily's eye settled on the middle of the lawn where the masked figure had stood, waiting for her to see him. Did he know the motion detector would reveal him via the camera?

After a minute or so Officer Michaels turned from his examination of the wall. 'Some of your flowers have been trampled here,' he offered lamely.

But what did she expect him to do? Reporting it didn't really make any difference to whoever had been here. And from the way the intruder had acted she felt positive it was a very deliberate attempt to scare her. If he wanted her to fear for her and Maisie's safety, he'd utterly succeeded. Would he come back?

'That he made no attempt to break in is one consolation,' the officer tried to reassure her.

Lily looked briefly back into the kitchen to check that Maisie wasn't lingering there and couldn't hear their conversation.

'If you'd feel better, I could have a patrol car drive by here tonight to make sure everything's OK.'

Everything's OK? Lily knew that things most certainly weren't and that, on the basis of what had happened, the police couldn't justify anything more than a gesture. Somebody had trespassed not broken in and it was clear the officer now believed it was Ewan, even though she was absolutely convinced it wasn't.

The officer appeared to read her thoughts and strolled back over the lawn towards her. 'Let me take a look in the alley at the back again. To be honest, it looks like you've been operating good security measures already, so I would advise you to keep—' His gaze shot up to the window above her and he halted. 'Who lives up there?'

'Clive Sargeant. He's away though.'

'I don't think so. Even though I knocked there earlier and there was no answer. Somebody was just at the window.'

Chapter 5

'You're sure you saw someone?' Lily asked Officer Michaels as she knocked Mr Sargeant's front door a second time.

He nodded and kept his attention on the battered green panel. 'There was definitely a face at the window.'

Mr Sargeant's door didn't have a bell and was a few feet to the left of Lily's but separated by a low wall. He also had a square of front yard, but it didn't have any potted trees like hers and was littered with cigarette ends. Their landlord didn't allow smoking inside the properties, which was a great relief to Lily. But it meant she often found Mr Sargeant puffing away on the doorstep. It was probably the only time she spoke to him.

He was sufficiently friendly, but she got the impression that as soon as he finished his cigarette, he was eager to go back inside. She'd never been in his home and had only glanced the flight of stairs that led up to the floor above hers. She occasionally heard his shoes dropping onto the floor when he got in and sometimes his TV when it was turned up. Other than that, very little else.

A creak from the other side of the door but it didn't open.

'Mr Sargeant?' Lily said after they both waited a few more seconds.

No reply.

Officer Michaels addressed the panel. 'It's the police. Would you mind opening the door.'

Still no response.

'Is he usually this sociable?'

Lily shook her head. 'Maybe it's not him. He's away a lot and I know he has somebody who comes in to water his plants.'

'They should still open the door,' the officer said loudly.

The lock clicked and the door opened wide. The diminutive Mr Sargeant was standing there in loose claret pyjamas. His grey hair was in disarray.

'Sorry to disturb you . . .' Lily began.

Mr Sargeant squinted. 'Hello, Lily. Sorry, I was catching up on some sleep.'

Lily noted that his nostril hair and eyebrows were looking more wild than usual. 'I had to call the police out because I had an intruder in the garden.'

Mr Sargeant's eyes darted between her and Officer Michaels. 'Today?'

'In the last hour,' the officer interjected. 'You didn't see or hear anybody? Or hear me knocking earlier?'

Mr Sargeant immediately shook his head. 'Sorry, I'd taken a sleeping pill.'

'But you saw me in the garden,' the officer pointed out.

'I've just woken up,' Mr Sargent replied, exasperated.

And it certainly looked like it to Lily.

'So why did you take so long to open the door?'

Lily didn't like the officer's tone but she wanted an answer to that as well.

'I had to quickly grab these pyjamas before I could come down. I sleep naked.'

That was more information than Lily needed. 'Well, if you didn't see anything—' she was about to apologise again.

'I didn't. Anything else?' He sharply directed the question at the officer. Before he could answer, Mr Sargeant closed the door.

'Thanks for your time,' Officer Michaels called mock gratefully after him. He turned to Lily. 'Well, I guess that answers that.'

The door opened again, and Mr Sargeant took a deep breath. 'Sorry, I didn't mean to be rude.' But he only regarded Lily. 'I'm trying nicotine patches but very unsuccessfully. Thought I'd attempt to sleep off the craving, so I'm not in the best of moods.'

'That's OK.' Lily held up a hand. 'Didn't mean to drag you down here.'

'Did they steal anything?' Mr Sargeant kept his gaze on her.

'No. It's just a little unnerving for Maisie and me.'

'With all your security I'd be surprised if they had.' He smiled briefly with yellow teeth. 'I'll certainly keep my eye out now though.'

'Thank you. I thought you were away.'

'I will be after today. Will you and . . . you two be OK here on your own?'

'Don't worry. We'll be fine.' Lily appreciated the question but could tell he wanted the conversation over with.

'OK. Give me a shout if you need anything,' he concluded glibly and closed the door again.

'Good to have neighbours looking out for you.' Officer Michaels projected the comment so Mr Sargeant could hear.

Lily waited for the thumps back upstairs to end. 'I feel so much safer now.'

Chapter 6

After Officer Michaels had left Lily found the number in her phone contacts. Even though Ewan was no longer in her life she knew they would always be inextricably connected. It went beyond their child and what they'd shared in the past, good and bad. It was Ewan's resonant voice she still heard encouraging or admonishing her after every decision she made in her daily life. She dismissed it as often as she had in their seven-year marriage, but the passing months hadn't diminished it. She wondered how much longer that would take.

Eight months and three weeks ago Ewan had given the number to her and every time her phone had rung since she'd anticipated seeing it in her display. But he hadn't been in touch in all that time and that told her exactly why they'd divorced. She understood that he was still bitter she'd got custody of Lily and that he was now attempting to set himself up lecturing mechatronics in a different part of the country, but he'd not once made contact in eight months and three weeks to find out how Maisie was doing.

Maisie had received a card on her fifth birthday in June but that had been it. He may now hate Lily but how could he possibly have severed his affection for their daughter? After several irresponsible incidents that had been instrumental in her winning full custody, she didn't trust him to look after Maisie at his home, but she'd never tried to prevent him from seeing her.

Now Maisie had stopped asking if she would hear from her dad, Lily didn't want her to overhear the conversation she was about to have. She wouldn't use it as an excuse to berate him. She would find out precisely what she needed to know and then hang up. But Lily was positive it wouldn't be as straightforward as that. As soon as she heard his voice, she knew the part of her she hated would immediately take over.

Lily could hear the sound of the TV that Maisie was watching in the front lounge. She closed the door and stood in her bedroom window to make the call. Her stomach muscles clenched as she dialled. She could see into the back garden and the lawn where the intruder had stood. That would remind her of the only reason for picking up the phone.

The number rang then stopped. There were three clicks and then it started ringing again. Perhaps he was forwarding to another number. She hoped he hadn't changed it.

'Lily?' It was him.

And it was like the intervening months hadn't existed. His firm utterance of her name speaking to a part of her she'd tried to shut off. 'Hi,' she said awkwardly and could hear a low hum in the background. A motor?

He was silent.

She'd called. She shouldn't expect him to talk. 'How are things?'

'Finding my feet,' he replied emotionlessly.

'How's . . . Christian?' Lily didn't want to know about his brother. She was stalling.

'What d'you want?'

'I thought you might be interested to hear about Maisie.' And there she went.

'You've done all you can to make sure I'm not part of her life,' he declared coldly.

What did she expect? 'I've never tried to shut you out.' She heard the air down his nose boom against his phone.

'No, not completely. Sorry I couldn't fit into those tiny slots you left for me.'

'Look, you don't want to get into this, I don't want to get into this.' But she knew both of them still did.

'Then why are you calling?'

Exactly. Lily focussed on the lawn. Should she tell him? Would he really care? 'I just need to know . . . whatever our problems are, I hope you'd never expose Maisie to any danger.'

There was a brief pause before he answered. 'What are you talking about? How could I *possibly* do that?'

Lily didn't like the way he'd said it. Was there a taunt lingering at the back of his reply? 'Just assure me . . .' She could hear the emotion bleeding through her voice. She'd promised herself not to do that. 'That you don't have some sort of game plan with her in the middle of it. You can think what you like of me, but I won't allow you to use Maisie.'

'What the hell has prompted this?' The mystification in his voice sounded genuine.

But all of his lies in the past had too.

'If you're planning to do anything then you'd better have a rethink.' She felt a rush of the usual hostility and simultaneous regret for its arrival.

He sighed, as he usually did. As if he were so used to her verbal attacks he could scarcely summon the energy to defend himself. 'Look, I count myself as fortunate now. I really do. Even though I'm living in the spare room of Christian's house and I have to wait for my nephews to finish in the bathroom before I can have a shave. The reason is, whatever's going on in your head right now . . . I don't have to care about it anymore.'

'Ewan.'

But he didn't allow her to interject. 'I've paid dearly for it. You've made that clear to me. But that is the one piece of compensation I've got out of this.'

'How can you not want to speak to your daughter?'

No response.

Lily suspected he wasn't about to justify himself to her. 'However you square that with yourself, fine. But if you want to punish me then just ask me to tell you what it's like to tell Maisie why her father has completely forgotten about her.'

'You know that's not true.' Ewan's voice suddenly sounded small.

But Lily's anger had properly taken over. 'Every time I have to make an excuse for you, honestly, you can chalk one up for yourself. I've told you before, I won't have my daughter endangered. I said that in the court and I'm saying it again now.'

But Lily knew he'd hung up before she'd finished speaking. She hit redial but it was engaged.

Chapter 7

'It's got Ewan written all over it.' Paulette dumped her denim handbag on the kitchen table and pulled out a chair.

'Ssshhh.' Lily closed the door so Maisie couldn't hear. She was in the bedroom on her tablet.

Paulette's normally spiky bleach blonde hair had been flattened by the rain. She tried to tease it upright again. 'He did some nasty stuff.'

'When he was drunk. Alcohol changed his personality. You can be the same.'

Paulette's gaze hardened.

'And like you it was all verbal . . . mostly.'

'Mostly. I did tell you to prepare for this, the day you won full custody.'

She had. But it was rich coming from her younger sister. Paulette lived her life by the seat of her pants. Her middle name was lastminute.com. The fact that she'd got soaked when the September downpour had been forecast for the last few days was testament to it. Lily watched the rain against the kitchen window as it suddenly intensified.

'Wow . . . let's hope that's not an omen.' Paulette took out her vape kit and put it on the table, caught Lily's expression and put it away again. 'You're sure he's definitely still in Dundee?'

'Who knows.' She really didn't. 'He said he was staying at Christian's.'

Paulette gingerly slid her soaking leather jacket off her brown arms. 'You could always call Christian.'

Lily had been tempted. But she was positive, after the divorce, that she was the last person Ewan's brother wanted to speak to. Particularly as Ewan had ended up sleeping in his spare room. 'I thought maybe you could.'

Paulette froze in the middle of hanging the garment on the back of the chair. 'Me?'

'You and Christian *were* an item.'

'Eight years ago.'

'I thought you said you stayed in touch.'

Paulette looked guarded. 'An e-card at Christmas. That's it.'

But Lily suspected there was more to it than that. She'd been obsessed by Christian, which was probably why the relationship had broken down. Paulette could be very intense. So much so she'd started taking medication for it when she was seventeen. Ten years later she was still taking it. As far as Lily knew though, Paulette hadn't found anyone significant since. There'd been a guy in 2016. A fireman, or had it been a policeman? But that had swiftly fizzled out. She didn't have children, went out of her way to declare she'd made the right decision about that. But she did love Maisie, even though she insisted she was always so happy to hand her back to Lily after taking her out for the day.

'So, any danger of a coffee?' Paulette looked pointedly at the kettle.

Lily acknowledged that she'd been eager to change the subject. She filled it and switched it on. They hadn't had the Christian conversation for some time but it was clear Paulette was still sensitive about it. They'd dated for about a year and Paulette had wanted to get serious. But Christian was a year younger than her and had been in no hurry. Lily had seen the crash coming. When the four of them had all gone out together it seemed a little too cosy, overpowering even. Two sisters out with two brothers. Paulette and Christian had met because of Lily seeing Ewan, but it almost seemed unnatural to Lily.

Paulette had initially joked about a double wedding. And then she kept on about it. That's when Lily had realised how immature she was, even though she was only two years younger. She'd been relieved when it had finished between Paulette and Christian. But she felt guilty that she'd never warned her. Never told her to dial it back because she might scare Christian away. She'd done that on purpose. Lily had been selfish and had waited for things to come to a head. Back then she'd thought Paulette would easily find someone else. But the intervening years had been hard on her. Christian had become highly successful manufacturing surgical components, met and married someone else and quickly had three children with her. When they'd spoken, Paulette felt as though he was deliberately rubbing her face in his life.

A year after Paulette's break-up both their parents had fallen ill, and Paulette had thrown all her energies into caring for them. Oesophageal cancer had claimed their mother first, and then their father had been diagnosed with Parkinson's. Watching a doctor of psychology degenerate so quickly had been heart-rending. Paulette had been so brave. Braver than she'd been. Lily recalled her father trying to speak in her ear the day he died and how it had alienated Paulette. He could hardly form words at that point, had lost control of his muscles, so what he'd said was indecipherable. They were his last words and, despite how much she'd cared for him, Paulette had been excluded.

'That's so creepy.' Paulette was watching the clip of the intruder on Lily's phone again. 'You haven't been seeing anyone else recently?'

Lily spooned some coffee into the cafetière. 'Someone I think would do that?'

Paulette raised a dark eyebrow. 'So, you *have* been seeing somebody?'

Lily didn't like to discuss her private life, what there was of it, and especially not with Paulette. 'Not really.'

'Not really?' Paulette's other eyebrow rose.

Lily knew she couldn't clam up. She'd called Paulette. Wanted her help. She dreaded going to sleep that night, so she'd picked up the phone to her even though she was sure Paulette might slightly revel in her misery. Paulette always thought that Lily had been dealt a better hand. 'One guy, Laurie, only for one date.'

'Laurie?' Paulette repeated as if the name were comical. 'When?'

'Few months ago. It was a mistake.'

'Uh-huh. Maisie know about him?'

'No. There was no point.' Lily willed the kettle to finish boiling so she could busy herself with their drinks. 'That's definitely not him in the clip. He was a nice guy. Just not right for me.' She picked up the kettle before it had clicked and filled the cafetière.

'Is this him?' Paulette was holding out Lily's phone with Laurie Campbell's face in the display.

'Do you mind not going through my photos.' Lily slammed the kettle down.

But she carried on scrolling through Lily's images. 'Why would you have a photo of him, if you only saw him once?'

'It was just off his Romanticlicks profile. I saved it . . .' Lily weakly protested.

'You've been doing online dating?'

'Just once; give me my phone.' She held out her hand.

Paulette pursed her lips, as if considering the request.

It was like when they'd shared a room at home. They'd always fought. Lily felt like a kid again. 'Give.'

Paulette handed it over. 'D'you think Laurie was stalker material?'

'No. Just a lonely guy.'

'I can see why.' Paulette nodded at the phone. 'And all stalkers are lonely guys.'

Lily briefly regarded Laurie's slightly pained expression. His square features were plain but he had the sort of thick dark hair and ghostly stubble she liked. But he'd lost his wife. He'd told her that within minutes of them settling themselves at the bar. It had only been five months since she'd been killed in a road accident and Lily had thought it was a little too early for him to be back on the singles scene. She knew she was being judgemental, but it had made her uncomfortable. He clearly wasn't over it. Had talked about 'his Helen' throughout the evening. When he'd asked to see Lily again, she'd politely declined. She closed the gallery.

'Sure it couldn't be him? You do have a knack.'

'What's that mean?' Lily had been considering asking Paulette if she minded staying the night, but now regretted calling her.

'Picking the high-maintenance ones.' Paulette shook her head in faux sympathy.

Lily got a flashback to a hundred arguments they'd had in the past. She could recognise the overture. Fact was, Paulette had liked Ewan. Lily couldn't blame her falling for his solid stubble jaw and the permanent mischief in his dark gaze. But Paulette had made a pass at him behind Lily's back in the early days, before he let her know he wasn't interested and hooked her up with Christian. Despite that, however, and even though it was difficult to endure the way Paulette occasionally sniped at her, Lily had got better at reminding herself that, bad times aside, she still had Maisie. 'You still on sweeteners?'

Paulette eventually nodded. She knew Lily wasn't going to rise to it.

Chapter 8

Lily woke and focussed on the ceiling. Had her phone just been ringing? It wasn't now. She'd caved into Paulette's advice and drank half a glass of red to help her sleep, and the room seemed brighter than usual. She waited a few seconds for the previous night's events to reassemble. That's right. She'd put a pizza in the oven for Maisie. Paulette had eaten most of it. Maisie hadn't been hungry and nor had Lily. Her stomach had been on edge because of what had happened that afternoon, and she'd chatted to her younger sister about anything she wanted until she'd left just after nine.

But when she tensed her neck muscles they ached and so did her temples. The pounding quickened. Had it really been half a glass? She tried to open her mouth, but her tongue was stuck to the roof of her mouth. What was the time?

The digital clock by her bedside said 06:06.

Thank God. An hour to collect herself before she had to rise and get Maisie ready for school. She closed her eyes again and listened to the percussion in her head. Maybe she was coming down with something. She often did in September. Hot days interspersed with wet and cold ones often kickstarted a cold. She listened for signs of rainfall on the window over the pulse in her eardrums but couldn't hear any. That was one small mercy.

She tried to busy her mind with the forthcoming audit they were expecting at work. The small strategy consulting company she worked for lived very hand-to-mouth and there were rumours of redundancies just before Christmas. Why was it always just before Christmas? If it was her how soon could she find an admin job that paid the same wage? Her savings wouldn't keep a roof over their heads for more than a couple of months. Normally she would have tried to ignore these thoughts, but today she was glad of them, if they could distract her from the man who had stood in her garden . . .

She couldn't fool herself that she wasn't terrified. If it had been an opportunist intruder it would have been disturbing enough, but to have gone out of his way to find a recent photo of Maisie, blow it up and then wear it like that.

Lily recalled the way he had calmly stared at her through the security cam and the holes cut in her daughter's eyes. Was Paulette right? Did she just not want to believe that Ewan could be capable of orchestrating something like that?

She wanted to look at the clip again. For the umpteenth time. She'd emailed it to the address that Constable Michaels had given her. Had they watched it or was it still sitting in someone's inbox? And had a patrol car come by to check on her last night or had she just been told that to make her feel more secure?

It was obvious Officer Michaels thought she was a victim of her ex and probably had more pressing incidents to deal with. The neighbourhood crime rate had risen rapidly since she and Ewan had moved into the property. More stabbings and drug-related incidents were what had made up her mind to get the security system installed now Ewan wasn't there. She hadn't even started to pay for that. But what she'd seen through her app was the last thing she'd expected. She reached over and grabbed her phone from the table and the action felt like a major exertion. Perhaps it was flu. All her limbs felt strained and her chest like somebody had been sitting on it.

Exposing her arms made her shiver. It was never usually cold in her bedroom, so it looked like she was definitely getting sick. She put her hand to her forehead but didn't have a temperature. She had no time to be ill. She had one of the best attendance records at work and hoped that would put her in good stead if they did decide to lay some people off. But it was more likely they'd keep on the new intern, Bridget Holby. She'd been shadowing Lily since July. Was that because they wanted Bridget to take on Lily's job? It wasn't a great place to work. Martin Pickton regularly hit on Lily but she always had fun with Julie Medlocke. Julie understood what it was like to be a working single mother.

One 'Missed Call'

Lily squinted at the number in the display. It wasn't one she recognised. Was that what had woken her up? Yes, it said 06:05. Bit early for the usual cold calls. She cursed herself for not turning off the ringer. She usually did, and if she had she'd still be fast asleep. That surprised her. After yesterday she hadn't expected to get a wink. She was about to call out to Maisie, as she often did. But it was still too early. She decided to slip across the hallway and look in. There was no window in Maisie's room, as it was between the front lounge and the kitchen. She'd locked the door to the kitchen the night before. She'd also locked the lounge, so the only way anyone could get in the hallway was through the double front doors and they were both solid wood.

Lily sat up but her head spun. She swung her legs out of bed and paused for a few moments on the edge of the mattress while the room came to a standstill. Her pyjamas felt damp against her skin. Check on Maisie and then grab some painkillers. She gingerly stood and her ribcage and legs felt tender as she crossed the tan carpet to the door, took her aquamarine robe from the hook and slipped it on. No sign of her slippers.

Her teeth chattered and she pulled the robe tight around herself and opened the door. Maisie's was sealed shut, so she crossed the dingy hallway and listened at the panel. No sound. She pulled down slowly on the handle. It usually creaked when it was fully depressed, but she managed to get it open without making any noise. She peered inside.

Her daughter's globe lamp was still on beside the bed and she watched Maisie's oblivious face, mouth open and eyebrows slightly frowning, and listened to her tiny snores for a few moments before pushing the door shut again.

But as she felt the cold wrap around her legs Lily came over faint and had to lean on the wall for support. What was wrong with her? Her sense of smell seemed to be heightened and an aroma of damp cement filled her nostrils. She staggered back to her room and flopped onto the mattress, quickly pulling the duvet over her as her frame trembled. She felt nauseous and her stomach gurgled loudly.

Let it pass and then fetch the painkillers.

Lily closed her eyes tight. Was this because she hadn't eaten and then drank the wine?

The phone rang and she realised it was still in her hand. It was the same number from earlier. Should she ignore it? But maybe it was Ewan on a new number.

'Hello?'

'Lily?' A small, unfamiliar male voice asked.

'Yes.'

'Are you secure?'

Lily pushed the duvet away and sat up. 'What? Who is this?' Her circulation beat against the earpiece. Was this the stranger from the garden?

'Do you feel safe?'

'Who is this?' Aggression in her voice now.

'You might want to check your app.'

The line clicked. He'd rung off.

For a few seconds, Lily remained motionless, staring at the display of her phone. Then she hit the security app icon.

It opened and Lily quickly scrolled through the black and white images to get to the view of the garden. But before she could she noticed something alarming in one of the others. It was the camera in the kitchen.

The hooded intruder was standing by the table.

Chapter 9

Lily's legs curled tight into her as she sat bolt upright and her exclamation caught in her chest.

He was wearing the Maisie mask and was standing motionless, his left hand by his side, the right clutching a phone to his chest.

Lily's first thought was for Maisie's safety. She'd locked the kitchen door. Hadn't she? She was on her feet, heart pounding as she stumbled dizzily into the hallway again. She pulled open her daughter's door and crossed the carpet to her bed. 'Maisie,' she said sharply and frantically squeezed her shoulder.

Maisie didn't wake.

'Maisie!' Lily glanced quickly back to the door behind her then shook her daughter harder.

Maisie remained impassive.

'Maisie!' Lily whisper-screamed at her and dragged her up the pillows.

Her eyes fluttered and cracked open and she frowned at her mother.

'Get up.'

'What is it?' she slurred.

Lily jammed her hands underneath her and levered her off the mattress. 'We're going.'

'Where? What's . . . happening?' But Maisie still seemed half asleep.

Lily carried her to the door and paused there, listening for sounds in the darkened hallway. She was positive she'd locked the doors. After what had happened the previous afternoon, she knew she'd double-checked. Kitchen door, then lounge and both front doors. The keys were in her bedroom.

She swung Maisie to the side and peered around the jamb. The kitchen door was still sealed. She held her breath. No sounds coming from behind it.

'I'm scared.' Maisie rubbed her eyes.

Should she call the police? Her phone was on the bed. No, she should grab the keys, get them out the front way first. Lily darted across the hallway and back into her room, lowered Maisie slightly so she could pick up her phone from the bed and then turned to the table beside it.

No sign of the keys.

Lily's gut froze. They weren't in their usual place. She always dumped them there after she'd locked up every night. She opened the drawer but knew she hadn't put them in there. Her eyes scanned the tan carpet. No trace. They couldn't leave without finding them.

'I want to get down.' Maisie started wriggling.

Lily gripped her tighter. 'Don't move.'

'You're hurting me . . .'

'Do as I say.' Lily quickly surveyed the dresser. Not there

either. She struggled her hand up from under Maisie and shifted her weight so she could look at the app.

The intruder was still standing in the same position by the kitchen table.

'Who's that?' Maisie whispered drily.

'Take this.' She gave the phone to Maisie. 'The moment he moves, you tell me. Understand?'

Maisie nodded.

Lily swung Maisie around as she tried to locate the keys. They'd vanished. How could she have locked the doors without the keys?

'Why is he in our kitchen?' Maisie's voice quavered.

They had to be here somewhere. She shouldn't have had the wine. Her mind felt foggy. She *had* locked the doors.

Lily had to be sure. She carried Maisie out into the hallway again, glanced at the still closed kitchen door and headed in the opposite direction to the front and lounge doors. She hefted Maisie and delicately depressed the handle of the lounge. Locked. That was a relief. It meant she wasn't going mad. The kitchen would be sealed as well. But it also meant . . .

She tried the handle of the inner front door, but it was locked too. They couldn't get out.

Her bedroom window, it was over the back garden. It opened at the top and she could at least feed Maisie through it.

Lily stumbled back to it. The bottle green blind was lowered, and she'd need to raise it before she could open the window and get Maisie out. 'You're going to climb out this way,' she told her.

Maisie shook her head.

'Listen. Climb out, get over the back wall and then go straight across the road to Mrs Unwin. I'll call the police.' And Lily would scream for help from the window if necessary.

'You have to come with me.' Maisie sounded terrified.

'I can't. I won't fit through the top window.' Lily reached for the tie that secured the blinds to the hook in the wall.

'No.' Maisie squirmed.

'There's no time to argue.' Maisie was too heavy. She started to put Maisie down, but she wouldn't drop her feet.

'He's moving.' Maisie's eyes widened at the phone.

Lily took it from her and studied the screen.

The figure stepped deliberately towards the door. The camera was positioned over it.

But he couldn't get to the hallway. If she'd locked the other doors she certainly would have secured that one.

Lily's and Maisie's breaths were suspended as the figure halted in front of the door. Then he opened it wide and strode through.

Chapter 10

Lily's attention shot to the bedroom door. 'Quickly!' She put down Maisie and raced over to it, butting her shoulder against the panel to close it. Once it had slammed, she looked down at the lock but knew there was no key in it. No way to secure it. She listened for the sound of footsteps in the hallway.

Nothing.

She checked the phone and saw him pace slowly halfway up the hallway and then halt.

'Help!' She screamed up at the ceiling, hoping Mr Sargeant would hear. But he'd said he was leaving that day. Had he got an early flight? Lily leaned her back hard against the door, but figured she wouldn't be able to repel the intruder for long. 'Go out the window,' she hissed at Maisie.

Maisie shook her head.

'Help!' She yelled louder and her eyes halted on the wooden chair beneath the dresser. Could she fit the back of it underneath the door handle and buy them some time? But she'd have to move from the door to drag it over. Would he bust through it in those few seconds? 'Maisie, do as I say.'

'No. I'm not leaving you.'

There was nothing for it. Lily bolted across the room and grabbed the chair. Tipping the clothes from it she carried it back to the door and positioned it there.

The back was too low for the handle.

Lily slammed her body back against the door and clenched herself in readiness for him to ram his way inside. 'Mr Sargeant! Help!' Now she had to call the police.

But her phone started ringing. Keeping her back solidly against the panel Lily glanced at the screen. On the security shot she could see the hooded and masked intruder standing still halfway up the hallway and holding a phone to his ear.

She answered. 'What do you want?'

'Don't worry about finding me. Worry about finding yourself.'

He hung up and Lily watched the figure drop his arm and slip his phone into his back pocket. But he didn't move from his spot.

'What's happening?'

'Ssshhh.' Lily held her hand up to Maisie. What the hell was he talking about? She kept her eyes on the screen, but he still didn't make a move towards the bedroom door. Lily scrolled down to the security cam image of her bedroom.

There was no sign of her or Maisie.

Lily looked over to where Maisie was standing beside the bed. The duvet was thrown back where she'd jumped out, but on the cam image the bed was still made. Were the cameras delayed? The intruder had obviously tampered with them. This had to be old footage of the bedroom. And if that was the case then there would be no recording of him attacking them.

She scrolled back to the hallway image. The intruder still hadn't budged.

'Has he gone?' Maisie whispered.

Lily shook her head and frowned. Why didn't he enter the room? Was he giving them ample time to realise that whatever he did wouldn't be recorded?

The intruder put his hand in his other pocket and produced something which he held up to the camera. Lily squinted. Her keys. Lily felt a chill pass through her. When the hell had he taken them, while she was asleep? But how had he got into the hallway when she'd locked the doors at both ends?

The intruder walked forward, and Lily rammed her weight against the door. 'Stay away from us! I've got a weapon! Help!'

The intruder didn't react to her threat but continued to the front door. On her phone Lily watched him stop there and very deliberately use the keys to unlock the inner front door. He swung it wide, walked through and closed it behind him.

Lily's attention remained locked on the screen.

Maisie scuttled across the room to her.

'Go back to the window.'

But Maisie clutched her arm tight.

Why hadn't she heard any footsteps when he'd passed the door? And there had been no sound of the keys or the door opening and closing behind him. What sort of trick was he playing? Whatever it was they needed to stay on the opposite side of the house to him. She didn't shift her eyes from the phone.

The front door had closed firmly behind him. 'We're going to run into the kitchen,' she whispered to Maisie. She saw her shake her head out of the corner of her eye. 'No arguments, we're going now. I'll carry you if you like.'

'We should call the policeman.'

'I will do. From the kitchen. We'll run in there and lock the door. Then we'll be safe until the policeman arrives.'

'We should stay here.' Maisie looked at the door fearfully.

'We can't lock this. Come on.' Lily took her hot hand. They couldn't afford to delay. If the intruder had the keys, he could let himself back in any moment. The kitchen door had a bolt the other side. They just had to get behind it. She'd call the police and they'd be able to see if he came back over the garden wall.

'No.' Maisie fought her.

'Now,' Lily said sharply and yanked open the bedroom door. She dragged Maisie with her and was relieved when she began to run to keep up. The kitchen door had closed behind the intruder, but he definitely hadn't locked it behind him.

They reached the sealed kitchen door and Lily pushed on the wood. It swung open and she ushered Maisie through. Lily immediately shut it behind them and shot the bolt at the middle of the door in place. It was usually quite stiff, so she was surprised that it slid home so easily.

She breathed again but didn't enjoy the relief for longer than a second before turning to the kitchen window. The hessian blind was still down, and she prayed that when she lifted it, she wouldn't find that he had slid around the back and was standing outside the pane.

She took hold of the string and yanked the blind all the way up.

There was no man outside, but Lily barely acknowledged that because there was no back garden outside either.

The familiar view from the window had completely changed.

Chapter 11

The walled garden had vanished, and Lily was looking down on a demolished building site from a drop of about two hundred feet.

Her hand went to her mouth and she almost buckled at the knees.

'Is he there?' Maisie asked with trepidation. She was too short to see over the draining board through the glass.

Lily shook her head but didn't tear her eyes from the new vista. The windowpane was smaller but afforded her ample view of the heaped rubble below. In the orange early morning light, she could see twisted metal poking up from red bricks and dirty cinder blocks. Beyond rusted white goods was the collapsed housing block. The distressed and shattered windows of the remaining eleven floors reflected the similar building she was in, and there were two blocks of the same dilapidated apartments to her left and right. The entire area was derelict and there was nobody in sight.

'Has he come back?'

She would wake up. Any moment. But the burning cold floor beneath her bare feet felt too real.

'What can you see?'

Still Lily didn't answer her daughter. The familiarity of her surroundings framing the condemned area before her made a response seem impossible. They had to be ten floors up. Maisie tugged her hand, but she still hadn't blinked.

Wake up. Please, wake up.

'Lift me up!'

Lily shook her head. She could feel a rushing in her ears blotting out every other sound. That smell was in her nostrils again. The drying cement aroma she'd picked up in the hallway. She gazed around at the kitchen. Tried to focus. Everything was in its place. Mr Gingerbread was eating disinterestedly from his bowl. But she knew her home couldn't have been ripped out of Fallstaff Gardens and dumped here. The cat looked up from its bowl and his green eyes met hers.

'What's wrong?' Maisie's voice was muffled.

Lily didn't reply.

Maisie released Lily's fingers.

She still had the phone in her hand. She dialled the police. Concentrated hard on the keypad and tried to ignore the window. What would she say when they answered? It didn't matter. This was too surreal. She was playing for time until she woke up.

No ring tone. She tried again. Lily had had dreams like this before, when she was shouting to people for help and everything slowed down. The recurring one was somebody walking away from her, her pace getting slower than theirs as she pursued them, her yelling for them to stop but not wanting them to because she was afraid of seeing their faces when they turned around. But she was scared enough already. Terrified enough to wake up. Let this be over now.

She dialled the police again, stabbed the screen hard with her finger. It felt as if concentrating on the task required every ounce of her strength. But the earpiece only buzzed in her ear.

Stay calm, stay calm . . .

She found her sister's number and dialled it. She needed to hear her familiar voice. Would be glad of her mocking Lily for having a stupid dream. But she could smell her own sour breath as she breathed erratically, and it bounced back from the mouthpiece. She clenched the handset hard as she waited. Briefly squeezed her eyes shut. No ring tone. And when she opened her eyes again the view from the window hadn't changed back.

Dirty sky over a forlorn broken place she'd never seen before. She could see rivulets of dirty dried rain droplets on the glass. Then she saw her own petrified expression dimly reflected there.

She tried to rationalise. It was what had happened yesterday afternoon that had triggered this. The intruder in the garden and Officer Michaels coming into the house. But suddenly remembering the intruder made her turn from her position at the pane.

Maisie had gone. The sound of the room trickled quickly back in.

Her daughter had shot the bolt and opened the door to the hallway. Back towards the intruder.

'Maisie!' Lily barrelled after her.

The hallway was empty. 'Maisie!' The front door was still sealed. Lily glanced into Maisie's room. No sign of her there. Could the intruder have slipped back into the hallway when her attention had been on the window? Lily jumped as Mr Gingerbread scuttled past her, brushing against her bare legs. She followed him into her bedroom.

Please wake up now!

Lily felt light-headed again, like she might faint. She wanted this nightmare over. But she already suspected it wouldn't be. It felt way too real.

Maisie was standing by the window where she'd pulled the green blind up.

'I needed to see.' She turned to the pane.

Beyond the glass there was no longer the view they had of the garden. Behind it was only rows of red bricks.

Chapter 12

Lily crossed the carpet and stared at the pane. But she knew the window couldn't have been bricked up while she slept in the same room.

'I want to go outside,' Maisie declared anxiously.

But Lily was beginning to realise that that was something they weren't going to be allowed to do. If this *was* a nightmare surely she would have opened her eyes by now. Their predicament was so convincingly real, and she dreaded that the next moments would confirm that beyond doubt.

She took Maisie's hand and led her into the hallway to the front door. Locked.

'What's happening?'

Lily knew she shouldn't display the escalating panic she felt in front of Maisie. 'I'm . . . just trying to work that out.' Was all she could offer. Was the intruder the other side of it? 'Let us out of here!' Lily banged her fist against the panel. 'Open this now!' Her voice rose an octave and she beat the wood harder.

Maisie took a step away from her.

But Lily couldn't contain her alarm. 'Let us out. I've called the police!' But she suspected he already knew she couldn't.

Maisie clutched herself.

Lily tried the lounge door again but that was still locked. She glanced up at the hallway camera positioned over the open kitchen door. Was he watching them? She returned her attention to the image of the hallway in her phone's security app.

There was no sign of either of them standing in the positions they were.

'Open it!' Even though she suspected she was wasting her time Lily thumped the door in frustration until her hand ached. When she eventually stopped there was no sound the other side.

They waited and listened. Nothing.

She had to calm down, breathe a few times. In through her nose and out through her mouth.

'Are you OK now?' Maisie asked nervously.

Lily nodded. 'I'm fine.' She tried to slow her circulation, but she could hear it beating in her temples. She had to focus. Process what had happened since she'd woken up.

And she *had* woken up.

'You've turned white.'

Lily could see fear bulging in Maisie's wide blue eyes and crouched in front of her. 'Listen, we're going to find out exactly what's going on. OK?'

Maisie nodded once, uncertainly.

She could see that Maisie didn't believe her. She had to stow her own fear away for her sake. She gulped drily. 'There has to be a reason for this.' But how could any of this even begin to make any sense? 'Whatever it is, we'll be OK. I promise.'

Maisie nodded again and shivered.

Lily rubbed her daughter's arms and felt how cold they were through her yellow pyjamas. 'You're freezing. Let's get your hoodie wrap.' Lily stood and quickly led Maisie to her bedroom. The faux purple fur garment was folded on the seat of the wicker chair beside her bed.

Too perfectly folded. Lily always left it draped on the back, and Maisie wouldn't have put it there so neatly. Had Paulette folded it last night? That wasn't something she could see her sister doing. She cautiously picked it up then opened it out.

She wrapped it around Maisie and put her nose to it. It wasn't Maisie's. It didn't smell of her. Lily frequently inhaled it. It was just as much a comfort blanket for her as it was her daughter. The truth of the situation seemed ludicrous. Had somebody replicated not only her home but also its contents?

Mr Gingerbread emitted a nervous meow.

Lily located the cat cowering in the corner beside the door. Maisie went to him.

'Wait!'

Maisie froze and turned back to her.

The cat hissed at them.

'Leave him where he is for the moment.' Lily could see he'd lost a lot of weight. Since last night. It was a different animal and it was clearly nervous of them both.

'What's wrong with Mr Gingerbread?'

'Just leave him.' Lily's mind raced. It was definitely a different cat. She could see its ribs poking through its fur. Who would have gone to these lengths? And where was their real cat now?

Maisie reversed her steps and cowered at Lily's legs.

The cat, the hoodie wrap, the bolt sliding so easily into place, the unfamiliar cement smell, the cold air and that view out of the window. She glanced at the camera positioned over the bedroom door and rapidly scrolled through the images on her security app. All of the rooms were empty. Including the one they were standing in. That was why the intruder had walked from the kitchen, along the hallway and through the front door without them hearing him. He was in their home. They weren't.

So, where the hell were they?

Chapter 13

Lily and Maisie were back in the kitchen, the door firmly bolted again.

Maisie was seated on one of the chairs at the kitchen table, her arms poking out of her hoodie blanket and protectively encircling her legs. From her elevated seat she could see through the window. She'd gasped inwards when she'd seen their new surroundings and Lily still hadn't heard her breathe out.

Lily couldn't begin to explain to her what was happening. Who had imprisoned them like this? And why? But she could barely comprehend the situation they were in let alone consider who could be responsible. What could their motive possibly be for doing this to a mother and child? Think. It seemed like a sick prank. But when she considered the intruder the previous day and took in their imitation home she suspected it was far from that. Who could have had access to so much that was private? Only one name suggested itself.

It seemed preposterous that Ewan would be part of this. Was this his punishment? Was that why he'd been happy not to see Maisie for so long and had this always been his plan?

At that moment, he was the only person she could believe would be gratified by this. But Maisie's distress? No. He loved his daughter. But now he had them where he wanted maybe he would try to take Maisie away from her. But it all seemed so outlandish.

Maybe they'd been targeted at random. Would a ransom be demanded? From whom? She only had Paulette left and she didn't have any money. But they were surrounded by the handiwork of someone who knew their lives intimately. Who else other than Ewan could it possibly be?

'Why did somebody move our house?'

Lily looked up at her daughter's pensive expression and wondered if it was better to let her believe that. Would Maisie feel more secure? But it was only a matter of time before she'd have to know the truth and perhaps the cat had already confirmed that to her. They'd left the animal locked the other side of the kitchen door.

Momentarily, she had to focus on keeping Maisie calm. 'Whoever did this obviously wants us to be at home.' That was the truth. If someone meant to harm them would they have constructed this space? She considered how they'd been relocated and the truth of that came thick and fast.

They must have been drugged. Someone had come into their home while they slept and physically removed them. They'd scooped her and Maisie up and driven them here while they were completely oblivious.

The intruder standing in the garden had been a brazen demonstration that this was to come. It must have taken some organization to snatch them and bring them here, so they must have planned to take them that night. Had whoever done it watched Officer Michaels surveying the flat? How had they got in? And how could they have unlocked the doors within to get to them?

To know so much about their home perhaps they'd been regularly coming into it when she'd been at work. Maybe Ewan wasn't in Dundee. He'd given back his key, but he could so easily have made a copy. She imagined him wandering around the empty rooms of their old marital home while she and Maisie weren't there. But her app would have alerted her. She'd only recently had it installed though. That definitely hadn't been Ewan standing in the back garden, however. Was there more than one person involved in their kidnap? It was the first time she'd thought that word. But 'kidnap' was what this was.

Before they'd locked themselves in Lily had swiftly checked the windowless bathroom was empty. Like Fallstaff Gardens it was the only room without a camera. She examined the seal of the window in the kitchen. It was their only view out of their reproduction home. There was no window in Maisie's room anyway and the one in hers had bricks behind it. The bay windows in the locked lounge were inaccessible. The kitchen window was now their only source of natural light.

The glass was set firmly in the wall and when she put her palm against it there was no give or rattle like her real one. It was rigid. She thumped it with her fist and it made a dull thud.

'What are you doing?'

It looked like it was unbreakable. She beat it again harder

and her wrist smarted. Lily moved to the wooden back door. She pulled down on the handle but knew it wouldn't open. The panel was simply a piece of set. There was no light around it. It was fixed to the wall.

There was the cat flap at the bottom but when she prodded it with her bare toe it didn't give. She bent to examine it. The flap wasn't translucent yellowing plastic like hers, it looked like it was solid yellow resin.

'How will the cat get out?'

Lily acknowledged that Maisie hadn't called the animal Mr Gingerbread.

'If he tries to go through there he'll fall.'

'It's OK, it won't open. He can't get out.'

Maisie frowned.

She knew that was going to be no comfort to Maisie.

'Like us?'

Lily didn't respond. 'Hello!' She shouted up at the ceiling. Mr Sargeant wasn't up there but perhaps there were other people in the building. She fought the impulse to shout 'help' again. She didn't want to frighten Maisie any more than she was.

Nothing.

But by the state of the structure opposite and what she could see of the one she was in, reflected in its shattered windows, she thought it unlikely that there was anyone above or below them. Maybe whoever was holding them captive was the only one who could hear her. But surely the intruder was still in their real home. How far away from there were they now? 'Hello!' she screamed louder, desperation fraying the word.

She gazed around the kitchen at all the familiar fixtures and contents. The shelves of pots stacked in the same way they were in her real kitchen, the slanted row of cookbooks on top of the cupboard. She opened it and it had all the same dried contents – packs of rice and pasta and noodles – as the one at home.

How long had this place existed and been awaiting their occupation? Lily closed the cupboard door, walked to the fridge and took one of Maisie's crayon drawings from under the familiar SpongeBob magnet. Had someone photographed the inside of her home then searched online for all the same contents? But how could they have Maisie's picture?

She put the magnet back and closely examined the crudely drawn orange car with the two of them sitting in it, Lily smiling in front and Maisie seated in the back. She ran her fingers over it but there was no texture, no waxy feel to the thicker strokes of crayon. It was a colour photocopy. The paper was shiny. It had been taken from their real home and duplicated. Cold bubbles fizzed up her spine.

'What's wrong?' Maisie had been watching her expression.

Lily fixed the picture back to the door. 'Just looking at how happy we are together.'

Maisie got up off the chair and came over to where she was standing.

Lily moved quickly to the window. 'Come over here.'

Maisie briefly regarded her drawing then followed her to the sink.

Lily picked her up and sat her on the draining board.

'I thought I wasn't allowed to sit up here.'

'Today you are.' She directed her daughter's attention through the pane. 'I want you to keep watch out here.'

'What for?'

'People.' Lily scanned the deserted rubble. 'If you see anyone out there, I want you to run and tell me straight away.'

'Where are you going?' There was sudden terror on her face.

Lily figured the kitchen was the safest room for Maisie to be. 'I'm going to search the other rooms. There must be another way out of here.'

Chapter 14

As she headed for the door Lily halted at the kitchen drawers. She slid the middle one open and was surprised to find the familiar contents inside. It was her tool drawer, and everything was present and correct, even if it looked slightly new.

The hammer and chisel were distinctly less grubby than the ones Ewan had left behind but they were the same make. Who else could have got inside her home without her noticing? Paulette was the only one with a spare key. They'd had issues in the past, but she couldn't countenance the idea that she had anything to do with this. Had Paulette misplaced her key at some point or had Lily? No, she always carried it around in her handbag and never had any others cut.

What about Mr Sargeant upstairs? Had he pretended not to be home when Officer Michaels had been there? Even if he wanted to get in though, how had he bypassed the security?

But she'd only recently had the cameras and alarm fitted. They'd lived there for four years without the system. Lily grabbed the hammer, chisel and her set of screwdrivers and turned back to Maisie. 'Eyes out of the window. You've got an important job to do.' She quietly closed the drawer.

Maisie nodded and turned to the pane.

Lily took a breath and unbolted the door. She opened it, tentatively made her way into the empty hallway and listened. No sounds of movement.

'Are you OK?'

'Fine. Just stay where you are.' Why had the intruder left her with the tools she needed to escape? Was this a test? By Ewan?

She took her phone out of her robe pocket with her free hand and checked it. The intruder hadn't tried to contact her since he'd walked through the front door of her house in Fallstaff Gardens. It wasn't even half six in the morning. Nobody would be missing either of them yet. And even when she did have a sick day the office very rarely rang her at home. What about Julie Medlocke? She had her back and would get in touch if she didn't appear, but would she do anything more if she didn't get a reply? She might try to call Lily's mobile.

A thought struck her, and Lily turned it over in her palm. Was it hers? She'd only just changed that wallpaper photo. It was of her and Maisie a few weeks ago after they'd had an outing to Brighton. It was an image of them together on the beach with the pier in the background. She examined the cheap black plastic case. It looked like hers. She went to contacts and hit 'This Phone'. That was definitely her number. Looked like it *was* hers.

Lily attempted calling the police again then Julie and Paulette. No dial tone. The last person she tried was Ewan. Why would she think his number would be any different to the others? Was it because of what Paulette had said about suspecting him? Was something jamming the signal? She went to her security app but now all the images of the rooms were black. Had he deliberately covered the cameras or was the connection severed? The app was working fine earlier.

'There's nobody out there,' Maisie reported despondently from the kitchen.

'Keep looking.' What about Maisie's school? They would soon be in touch if she didn't attend. But even when they were both missed, and the alarm was eventually raised, it didn't matter if the police kicked down the front door. Where would they begin to start looking for them? They could be miles from Fallstaff Gardens.

Pocketing the phone, she circled her red hair behind her ear and listened at the front lounge. The TV was in there. If it was even a room. She carefully pulled down the handle. Still locked. She tried the inner front door. Locked too. There was no noise coming from the other side, so she examined the hinges. Weren't you supposed to be able to lift a door off from that side? She put the hammer and chisel on the floor and opened her screwdrivers.

The phone rang and she jumped and swiftly pulled it out. Lily looked along the hallway to Maisie who immediately tried to slide back down the sink cupboard. 'Stay there,' she hissed.

Maisie froze and then reluctantly pulled herself back up.

'Window.' Lily gestured at the glass and Maisie turned back to it.

Lily looked up at the hallway camera over the kitchen door.

Had he seen her with the tools? And did he have the same security app as her so he could watch her from anywhere? She answered and held the phone to her ear.

'You're wasting your time.' It was the same male voice from before.

'Why are you doing this?'

'Isn't it time you both had breakfast?' he said flatly.

Lily swallowed and turned to the front door so Maisie couldn't hear. 'Where is this place?'

No response. Only light breathing.

'Please . . .' she whispered, 'I'll do whatever you want. Just let us out.'

'There's cereal, fresh milk and eggs too.'

'What do you want?'

'I told you. Eat. You both need to sustain yourselves.'

Lily hesitated. Didn't want to ask. 'For what?'

'For the day ahead. There's cat food there too. Don't let Mr Gingerbread starve.'

'That's not my cat.' Aggression filled out her voice. 'Why would you do this? If it's a ransom you're after—'

'No. This isn't that sort of scenario. You can use the tools you have. Try the window with the hammer and chisel; if you feel the need. It's reinforced though, so you'll barely scratch it.'

'Just tell me what you want.' Lily gripped the phone tighter.

'You'll probably have no problem removing the door to the porchway but beyond that there's no way through. It's plate steel. Be my guest but, take my word for it, you *will* be wasting your time.'

'Please, stop this. Let us out now and I promise I won't breathe a word of this to anyone.'

'That will be the case . . . regardless of what you do.'

Lily flinched and closed her eyes. 'You can't lock up a child.'

'No?' He paused. 'Is that right?'

'Tell me who you are. Tell me what you think I've done to deserve this. I promise, I'll do whatever you ask.'

'That's a very rash promise.'

'Just let Maisie go.'

'Shall we just take this conversation as read? I think you already know the answer.'

Lily opened her eyes, inhaled and swallowed her anger. 'We'll have breakfast.'

'Good. I've already eaten. Top right cupboard. Cornflakes were running a bit low but you'll find a full box in yours.'

'You're in my kitchen?' she said incredulously and imagined him standing there. Would Mr Sargeant hear him moving around? But surely, if he hadn't jetted off yet, he'd just assume it was her.

'Don't forget to keep your phone charged so I can contact you. Charger's in the usual place. I have to go now.'

'Wait!'

'You've got everything you need.'

'Tell us what we need to do.'

'To curry favour you mean?'

Lily gritted her teeth. 'Yes.'

'Eat, drink, sleep. Keep yourselves healthy. Keep yourselves sane.'

'And when will you explain?'

'The reason you're there?'
'Yes.'
'Maybe never.'

Chapter 15

She prayed he was toying with her. 'And what if we refuse?'

'Refuse to keep yourselves alive?' he eventually replied.

Lily thought he might have hung up. She didn't know how to respond.

'If you go on hunger strike, you die. If that's your choice, so be it, but is that what you really want for Maisie?'

She didn't like him using her daughter's name. 'Please . . . give me something.'

'I have. A full box of cornflakes.' He cut the call.

Lily took a deep breath before she walked slowly back to Maisie in the kitchen.

'Was that the scary man?'

Lily nodded. She found the number in her recent calls and hit redial. No dial tone. He'd clearly jammed the signal again. 'Just keep looking out of the window.' She made her way back to the inner front door.

'Didn't you tell him we'd have breakfast?' Maisie called down to her.

'Yes. I did.' Was there any point in trying to remove the

door? He'd be watching her through the hall camera. He hadn't forbidden her though. 'Are you hungry?'

'No.'

'Keep watch then.' Could he really be standing in her kitchen? If so, how far away was he from them? A few miles or were they in another part of the country? Was someone else standing behind the front door before her, listening to their conversation? She picked up the hammer from the floor, gripped it tight in her hand and barely restrained herself from swinging it at the door. She couldn't lose control in front of Maisie again.

Quarter of an hour later she'd managed to unscrew the hinges from the door and grunted as she attempted to lift it. It weighed a ton.

'Can I help?' Maisie was standing behind her.

She couldn't banish her to the window again. 'Just stand back.' Lily supported the weight by the handle, but it was too heavy and, as it came off, she staggered and then jumped back. It slammed onto the black and orange tiles of the hallway floor.

'Are you OK?'

Lily nodded. It had nearly landed on her bare foot. 'I'm fine.' But her attention was already on the front door beyond. There was no light around it. She bent to the letterbox halfway up it, lifted the aluminium flap and looked through.

He was right. Through the slot she could see dull, silver steel. She pushed the head of the hammer inside and butted the head against it. The wall the other side emitted a heavy thud. Lily exhaled and her shoulders sagged. She clenched her teeth, closed her eyes.

'We're locked inside, aren't we?'

Lily turned to find Maisie standing in the porchway. 'I told you to stand back!' She couldn't keep the anger from her voice.

Maisie recoiled, as if she'd been struck.

'I'm sorry.' Lily hugged her and put her nose against the side of her hot face. 'I didn't mean to shout.'

Maisie put her arms around her neck. 'It's OK. We'll be OK.'

Lily felt the burn of tears but fought them back. 'Of course we will be.'

After a few moments, Maisie released her. 'What about the lounge?' There was still hope in her eyes.

Lily nodded and quickly rose before any tears rolled down her cheeks. 'Let's check it out, shall we?' But she knew it would be pointless. Was their watcher enjoying this? She took Maisie's hand and led her out of the porch. She put her eye to the gap at the hinges of the lounge door but there was no light. Peering through the keyhole gave her the same result. 'Move behind me.' Lily raised the hammer.

Maisie obeyed.

She swung the head hard at the panel, but the wood was solid and the hammer bounced off it. The door at home was lightweight, but this was obviously made of something sturdier. Was there any point trying to take this off at the hinges if it was set against steel like the front door? He'd told her she'd be wasting her time. Now she believed him.

Maisie examined the tiny dent in the wood. 'What do we do now?'

It was a good question. But Lily knew she had to keep making decisions. 'First, we're going to get dressed. Then we have breakfast.'

'Because the scary man said?'

Lily glanced briefly up at the camera. 'No. Because we do need to eat.'

'But I said I'm not hungry.' Suddenly Maisie's stomach bubbled and grumbled in contradiction and it echoed down the hallway. She smirked slightly.

Lily smiled too, for her benefit. But she had no idea what they would do after that. It was clear that the space that had been created to trap them in was designed to be anything but temporary. 'We'll feel better once we've eaten. Then we'll figure this out together.'

Maisie nodded and turned to go to her bedroom.

'Wait.'

Lily stopped and turned.

'Let's just listen a moment.'

'What for?'

'Ssshhh.' Lily held up her palm and tried to let her heart rate slow down so she could hear.

They both stood still.

Nothing. No sound of traffic. It didn't appear they were anywhere near a main road.

Maisie opened her mouth to say something, but Lily held her hand out firmly.

They stood like that for three minutes and only then did they just hear a sound. Wind mournfully blowing through one of the upstairs rooms. Were they really all alone?

Chapter 16

Lily flipped open the lid of the see-through kettle. It was identical to hers but pristine inside. The bottom of the one in Fallstaff Gardens was coated with chalk. She sniffed the interior and then took it to the sink. She turned the familiar tap and suddenly a loud clunking noise emanated from behind the splash tiles.

A few seconds later, water squirted harshly from the mixer but then stopped. Pressure built again and it started sporadically flowing down the plughole. It looked slightly brown. Where was this coming from, the original plumbing or had a pump been set up specifically?

She positioned the kettle under it and let it fill. She held it up and examined the water through the glass. There were no particles, but she still didn't trust the colour. Could the water be drugged and would boiling it make any difference? She poured it away and let it fill a second time. The brown wasn't as vivid this time. She repeated the process a few times until it was clear and then switched it on.

She watched the kettle glow blue as it started to grumble. Electricity, water, what about heating? She touched the duplicate radiator on the wall. It was cold to the touch. Would it work? The rooms seemed to be warming up now the sun was out though, plus she had on a navy sweatshirt, jeans and socks. Maisie was in a red and green striped jumper and dungarees. The clothes were the same as in their real wardrobes but brand new. Despite their surreal circumstances, however, Lily knew she had to keep things as normal for Maisie as she could. If that was possible.

Again, her mind repeated the same circuits. Was she missing something? Did she have to look further into her past to explain why this was being done to them? But she couldn't recall any slight she might have committed against anybody that would have engendered the sort of hatred to fuel this sort of campaign. What about Laurie Campbell, the man she'd dated once who'd lost his wife in a car accident? She recalled his flinching expression when she'd politely refused his request to see her again. Paulette had said he was stalker material, but it seemed unlikely he could have developed an attachment to Lily if he'd only spent a handful of hours with her in a bar.

She kept coming back to Ewan and, the ironic thing was, she could hear his voice dismissing her suspicions. But she couldn't think of anyone else who could harbour the sort of animosity required to inflict torment in this way. But Ewan's world revolved around Maisie. That was why she couldn't fathom why he'd withdrawn affection from his daughter. Did he really want to spare himself the pain of reminding himself of the family he'd forfeited? He'd never admitted blame after what had happened. But they both knew that their daughter's transformation from the bright girl they'd brought up to the shy introvert she was now was a result of the slow burn of acrimony that came to a head and exposed her to it so completely that one awful day.

Lily went to where Maisie's copied picture had been fixed and opened the fridge door. The shelves were full of the food she usually had in – eggs, broccoli, carrots, bananas, Cokes, string cheese and a multipack of the mini yoghurts Maisie loved – plus a large carton of milk was tucked in the door. She took it out and placed it on top. There was a greaseproof paper package on the bottom shelf and when she unwrapped it found some bacon inside. There was no label on it or the plastic milk carton. No clue as to where any of the provisions had been bought.

She opened the freezer drawers and found their favourite brands – chicken nuggets, lasagne, Swedish meatballs, potato waffles and fishfingers. Had the boxes been tampered with? She examined their seals. If they had they'd been glued back in place. She replaced them and tried not to consider that there was enough food to last them a good few weeks.

'I'm still not hungry.' Maisie was hovering beside her.

'We have to eat.' That was the truth. Whatever had been provided for them was their only option.

Lily closed the freezer, carried the milk to the kitchen table and then grabbed the cornflakes from the cupboard. It *was* a full packet. She found corresponding yellow bowls in their customary place inside the china cabinet and set them on the table before looking up at the camera. Doubtless, he was watching them. Would he release them sooner if they did as they were told or did he plan to keep them imprisoned regardless? There had to be another way out of their prison, but she would go along with what he said in the meantime.

'I don't want anything,' Maisie grumbled.

'Just sit.' Lily went to the drawer to get some spoons and noted the sharp knives were all present. With those and the tools in the other drawer she had enough weapons to defend them. But she got the impression that he'd already made allowances for any moves she would make.

How long must he have been watching and researching them and setting this up? Had he scoured for locations which had the exact layout of her home or had this been constructed inside a larger space? She poured out the cornflakes into the two bowls and opened the milk, sniffing it first. It smelt fresh but she paused the carton over the first bowl. She sensed him watching her, waiting for her to continue.

She put it to her lips, hesitated and then took a little against them. She lowered the carton, tasted the tiny drop there with her tongue. It seemed OK. She swigged a little more and swilled the trickle around her mouth. Why would he poison them if he'd gone to all this trouble? But again, she considered that he could drug any of the groceries he'd provided and wouldn't have to worry about her trying to defend them with a knife.

Lily poured the milk into one bowl. 'OK, if you're not hungry, I'll eat.' She tried to imbue the statement with a degree of irritation to mask the fact that she wanted to try the food first.

Lily sat at the table and Maisie squeaked out a chair and seated herself as well.

Lily peered into the bowl at the cornflakes getting soggy from the milk. What if they were drugged and she passed out leaving Maisie at the mercy of their captor? But she certainly didn't expect Maisie to try them first and they had to eat sooner or later. She glanced at the camera.

He knew that. There was no choice.

She stood, took both the bowls from the table and tipped them in the identical swing bin by the kitchen dresser.

'What are you doing?' Maisie regarded her uneasily.

'I don't fancy them. Let's have some eggs.'

'But I don't like eggs.'

'You like pancakes.'

'That's not eggs.'

Damn. That was a fact she'd withheld from Maisie. She wouldn't touch fried, scrambled, poached or boiled because she knew eggs were baby chickens, so Lily had taken to making pancakes to make sure she got her protein and had kept the key ingredient a secret.

Maisie frowned hard and her head followed Lily's return to the refrigerator.

She opened the door and took out the box of eggs. She carried them to the hob and opened it, examining each one carefully. How could he tamper with these?

'What are you doing?' Maisie asked warily.

'Just making sure they're fresh.'

'Why didn't you tell me there were eggs in pancakes?'

'You didn't ask me if there were.' But Lily knew that wouldn't work.

'I wouldn't have eaten them if I'd known that,' she lamented

Lily turned on the hob. 'But you love pancakes.'

Maisie didn't reply.

'And what about cake? You like that.'

'That hasn't got eggs in it.'

'It most certainly has.' She may as well know the whole truth. Lily put some oil into the pristine pan resting in its usual position on the back-right ring and sparked it up. So they had gas as well.

'I won't eat those, even if you make them into pancakes,' Maisie stated flatly.

Lily cracked two eggs into the pan. 'I'm having some, so you'll have to as well. It's all that's for breakfast.'

'I saw fishfingers in the freezer.'

'They're not for now, you're having eggs.' It seemed ludicrous having such a familiar argument.

'I don't want them.'

'Just eat what I give you!' Lily took a breath. It was the second time she'd lost her temper. She rarely shouted at Maisie and, when she did, she always felt a little sick. Maisie wasn't naughty, never behaved as badly as Julie Medlocke's twin boys. But she had an aversion to eggs. Just like Lily had when she was a girl. 'I'm sorry.'

Maisie turned away from her.

'I'm sorry. I really didn't mean to shout.' Lily could see her daughter's body tense and knew the tears were about to flow. 'You're obviously hungry. You need to eat. We both do. That's why I lost my temper.'

'Why can't I have cornflakes?'

'They're stale.'

Maisie wailed. 'I want to be in our real home!'

Lily crossed the room and put her arms around her, felt the sobs in her shoulders as they racked her body. 'I'm sorry. That was my fault. Ssshhh.'

'Why . . . don't we . . . call Daddy?' Her little chest pumped out the words.

'We don't need to do that.'

'I want . . . to . . . see . . . him.'

'I'm here to look after you.' Lily felt her own tears start to burn but clenched her eyes against them. 'It's going to be OK. I promise you.'

'But we can't . . . get . . . out.'

'We'll find a way. Ssshhh.'

'I'm scared.'

So was Lily. But it was at that moment that she knew she had to be an even better mother than all the times she'd guided her daughter around the edges of Ewan's self-destructive behaviour. Lily glared up at the camera positioned over the door. 'We're going to get out of here,' she whispered.

Lily held Maisie and comforted her until her crying had subsided and her erratic breathing began to slow down. 'You and I are going to be a team.'

'We are a . . . team.'

'But better than that. We're going to be a super team from now on.'

'Can I sleep in your bed tonight?'

Lily could hear the fear in her voice. 'Of course. We'll have a pyjama party.'

'Yes.' She nodded.

Lily swallowed her emotions. Would they still be here by evening or would the intruder be in touch to let her know exactly what he wanted? But judging by what he'd said to her on the phone and all the well-stocked shelves she got the impression that he was in no hurry to answer that question.

A loud beeping interrupted her thoughts.

She released Maisie and looked upwards. It was a smoke alarm, just like hers. The eggs were burning in the pan. She darted over to the hob and slid the pan off the heat. Fumes filled the kitchen. She instinctively grabbed a tea towel from its customary sucker hook and waved it up at the detector.

Maisie was on her feet, watching and coughing.

The alarm stopped, but when Lily ceased waving the towel it started again. She couldn't open a window. 'The extractor.' She thought out loud and easily located the switch in the hood over the hob. It started buzzing and sucking out the fumes.

Maisie kept coughing.

'Just give it a minute.' But it suddenly struck Lily that if there were a more serious fire, there was no escape.

No window to open, no door out of there.

Chapter 17

While they waited for the smoke to clear Lily led Maisie to her bedroom and tried to distract her. 'OK. Gather whatever things you want, and we'll carry them over to my room. No reason why we can't have a pyjama party now.'

'But we've only just got up,' Maisie pointed out.

'Does it matter? We can put our pyjamas on over our clothes so we can keep warm.'

Maisie beamed and appeared to like that idea.

'What toys d'you want to bring over to my room?'

Maisie put her hands on her hips and surveyed her toyboxes. 'I don't want any of these.'

Lily wondered if it was because her daughter knew that none of the toys were the ones she'd played with before.

Maisie turned and walked out.

'OK, I'll bring your PJs and we'll get cosy on the bed,' she said breezily.

In Lily's room they pulled their nightwear on over their clothes, and Maisie slipped under the double duvet and pulled it up to her chin.

Lily remembered the kettle had boiled. 'Wait, I fancy some

coffee. Just going to grab some first.' The truth was, she already felt exhausted and didn't want to fall asleep.

'I'm coming with you,' Maisie exclaimed and leapt out of the bed.

'OK.' Lily thought Maisie was clearly scared to be left alone and let her accompany her back to the kitchen. 'You want anything?'

Maisie shook her head emphatically.

She quickly made herself some instant coffee. It was a new jar and the seal hadn't been broken. Could she trust it though? Lily had it black. She picked up the yellow mug and checked the window. No sign of movement amongst the rubble.

Maisie stood on tiptoes to see over the sink. 'Anybody?'

'No. Let's take five.' She surreptitiously slipped a paring knife into her robe pocket as they left. She looked up at the camera above the kitchen door and hoped he saw her do it.

They returned to the bedroom and Lily closed the door before they both got onto the mattress.

Maisie slid under the cover again and put her head on Lily's left breast. 'I can hear your heart beating fast.'

'It's because the smoke alarm made me jump,' Lily mitigated. She gently stroked Maisie's head and hoped that might slow it down. Did they really have to spend a night in this weird facsimile home and would either of them be able to sleep with the prospect of the intruder gaining access at any moment? He would have to get in through the sealed lounge or front door though, so surely she would hear him.

Recriminations that Lily had been trying to hold at bay kicked in. How could she have allowed this to happen to

Maisie? She'd let them be taken. The intruder had audaciously walked into their garden and demonstrated that he was deliberately targeting them by wearing Maisie's face.

That had been a warning she should have reacted to more fiercely. She should have taken Maisie away. Stayed somewhere else. But nobody would have believed that locking all the internal doors, as she had, wouldn't have kept them safe. Nobody could have conceived of waking in a place like this.

'Why don't you want Daddy to help us?'

Lily considered how to answer. 'I do.'

'Doesn't he care about us anymore?'

'Of course he does. I've tried to phone him already. And Auntie Julie and Auntie Paulette.'

'What about the policeman?'

'I can't get through to anyone.' It was pointless withholding the truth from her.

'Why?'

Lily shook her head. 'Whoever wants us here has done something to my phone.' She took it out and checked. No coverage. The only thing that had been working was the security app and when she scrolled through the various cameras they were still all black.

'Is the scary man going to hurt us now?'

Lily swallowed silently. 'No. I won't allow that.' She spread her fingers protectively over Maisie's head.

'You're only saying that,' Maisie said offhandedly.

Lily stiffened. 'No, I'm not,' she replied categorically. 'Nobody will be able to harm the super team.'

'You haven't always been able to stop me from being hurt.'

'I got my share of bumps and scrapes in the playground,' Lily comforted.

'At home, I mean.'

Lily briefly closed her eyes. She knew which occasion Maisie was referring to – when she'd been arguing with Ewan and Maisie's arm had been jerked in the struggle. She'd torn a muscle but she so easily could have broken it. That was the last time she'd allowed Ewan in the house. 'That was an accident, Maisie. This is different.'

'How?'

'Because I'm going to be on guard every second.'

Maisie didn't reply.

Lily tried not to let the exchange upset her. 'That was Daddy, this is different.'

Maisie nodded once.

Was she really defending herself against someone different? But Ewan had been sacked from his teaching job because of his alcoholism. He was penniless when he'd left for Dundee. But maybe he'd got the money from his wealthy brother.

Christian hated her for insisting on full custody and had told her so in his last phone call to her. It seemed so fantastical, but as she gazed around the room at the fixtures and fittings that had been recreated so faithfully, Lily couldn't dismiss the only men she could think of who might revel in her suffering.

Chapter 18

Half an hour later Lily had cajoled Maisie into painting her nails with grown-ups' varnish, and while her daughter was absorbed she got up off the bed and wandered casually around the room. She'd assumed that the only ways in were through the front and lounge doors but, if the apartment had been created within another space, could there be other entrances to allow him easy access? She wanted to make doubly sure that he couldn't enter the bedroom if they'd barricaded themselves inside.

Glancing up at the camera first she pretended to be studying the bookshelf. She took a paperback off. It was her copy of *Confederacy of Dunces* resting in its customary position along the tops of the others because she'd run out of space and deposited it there some years ago. She flicked through it but it wasn't hers. It looked to be second-hand and, although it was the right edition and the pages were aged yellow, Lily knew it wasn't the book she'd read.

Whoever had imprisoned them must have sought out every book here and carefully collated them. She ran her eyes along their spines but, although they were all in place, Lily's instincts said they didn't belong to her. Why was that? She supposed that was how Maisie had felt about her toys. An overriding sensation that a history of personal interaction was missing.

Lily carefully examined the wall beside the shelf for any slits in the mauve painted wallpaper. She moved to the next bookshelf and analysed the wall there. Nothing. Lily completed a circuit of the room until she was back at the first bookshelf and her attention settled on her photo albums. Lily had so many images of Maisie on her phone and was always promising herself to download and print off the best ones. However, she never found time to get around to it and felt guilty that there weren't more recent pictures of her framed on the walls.

But she'd scrupulously filled two albums with Maisie's first couple of years. She considered the crayon drawing of Maisie's in the kitchen. Would she find copies of every photo inside? She reached up to the top shelf, but her hand hesitated an inch from the spine of the first album. Lily didn't want to look but knew she had to.

She took the heavy album down, filled her lungs and opened it. The first photo was identical to the one in her album and was a picture of Maisie lying on her back in her crib when she was only a few days old. But she'd had that one printed on glossy photo paper and this was dull. She put her finger on the plastic sheet covering it and skimmed it aside. She peeled the photo from its sticky backing page and saw how flimsy it was. Looked like another photocopy.

She turned the next pages depicting Maisie's infancy and found more of the same. But the most disturbing notion was that someone must have taken her real album and removed each separate photo, copied it and then put it back. When had that been done? How long had they been walking in and out of her home, taking what they wanted and then replacing it without her noticing? Lily racked her brains, tried to recall any significant moments when something had vanished. But the truth was her life was so busy she probably wouldn't have noticed if anything had gone astray.

She scanned the books again. Had somebody stood in her bedroom, taken a photo of her shelves and then meticulously recreated every book she'd read since she was a teenager? She shuddered.

'Why are you looking at those?'

Lily glanced over to where Maisie was sitting cross-legged at the head of the bed. 'Just reminding myself how big you've got.' She tried to back up the excuse with a smile and a shake of the head, but her expression froze when she turned the next page.

'What's wrong?' Maisie instantly picked up on her alarm and put aside her nail varnish.

Lily shook her head. 'Nothing . . . just . . .' But she couldn't conceal her shock.

The next page contained photos from Maisie's first birthday party. They'd had a small gathering that included Julie Medlocke and her boys, Paulette and a few of their new neighbours.

Mr Sargeant hadn't attended but had left a bottle of red wine on the doorstep with a card and his best wishes. It had been a gorgeous June day and it had given them an excuse to use the walled garden. Ewan had laid out the folding chairs and been on his best behaviour. He'd shown Julie's boys how to rugby tackle. Maisie had woken up crying in what was then the nursery and Lily had put her in the pushchair and taken her out to the garden. Everyone had held and made a fuss of her and then Lily had put Maisie back in the chair with the hood up to protect her from the heat. That was when she'd taken the photos and Ewan had said how good they were.

But the photos in the album weren't those.

'What have you got there?'

Lily hadn't noticed Maisie climb off the bed. Her eyes were still fixed on the two photos before her.

'Let me see.'

Lily looked down to see Maisie gazing up at her. 'I said, it's just the photos . . .'

'Let me see then.'

Lily showed her and she looked bored. 'Oh, those again.' Maisie turned away, disinterested, and returned to the bed.

Lily flipped to the next page where there were more of the same. Photos of Maisie in her chair with a subtle difference that her daughter hadn't noticed. The pictures she'd put in the album were ones she'd taken with her camera. It was an old Nikon she'd had for years that she'd been determined to use because it would make her develop photos and get prints done of Maisie. But in these images Lily was in shot, peering at her baby through her camera.

Who had taken them? Ewan certainly hadn't and nor had Paulette. In fact, she couldn't recall anyone else taking pictures that day. None that had been shared with her anyway. Until that moment she'd thought that only she'd recorded the occasion. But someone else clearly had.

Chapter 19

Who else had been there? She studied each photo. They appeared to be captured by someone who had stood right beside her, but the angle was slightly elevated. Could it have been shot from a distance? Had a zoom lens been used or had the photographer actually been at the party? Ewan definitely wasn't responsible. He'd been too busy with the guests and the Pimm's. That's right. The tennis had been on and he'd been in and out of the lounge to check on the score. Paulette didn't take any snaps and Lily was sure Julie Medlocke hadn't. She'd spent the whole day trying to corral the twins.

Which neighbours had been there? Mrs Unwin, the elderly lady who lived opposite, had sat in her chair and refused everything but a cup of tea. She'd been in a wheelchair even then. Arthritis in her legs. She hadn't had a camera.

Why not just replicate Lily's photos of Maisie? This was a different image that had been deliberately included. Was it an illustration of just how long she'd been watched? A cold current trickled upwards from the nape of her neck. Lily turned more of the pages. The following pictures were, again, duplicates of hers. No subtle shift of angle in any of them.

Lily took the second album down and opened it. Filling her chest, she rapidly flicked through it. Maisie sitting in her highchair in the kitchen; Maisie asleep with Ewan in bed; Maisie stroking Mr Gingerbread; Maisie sitting naked in the kitchen sink. She reached the final pages depicting Maisie's second Christmas. Lily immediately acknowledged how one of the photos differed from the ones she'd taken.

They'd been at the German Christmas market and Ewan had wanted a photo of Maisie on Santa's lap. Lily hadn't been sure. She'd only been a year and a half but Ewan had said it would be great to show her the snap when she was old enough to know who he was. That maybe she wouldn't be nervous of sitting on his lap if they could show her she'd already done it. But Lily had panicked when he'd lifted Maisie from her and handed her over to a complete stranger in a costume. She'd taken the photo as quickly as she could and been relieved to get her daughter back.

But here she was in shot again, pointing her camera at Maisie being held gingerly by Santa while a beaming Ewan stood off to the side. She was positive nobody else had been with them. Somebody had taken this photo the same time as her. They must have been following them as they wheeled Maisie through the market. How many occasions had they been monitored and photographed and been completely oblivious to their watcher's presence?

Lily's arms trembled but it wasn't anything to do with the weight of the album. She could see the anxiety in her expression and remembered how she desperately wanted to snap the picture and have Maisie returned. If only she'd noticed who was standing on her left-hand side . . .

Lily's eyes were drawn to the area behind Ewan. It was the outside of Santa's workshop and there was a plastic window of toys behind him. She squinted at the reflection in the Perspex pane and could vaguely make out the crowd that the photographer would have been amongst. How close had they been standing?

Lily peeled the plastic page off the photo so she could study the reflection more closely. But there was no detail and all she could make out was the dark outlines of people's heads she assumed were other parents waiting in line.

'I want to go to bed now,' Maisie stated.

Lily looked up from the album. Her daughter was stacking pillows.

'It's not even lunchtime.' She closed it but took it to the mattress with her.

'I know. But maybe if we both go to sleep, we'll wake up back at home.'

Lily got on the bed beside her. 'I really wish that would happen too.'

Maisie lay down on the pillows, pulled the duvet over herself and shut her eyes tight.

'But it might not.'

'We have to try though.'

Lily put her hand on her cheek. It was cold. 'We'll try later.'

'I want to go now. I don't want to be here any longer.'

'Nor do I. But you're not sleepy. You won't drop off yet.'

'I will. And if we can fall asleep at home and wake up here it might work the other way around.'

Lily wanted to believe that. But having just realised how

long her life had been under scrutiny she was positive that the years that had led to this moment meant that the place they found themselves in was to be their home for longer than either of them wanted. She got under the duvet as well and pressed her body to her daughter's.

'Just fall asleep,' Maisie said without opening her eyes. 'You'll see.'

'OK. Let's try.' But she wasn't about to let her guard down. She gripped the knife through her robe pocket.

Maisie started making false snoring noises.

Lily's position allowed her to keep an eye on the camera over the door. She slid her phone out of her pocket and placed it gently on top of the duvet cover. No reception and the app showed all the security cameras at home were still black. What was he doing there, if he was actually there? They still had no choice but to wait for his call.

Could she cover the cameras while they tried to escape? But escape how? Whoever he was, he'd had time to second guess every move she'd make.

'You're not trying.' Maisie had her eyes open again.

'I will. I promise.' Lily looked around for the impostor cat. Was it in the room with them?

'Shut them tight.' Maisie put her cold fingers against Lily's eyelids.

'OK, OK.' Lily closed hers. After a few moments she opened them again, but Maisie was watching her.

'Go to sleep.' Her daughter frowned hard.

Lily obeyed.

She listened to her daughter's breathing and the faraway

sound of the wind blowing through the upper floors of the building and tried to identify any other noises behind it. Maybe somebody was only feet away from them, just the other side of the wall.

'Keep them closed.' Maisie sounded as if she really was about to drop off.

'OK.' Lily squeezed her eyelashes. Was he watching them now? Lily decided to give them ten minutes, let Maisie realise for herself that they weren't about to wake up safe at home. It would be a tough lesson, but she would be waiting to comfort her.

They had to eat, had to keep themselves healthy like he'd requested. But she wanted him to be in no doubt she'd do anything to defend Maisie. Lily sincerely hoped he saw her pocket the knife and that he knew she was deadly serious about using it. If he tried to get inside, he'd know that for sure.

Chapter 20

Maisie fell properly asleep and Lily watched her oblivious face, dreading the moment she opened her eyes again.

Less than five minutes later she did. She fixed her gaze on her mother and then looked around them. The expectation drained out of her expression as she acknowledged they were still in the same room.

'You OK?'

Anger registered on her daughter's face. 'Did you fall asleep?'

'Yes, I've just woken up,' she lied.

'Promise?' Maisie asked sceptically.

Lily was about to answer but her mouth froze.

A soft tapping sound.

'We have to try again—' Maisie insisted.

'Ssshhh.' Lily raised her head from the pillow and held up her hand.

'What is it?'

'Quiet.'

Maisie lifted her head from her pillow too. 'I can't hear anything.'

'Listen.' Lily waited. Her circulation loud in her head. Was that what she'd heard? There was nothing now.

But a few seconds later it came again. A soft tapping noise. Six in a row.

'I can hear it too.' Maisie sat up.

Where was it coming from? Lily put her fingers on her daughter's arm to restrain her. Was it in the room?

More taps. And they didn't sound like they were against any of the walls around them.

'It's out there,' Maisie whispered and pointed to the sealed door that led into the hallway.

Was somebody trying to get their attention? Was somebody already inside? 'Stay here,' Lily whispered too.

Maisie shook her head exaggeratedly. 'I'm coming.'

'Don't move from this bed.' Lily swung her legs off it and placed her socked feet on the carpeted floor.

Maisie did so as well, dropping silently onto her side.

'Get back on there. I won't tell you twice,' Lily hissed.

More tapping turned both their heads to the door.

'I'm going to look.' She slid her hand in her pocket and felt the blade of the paring knife.

Maisie looked terrified. 'Don't go.'

'I have to.'

Maisie suddenly ran from her side of the bed to Lily's and clutched her leg. 'Stay here.'

Lily put her palm on her warm head. 'I'm just going to take a peek and then I'm coming right back.'

'It's the scary man.'

She could feel her daughter trembling against her. 'I won't be long.'

Maisie shook her head once.

'I promise I'll come back.' But what if he was waiting for her out there? What if he attacked her or subdued her? Maisie would be left alone.

Tap, tap.

Both their attention shifted to the door again.

Lily figured that if he'd really wanted to harm them, he could have done so very easily when he'd relocated them unconscious to their prison. But she still wondered if there was just one man behind their ordeal. Was there another watching them who was getting bored and now thought he'd have some fun tormenting them, or was this all part of the plan?

Maisie dug her nails into Lily's leg.

Tap.

Was the sound metallic? Lily bent to Maisie. 'You can walk me to the door, but when I go through it, you're to hide under the bed.'

Maisie looked as if she were in pain, her mouth askew as tears glistened in her eyes.

'Do it. Then count to twenty in your head. When you get to twenty, I'll be back again.'

Tap, tap, tap, tap.

Lily stood abruptly, so Maisie would have to let go, and then took four paces so she was standing in front of the door. She turned back to Maisie who was clutching her hands. She could tell her daughter was about to release a sob. She put her finger to her lips. 'Don't.'

Maisie's chest pumped but she kept her lips sealed.

'Twenty seconds.' Lily put her fingers on the handle. She didn't want to delay the moment any longer. She turned the handle, opened the door just wide enough for her body and slipped through.

She looked first to the sealed front and lounge doors. Nobody there. Her attention darted the other way to the open kitchen door. No sign of anyone there either. At least, not that she could see from her vantage point. Maisie was peering at the crack. She pushed the door quickly shut behind her. 'Hide.' She waited. Nothing. 'Maisie,' she whispered sharply.

Maisie's soft footfalls headed back to the bed.

Lily returned her attention to the open kitchen doorway, but she didn't take another step forward. She waited, body pumping, and took out the knife.

The irregular tapping came again a few moments later. It was definitely coming from the kitchen. Lily edged along the hallway and paused at the threshold.

The kitchen was empty. She released half a breath. Had it been the water pipes? She didn't move from her position at the doorway. Maybe this was a test and their reactions were being monitored. She imagined her daughter under the bed, counting. She'd reach twenty soon.

Tap, tap, tap, tap, tap.

Lily's eyes shot to the window. Was that coming from outside? She crossed the floor to the kitchen sink and looked through the dirty pane at the rubble below.

Her pupils darted about the bricks and twisted metal until they located a movement to the right-hand side of it.

Somebody was standing there.

Chapter 21

The tanned, male figure was wearing a dark blue baseball cap, a dirty white shirt rolled up at the sleeves, a pair of tight black jeans and white trainers. He was standing beneath a stack of rusted white goods and was attempting to extract a tall freezer from beneath the two washing machines above it. He'd managed to tip the freezer forward so half of its top was exposed but the weight above was holding it in place. He had a sledgehammer in his hand and was trying to bash the washing machine restraining it back far enough so he could pull it out.

Lily immediately started banging on the window. 'Help! Help!'

But her fists only made dull thuds on the reinforced glass.

She beat it harder. 'Up here! Help!'

The figure couldn't hear. He swung the sledgehammer again at the washing machine and its blows drowned out hers.

'Who's there?'

Lily swung round to find Maisie standing behind her. 'I told you to stay in the bedroom.' But it didn't matter now. She rushed to the tool drawer and grabbed the hammer.

Maisie climbed up onto the sink. 'Who are you shouting at?' But then she spotted him. 'Hey!' She pounded her small fist on the window.

'Stand clear of the glass.' Lily hefted the hammer.

Maisie shifted herself back.

'Right back.'

Maisie pressed herself up against the wall to the right of the sink.

Lily could see the figure was still swinging his sledgehammer.

Tap, tap, tap, tap. Its heavy percussion on the housing of the washing machine barely filtered through to them.

The figure stopped to catch his breath, and Lily immediately swung her hammer at the pane. It struck the window with a solid 'thunk' and it resonated painfully in her arm.

The figure didn't turn. He still hadn't heard. He took off his baseball cap to reveal a shaved head and ran his palm over his scalp.

Lily could make out his features. He looked to be in his mid-twenties and had a long beard dangling off his chin.

Maisie examined the vague white graze the hammerhead had left on the thick glass. 'Do it again!'

The figure put his baseball cap back on.

Lily swung the hammer. Once, twice, three times. Each smash trembling her whole frame but only making a damp impact against the window.

Maisie watched the figure. 'He still hasn't heard.'

Lily ignored the pain shooting through her shoulders and squinted at the man below. He dropped the sledgehammer and gripped the top edge of the freezer with both hands. His body jerked as he tried to yank the frame from under the washing machines.

'Get down from there.' Lily held out her hand and helped Maisie off the draining board.

'Hurry!' Maisie stood behind her.

Lily didn't grip the handle of the hammer so tightly but swung her arm harder at the window.

The hammerhead hit it with more force but bounced back at her. Another white dimple was left in the pane.

The figure struggled with the freezer, still oblivious.

'Look . . .' Lily swung the hammer. '. . . up!'

She seized the handle in both hands and repeatedly buffeted the steel head against the middle of the window.

The figure froze.

Lily stopped. Her whole frame trembling.

The man turned in the direction of their building.

He might only look up briefly and, in that split second, Lily had to make sure he saw her. She went to the window and pulled her knees up onto the draining board. She frantically waved her arms. 'Up here!'

But his gaze was directed along the ground. His head scanned the rubble from left to right.

Lily furiously pummelled the glass. 'Just look up!'

But the peak of his baseball cap was between them. He'd have to remove it or tilt his head up to see her.

Maisie was beside her; she had a metallic mixing spoon that she'd taken from the utensils pot and joined in.

The figure's head turned from side to side as if he was trying to pinpoint the noise.

'Look up, look up!' Lily's arm was a blur. It felt like her wrist was about to break.

The figure backed away from the freezer.

'Where's he going?' Maisie rapped the spoon harder.

Lily didn't answer. It looked like they'd spooked him.

'Don't go!' Maisie screeched.

The figure scuttled back down the pile of bricks and hesitated at the bottom.

Lily and Maisie shouted and assailed the pane but, after his head darted around a few times, the figure headed off to their right.

'He's leaving!' Maisie sounded hysterical.

The figure picked up his pace.

Lily wondered if he was trespassing. Did he think he was being driven off?

He quickly dodged his way through the debris and kept his head low.

'Help us, please!' Maisie yelled.

Lily could hear the tremor of desperation in her daughter's voice. Her arm ached and her buzzing fingers could hardly grip the hammer.

But they both only stopped battering the glass when he'd completely disappeared from sight.

Chapter 22

'He heard us,' Maisie said, crestfallen.

Lily's knees and shins ached against the draining board as she pressed her forehead to the cold window and briefly closed her eyes.

'Has he gone forever?'

Lily exhaled. 'Maybe not.'

'Why did he run away?'

'Perhaps he wasn't meant to be here. I think he was trying to steal that freezer.' Lily straightened. 'So he might try and come back for it.'

Maisie brightened at that. 'So . . . should I watch out the window, like before?'

Lily nodded and put her hand on Maisie's shoulder. 'That's a great idea.' But even if he did come back would their attempts to attract his attention send him scuttling away again?

They both waited silently at the pane but after fifteen minutes there was still no sign of him.

Lily turned to the camera. Their captor knew what had happened. Would he ensure it didn't again? She wondered if he might try to intercept the trespasser. How secure was the site and would other scavengers come? If they did, how could they possibly alert them to their presence? The glass of the window was sealed and unbreakable. They'd have to rely on them looking up and spotting them at the pane and that was highly unlikely. Again she speculated about exactly where the building was. In London or were they on the other side of the country?

'I'll stay here all night tonight and keep watch while you get some sleep,' Maisie offered.

Lily felt a surge of affection for her daughter. 'You don't need to do that.'

'I want to.' She nodded solemnly.

'There'll be little point. There's no lights out there. You won't be able to see anyone in the dark.'

Maisie turned back to the barren site to confirm it. 'So, it'll be black out there?' There was trepidation in her voice.

'But we'll be safely locked away up here.'

Maisie nodded but didn't seem convinced.

'If we can't get out, nobody can get in.'

Maisie nodded again.

Lily could tell from her frown that her brain was turning over. 'What are you thinking?'

Maisie's features set in determination. 'We should leave this light on. All night.' She pointed to the orange shade above her head.

Lily looked up at it. 'Yes.' Her daughter was right. She climbed down, crossed the tiles and switched it on.

'That way, people will see us. If we hear the noise again, we can wave out of the bright window.'

'That's a very good idea.' It was. Lily looked to the building opposite. It would block anyone from seeing the bulb on from a distance. She didn't want to point that out to Maisie. But if anyone did come back to help themselves to what was buried in the rubble, they'd have to wonder why there was one solitary light glowing in a derelict housing block.

'We should never ever switch it off.'

'Absolutely.'

'It will be like a star.'

Lily could see how excited Maisie was becoming. 'A star so people can find us.'

'Yes.'

Lily didn't want to deflate the moment. Would the intruder really allow them to use the light to their advantage?

'Do you know that code? You know, that sailors use?'

'Morse code?' But Lily didn't. She shook her head. 'But we can still flash the light if we see anyone.'

'Somebody will have to come when they see it.'

An idea occurred to Lily and she went to the drawer below where she kept the tools and yanked it open. It was more ordered than hers, but the disparate contents were unsettlingly familiar.

Maisie didn't budge from her position. 'What are you doing?'

Lily scrabbled through the packets of screws and wall plugs, dusters and sponges and found two new long-life bulbs that would fit. 'If it goes out, we can change the bulbs; these will last for months.' She walked into the hallway and confirmed the one there was the same. 'We can use the bulbs from the other lights too. Even if we just keep this one going.'

Maisie grinned and nodded, pleased to have thought of it first.

It was something to cling to. But again, Lily assumed their captor wouldn't have overlooked it. Did it matter if they had enough bulbs to keep the light going?

As if to negate the hope, the light went out.

Chapter 23

Lily heard the breath catch in Maisie's chest then walked to the wall switch and flicked it up and down and up again. Nothing.

'Is he listening to us?' Maisie whispered in alarm.

It was the first time it had occurred to Lily. She'd assumed that, because everything else in their prison was identical to what they had at home, the cameras were the same as hers too. They only recorded images and not sound. She looked up at the one over the kitchen door. It was exactly like hers but maybe there were microphones hidden elsewhere. Her eyes shifted to the air vent in the wall above the cooker. Just like in her real kitchen. Was one planted there? Lily grabbed one of the chairs from under the kitchen dining table.

'What is it?'

Lily didn't reply but positioned the chair in front of the cooker, stood on it and peered through the thin slats of the metal grid. They were at an angle, so it was impossible to see through to the darkness the other side. Then she considered that maybe there was no reason to conceal a microphone.

Perhaps someone was actually hiding there listening in on their conversation.

She got down from her perch, opened the tool drawer and took out a dumpy Phillips screwdriver. It had the same green handle as her trusty one, but there was no ingrained dirt on it. She got back on the chair and quickly removed the four screws holding the grill to the wall.

Maisie clambered down from the draining board and held the back of the chair Lily was standing on. 'Careful you don't fall.'

'That's it. Hold me steady.' Lily took out the final screw and then gripped the edges of the plate. It had been fixed so firmly to the wall that, when it came away, she could see the indentation it had made. But there was nothing behind it. No microphone, no fan, no recess. Just plaster wall.

'What have you found?'

Lily looked down at her daughter's face squinting hopefully up at her. 'Nothing.' She got down, stamped the pedal bin and dropped the plate into it. She looked around at the other walls. Was the cooker fan the only ventilation in the room? She couldn't see any in evidence. The kitchen window was sealed and so was the cat flap. The room was just a façade and a dangerous one. Again, she considered what would happen if there were a fire. Would they die of smoke inhalation? Would their captor release them?

The phone buzzed in her back pocket.

Lily fumbled it out and answered.

'He's gone,' the male voice said bluntly.

'Who?'

'If you see anyone else, I don't want a repeat of that performance.'

So, the trespasser had clearly been unexpected. 'Please, I'm ready to do whatever it is you want.'

'Are you?' The voice at the other end snapped back. 'Really?'

Lily moved a step closer to the wall by the cooker. 'Just tell me what it is.' Could she hear his voice the other side of the wall as well as in her ear?

'The only time you can use the light in the kitchen is if you drop the blind.' He lowered his voice.

Lily edged closer to the wall. Was he standing only feet away?

'Understand?'

'Yes.'

'Then let's have a little practice.'

Lily sighed and crossed to the kitchen window.

'That's it. Just tug the rope.'

She untied the hessian blind and allowed it to fall into place.

'Good. It has blackout backing. I'd like you to impress upon your daughter how vital it is she doesn't lift that blind when the light's on.'

'I will.'

'Try the switch now.'

She went to it and flicked it down.

The light came on and buzzed overhead.

'If you forget to pull down the blind, just once, then I remove privileges.'

The light went out again.

'Not just the lights but your gas, your water, your heating. I control it all. Do you understand?'

She nodded.

The light came on again.

'Understand?'

'You can see me nod through the camera.'

'I need to hear you say it.'

'Why over the phone? You can hear me anyway. Where are the microphones?'

'Let's just agree that I see and hear everything. But I still need you to say it.'

'I understand.'

'I'm afraid I still have to remove privileges though.'

'What for?' Lily's fingers tightened on the handset. 'You didn't tell us about the blind.'

'True but you attempted to attract the attention of our visitor.' He remained silent as he let her take this in.

She wondered if he'd caught the trespasser. Had he been waiting for him as he'd hurried away from the rubble? 'I'm sorry.'

'This is where I say I understand. You want to get out of there. You did what you thought was necessary. But you had to know that the action you took was contrary to the way I expect you to behave.'

'What is he saying?' Maisie hissed up at her.

'Just tell me what you want me to do.'

'I have done, and I can't stress how much we both need Maisie to cooperate when it comes to the blind.'

'I'll tell her.'

'Good. Replace the grill where you found it and we'll overlook that. But privileges will still have to be lost for your conduct.'

Lily looked up at the glowing light and anticipated it going out again.

It remained on.

'What privileges?'

'Don't expect there to be many other visitors, but if anyone else does come then you're both to ignore them.'

'I understand,' she said before she was asked. Perhaps the trespasser had escaped. 'Which privileges are you taking away?'

He hung up.

Chapter 24

'Speak to me!' Lily hit the number that had just called her and listened. It rang.

And as it did, she took a few paces back towards the cooker. Could she hear a phone in the room next door?

Nothing. She strode into the hall and straight into her bedroom. No sound from there either. He was probably watching her via the camera and knew exactly what she was doing.

Maisie followed her in. 'What did he say?'

'Ssshhh.' Lily waited a few moments longer and strained her ears. No muffled ringing. Perhaps he had his phone on silent mode though. The line was cut. When she tried again there was no dial tone. He was blocking the signal again. She hung up and sat on the bed so she was facing Maisie. 'Listen, that was a really great idea about leaving the light on, but we're not allowed to do it.'

Maisie nodded forlornly. 'Because he can turn it on and off?'

'Yes, but more important than that, we have to put the blind down before we can switch it on.'

'Was he angry?'

'Yes, he was. And he said that once the blind is down it has to stay down.'

'We can't even lift it if we hear someone?'

Lily shook her head emphatically. '*Especially* if we hear someone.'

'OK.' Maisie's eyes shifted left.

'Do you understand?' Lily didn't like using the same words as he had.

Maisie nodded.

'I need you to promise.'

'OK.' Her gaze eventually returned to Lily's. 'I promise.'

'We have to do everything we're told.' She hoped he was listening to this conversation. 'If we do, the sooner we can get out of here.'

'Is that what he said?' Maisie's deep blue eyes were full of hope.

'Yes.' Lily didn't want to lie to her but knew she had to give her every reason to behave. She wondered if he was enjoying watching her deceit. This was a conversation for the camera now, though, and she had to silence her questions. 'He knows wrong from right.'

'But if he knows that, why has he locked us in here?'

Lily considered how to respond. 'He'll have his reasons. And I'm sure, when he's ready, he'll tell us what they are. In the meantime, we have to show him that we're thankful for him looking after us and keeping us safe while we're here.' Lily wondered if he saw through this. Or was someone capable of doing what he had so delusional that it was exactly what he wanted to hear?

Maisie frowned. 'But he shouldn't have taken us away from home.'

Lily gripped Maisie's wrists where they hung at her sides and gently squeezed. 'We're here now though, but I don't believe he'll let us come to any harm.'

'Why?' Maisie asked.

'Because we've done nothing wrong. How old are you on your next birthday?'

Maisie looked mortified. 'You know that.'

'Just remind me.'

'Six.'

'But that's a long way away. You're still five for a while yet.' She had to stress to him just how young Maisie was. 'And where do you want to go for your sixth birthday, when it comes?'

'I want to go to Ireland,' Maisie replied, slightly irked that she was being asked to prompt Lily after all the conversations they'd had about it.

Lily had thought that, by now, Maisie would be craving the usual trip to Florida and Disney World, but she didn't appear interested. 'And why d'you want to go there?' But she already knew.

'To see the Giant's Causeway.'

'Yes. There's so much you want to see. I want to travel with you to those places too.'

Maisie fixed her with confusion.

'We have to keep looking forward to it. There's so much we have to do.'

'I'm really hungry now.' Maisie turned towards the doorway.

But Lily held her firmly. 'Remember what we've been told about the blind.'

'I will.' She tried to pull her right wrist from Lily's palm.

'He makes all the rules. We stick to them and he looks after us.'

'I know. I need something to eat.' Maisie struggled free.

'OK.' Lily watched Maisie disappear through the door. 'I'll come and make something for you now.' She got up off the bed and didn't acknowledge the camera as she followed her daughter back to the kitchen.

'He's starving.' Maisie tipped some more cat biscuits into the bowl.

'That's enough.' Lily took the box from her.

They both watched the cat noisily chomping his way through the food that Lily had just emptied out of a tin.

Lily caught Maisie's scowl. 'What shall we call him?'

'Cat.' Maisie said flatly.

Her daughter was clearly uncomfortable with the lean replacement pet and so was she. 'At least he's fed now. What about you now? How about some fishfingers?'

Maisie nodded and Lily got some out of the freezer and examined the seal. 'Come and sit at the table.' Lily didn't want her anywhere near the blind.

'They're not ready yet.'

'Just come and sit at the table.'

Maisie sighed and slid out her chair.

Lily had replaced the vent plate and slid her chair back

under the table. She put the fishfingers under the grill and was relieved when the gas hissed as she turned it on.

She cooked them thoroughly and put them on a plate on her side of the table.

'I'll get ketchup.' Maisie was about to leave the table.

'No ketchup.' Lily didn't trust that.

'Why not?'

'Just eat them on their own. No more talking.'

Maisie pouted and reached out to take one.

Lily dragged the plate back further from her reach and sat. 'I'll try one first.'

'You don't like fishfingers.'

'I do.' She didn't. But she knew what they were meant to taste like. She examined the fishfinger, blew on it and held it to her lips.

Maisie waited.

She doubted it was poisoned. Rules had been set out for the days ahead. But she wasn't about to trust anything he said. Lily took a small bite off the end of the fishfinger and tentatively tasted it. It was bland stodge. Could it really have been laced with something? She chewed the morsel, hesitated and then swallowed.

Chapter 25

Maisie being dragged away from Lily was like the worst, most vividly detailed tableau. Lily's fingers clasping the shoulder of her daughter's tee shirt, the cotton stretched, Maisie's expression of shock and pain as she was yanked from her mother's grip.

'Let her go!' he growled through his teeth. His fingers were locked tight around Maisie's arm and briefly her daughter's feet lifted from the floor. 'Maisie, come with me!' He angled his body towards the door.

It had become a tug of war.

The scream Maisie emitted branded the moment on Lily's brain. The cry not just a sound of alarm and pain, but of permanent injury. Maisie's expression wasn't just frightened. There was a new confusion there; she was part of a moment she couldn't comprehend.

But Lily could see that he was unperturbed. Taking Maisie was his only agenda, whatever damage it caused. She maintained her grip on Maisie's other arm. She wouldn't allow him to take her. Not now. Not ever.

But then something worse happened. The sound that

silenced the struggle. The low click as Maisie's arm had been pulled on too hard.

They both froze then, knowing it had gone too far.

Ewan released Maisie's hand as if she'd given him an electric shock. But more like he didn't want to be blamed for what had just happened.

It was that expression that made Lily's mind up about removing Ewan's right to be Maisie's father. When things became ugly, when the courts entered the picture, Lily told herself she should picture that exact moment. But she never had to because that sound and Maisie's expression never left her.

All the anger left Ewan's face in an instant and he became a frightened child too. He retreated from them both, distancing himself so nothing that had transpired could possibly be anything to do with him.

Maisie hadn't cried. She'd been suspended in that moment when her parents had almost broken her. She didn't speak until the following day. A week later Maisie's therapy with Doctor Hart began.

Lily opened her eyes. She was staring at the mauve wall beside her bed. Momentarily she'd forgotten her situation and closed her eyelids against the sickening memory. But the present pushed it out. There was a new threat to deal with. The previous day's assault on the window still ached in her arms.

Her back was cold. Maisie. She turned quickly to find the space in the mattress next to her was empty.

Her daughter's half of the duvet had been thrown back.

'Maisie?' She immediately swung her legs out of bed but had to pause. The room rocked before her. Lily didn't wait for it to settle before staggering across the carpet to the door. 'Maisie, answer me!'

No response.

Lily stumbled across the hallway to Maisie's open room door. Her bed was still made. When exhaustion had overtaken her Lily had settled her into her double bed and eventually fallen asleep beside her.

She'd put the hammer and knife under her pillow, fought drowsiness as long as she could. What time had that been? What time was it now? She was still wearing her nightwear over her clothes and pulled the phone out of her robe and squinted blearily at the screen.

06:23

'Maisie!' She checked the bathroom. Empty. Lily dizzily zigzagged down the hallway. It was how she'd felt when she'd woken in her prison the morning before. Only worse. She entered the kitchen, breath awaiting its release from her chest. No Maisie. 'Maisie, answer me!'

Lily's heart punched her ribcage as she waited. But she could only hear the low howl of wind blowing through the floors above her. She swung to the camera over the door. 'Give her back to me!'

I'm afraid I still have to remove privileges though.

When had he taken her? How had he? Lily's mind raced and the room swung. He'd drugged her.

She found the number he'd contacted her on and dialled.

It rang four times before it was answered.

'The person you are calling is unavailable at the moment. Please leave a message after the tone,' the recorded female voice said.

Lily waited for it to beep and looked up at the camera, concentrating, keeping her tone level. 'Please, please, please, give her back.' She felt her legs shudder and wobble. 'I don't care what you do to me. Please, don't harm her. I'll do anything you want. Anything. Don't touch her, please.' She continued to plead, her words becoming a blur, spittle flecking the mouthpiece.

She eventually heard another beep.

'If you wish to re-record the message press one.'

He was torturing her. She stared unblinking at the camera. 'I know you can hear me. This is punishment enough. You've made your point. I won't touch the window again. Just give her back to me!' She wanted to fall to her knees. Wanted to curl up on the floor. Whatever was in her system spun the kitchen around her. But she remained upright, her body trembling and swaying.

She waited for a reaction, anticipating the phone buzzing in her hand. But the only sound was the rushing in her head. 'Bastard!' She hurled the phone at the camera, but it missed and struck the top of the door frame and landed on the kitchen tiles with a crack.

Lily ran to where it lay and quickly picked it up. The screen was fractured but the display was still illuminated. There was no dial tone. He'd jammed the signal again. Or had she broken it? Who could she call anyway? Nobody could help her. She looked directly up at the lens, her chest pumping as she fought for breath. 'I'm sorry, I'm sorry.' She squeezed her eyes shut but the room spun faster.

You have to calm down.

But her breathing became more erratic. Where was Maisie? Who was she with? She couldn't begin to imagine how frightened she would be. 'Ewan, if this is you, let her come back to me.' A tear trickled from her left eye. 'You can do anything you want to me but just let me know she's all right.'

She dropped. Fell onto her knees beneath the camera. Her strength was gone. Whether it was the drug or the feeling of total powerlessness she didn't know. At that moment, she felt everything drain out of her.

Lily screwed her eyes shut, let the tears drop onto the tiles and wished she could wake from this nightmare back to the one she'd already been inhabiting.

Chapter 26

When Lily got up off the tiles, she looked at her cracked phone.

06:47

It felt like a couple of hours had passed. Her accelerated thoughts had conceived of every horrible scenario she could do nothing about. She wiped the moisture from her eyes with the back of her hand and sniffed harshly. She had to pull herself together.

She marched to the front door and thumped it. 'Let me out of here! Let me see her now!' Her arms still ached from yesterday, but she beat on the panel harder. 'Open it!' She didn't wait for a response, just kept pounding, felt the solid pain in her fists and shoulders. She was punishing herself.

Lily stopped when she felt light-headed and stumbled back a few paces from the door. The veins beat in her head, but she didn't want them to slow down, didn't want to let the silence back in. Had Maisie been taken away from the building? Could she be imprisoned in a floor above or below or in a room next door?

'Maisie!' She yelled as hard as she could. 'I'm here, sweetie! Don't worry! I'm right here!'

Her words reverberated around the rooms of her empty prison.

Images popped into her mind. Unbidden pictures of where she could be. Lily couldn't shake the clip of the intruder in the garden wearing a mask of her daughter's face.

She tried the phone again. No dial tone. Please God he was making a point about her obedience in the future. Or was this her ultimate punishment? She couldn't swallow.

She slid her back down the lounge door, closed her eyes and gritted her teeth against a feeling of hopelessness so overwhelming she thought she might pass out. 'I've learnt my lesson.' She nodded for the camera. 'She's just a child. Don't use her to—' The words died in her throat.

She tried to inhale and breathe out, but the idea of being unable to reach her daughter when she would be so obviously petrified kept jump-starting her heartbeat.

Lily could feel his eyes on her. How could he watch this? She wondered if he'd always planned this moment, irrespective of her behaviour. She wanted to trash her prison. Smash up every single item that he'd painstakingly replicated. But she couldn't afford to endanger Maisie any more than she was. All she could do was plead.

'Please, let her go.' She repeated the words, her eyes still closed.

Lily remained against the door for twenty minutes saying the same over and over. Then the phone buzzed in her hand. Sitting bolt upright, she immediately answered. 'Hello?'

There was nobody the other end. She examined the display. A message had arrived. But when she opened the text there were no words.

It was a dark photo image.

Lily could see that it was Maisie's face. At least, one half of it. The camera had been held very close to her so only her eye, her nose and her top lip were in shot. Her eyelid was closed.

Her fingers went to her mouth and her palm blocked her exclamation. The hallway canted but it was nothing to do with what she'd been drugged with.

Had the camera caught Maisie mid blink? Was she asleep? Had she been drugged too and was unconscious? She'd rather that be the case than think of her daughter aware of the situation she was in and knowing that her mother couldn't help her.

Lily tried to repel the question that begged to be asked. Her fingers shook as she wiped at her tears and tried to focus.

The phone buzzed again. A text message this time.

Lily quickly opened it.

More images to follow. If you behave.

Chapter 27

Several hours passed and Lily didn't budge from her position at the lounge door. She'd considered moving to the blind spot under the kitchen doorway so her captor couldn't watch her on either of the cameras, but figured he wanted to observe her mental anguish. She wouldn't deprive him of that, not if it meant he might return Maisie to her.

Lily's fingers gripped the phone tight, her knuckles white and arms still painful from the impacts on the door. Her legs jumped and twitched, the idea that her daughter could be getting further away from her burning in her stomach and triggering the spasms while she kept telling herself to remain calm and that all she could do was wait.

She continued to count the seconds of each minute and anticipated another image arriving, willing the phone to buzz but not wanting it to either.

Her dizziness had passed but that made her reality seem even more raw. How could somebody detest her so much that they'd want to put her through this? Could this really be Ewan? Would she rather that be the case than consider it could be a stranger? Lily knew Ewan could never harm Maisie. Never again. That was something she could cling to. Ewan had wanted a second child. They'd been trying for one when everything had fallen apart.

Could the man on the phone really be in her ex-husband's employ? Maybe what she'd seen in his eyes the very last time she'd spoken to him should have been a warning.

She'd been taking Maisie to swimming on a Saturday morning and Ewan had been standing on the other side of the road. At first, Lily had scarcely recognised him. Had thought he was a homeless man. He'd lost a lot of weight and had grown a beard. He'd never had a full-grown beard before. His normally neatly cut auburn hair had grown down over his ears and hung in his eyes. He was wearing his old army fatigue jacket, jeans and boots.

He'd held up his hands as soon as he'd known she'd recognised him.

'You're not allowed to be here.' Not within a mile of them.

He started crossing the road. 'Please. It's just us now.'

Lily turned back to the front door and Maisie was standing frozen on the step, her expression pensive.

'Hey, Twinkles. How have you been?'

When Lily returned her attention to Ewan he was quickly crossing the road. 'Wait,' she said firmly to him. But Lily didn't want to spark an argument in front of Maisie.

Ewan met her eye as he reached their side and there was pleading there. 'Please, just a minute.'

What could she do? But why was he breaking the terms of his restraining order?

'I just needed to see how you were doing.' His gaze was on Maisie again.

'I'm OK.' She remained in front of the door.

He opened his arms, but she didn't move. 'Come on then.'

Maisie looked to Lily and she nodded that it was OK.

She went to him and he embraced her and kissed her cheek.

Lily noted that Maisie remained stiff but then returned the hug. It had only been four months since the incident. Maisie had been examined by the doctor immediately afterwards and he'd said she'd only pulled the muscle in her shoulder. Lily had told Ewan to stay away from them, that he should find somewhere else to stay until she was ready to talk to him. He'd obeyed, but had phoned every day to find out how Maisie was.

He'd spoken to Maisie and his daughter's attitude towards him had markedly changed. It was clear to Lily that she was frightened of him. Maisie never got to see him coming in drunk from work, but as soon as it had impacted on her safety Lily knew she couldn't make excuses for him. She'd seen it happen with her friend. Julie Medlocke had given her ex so many chances and told Lily she regretted not picking up the phone to her solicitor three years earlier.

'Where are you two going?' Ewan asked Maisie breezily.

'Splash Zone,' Maisie said to her shoes.

'Cool. Do you want me to come?'

What was he doing?

Maisie turned to Lily and there was panic in her eyes.

Ewan caught it. 'Maybe next time.'

Even though Lily was aghast at what he was trying to do

she could see how mortified he was by how Maisie had reacted. 'Why don't you get in the car. I'll just talk to Daddy for a minute and then we'll get going.'

Maisie nodded, scurried past Ewan without looking at him and got in the back.

Lily closed the door and moved away from the car.

Ewan followed and was looking at the pavement.

Lily had been about to placate him, was going to tell him that it would take time for Maisie to trust him again. At that point she'd believed her daughter would. She knew they were over but she wanted Ewan to be part of Maisie's life, however they negotiated that.

But when Ewan looked up at her there was only undiluted enmity in his gaze. 'You've turned her against me then,' he stated with finality.

'No.' But his contemplation of her was just so ugly. 'No. She just needs time.' She wanted to step away from him.

'More time with you? Yeah, I can see why you'd say that.'

'Listen . . .' He'd caught Lily off-guard. It was what he'd planned. 'I just need her to feel secure before I ask her to be part of this again.'

'Secure? Are you saying I'm a danger to my own daughter?'

'No.' But she paused before she answered.

He shook his head at her in disgust, hooded his eyes as if he couldn't look at her. 'And what *is* "this"?'

Lily darted her eyes to the car. Maisie was looking out at them through the back window. 'You're upsetting her again.'

Ewan didn't turn to look at her. 'Don't use her so you don't have to speak to me.'

'What are you talking about?'

'The restraining order. That's not about what happened with Maisie.'

'Isn't it?' Lily raised her voice. She lowered it again. 'So tell me, what is it about, if it's not me having Maisie examined at the hospital.'

'Don't use that either.'

'Did I pull Maisie's arm?'

'Yes, you did. You were pulling on her other arm while I was trying to leave.'

Lily glanced over at Maisie again. 'Look, we can't do this here.'

He shook his head. 'Or anywhere else. That's very convenient for you, isn't it?'

'You have to go.'

He leaned closer to her face. 'And when are we going to talk about the real issue here?'

She could smell the stale alcohol. 'There is only one issue. Our daughter.'

'No, that's what you want it to be. What you want everyone to think it is.'

'And what do you think is more important to me than Maisie's welfare?'

'The life you want. The one you'll have next. With him.'

Lily opened her mouth to reply but the contempt in his eyes dared her to deny it.

Chapter 28

'How stupid d'you think I am, Lil? And take *that* look off your face.'

Lily checked on Maisie. She was still observing their dialogue through the back window. 'We need to have this conversation another time,' she said categorically.

'What's the matter, worried Maisie will hear? You'll have to introduce him to her soon enough so why not now?'

'You're being paranoid and spiteful. I can't talk to you when you're like this.'

'And you always accuse me of not wanting to talk things out.'

'Go home and I'll call you later.'

'So when's he moving in?'

'I'm not even going to qualify that with an answer.'

'Which is an answer in itself.'

'Is that what you really think? That all of this is about Sam Castle?'

'Is it?'

'You're being ridiculous.'

'I think you've been looking for an excuse.'

Lily rounded on him but turned her back to Maisie and kept her voice low. 'This is no excuse. This is our daughter in the hospital because you can't control your temper.'

'I expect that's what you told them. That it was my fault.'

'No, although I should have. Because it *was* your fault. The only reason I didn't is because I know how sickened you would have felt for what you did.'

'Probably as sickened as *you* felt. There were two people in that argument. How does Maisie remember it? Or are you guiding her in that respect?'

Lily closed her eyes briefly and took a breath. 'We need to take a step back.'

'You've already made me do that, remember? One mile to be precise.'

'I have to protect Maisie.'

'From me?' He stabbed a finger into his chest.

'Yes. I can't allow that to happen again . . . ever.' She held his gaze. 'Do you understand? Now turn around and leave. You're upsetting her.'

'And I suppose you'll be using this against me as well.'

'We'll pretend this never happened.'

'Of course you will. I just wanted to see her.' The animosity in his eyes hadn't waned. 'But I suppose you can always discuss this with Sam.'

'There is nothing between us.'

'On Maisie's life? Nothing ever happened?'

Lily's response stalled.

'You're all about telling the truth. How about being honest about that?'

'I'll tell the truth when it matters,' she retorted angrily.

'Oh my god, there it is. You really are going to make it look like my fault. I imagine Sam would advise you to do that.'

'He's got nothing to do with this.'

'Not even a little bit? At the back of your mind are you not thinking about what happens when you've got me off the scene?'

Lily fought back emotions. Did he really think she wanted to remove him, just like that; that what they'd shared for eight years meant nothing to her? How could he really believe that she was so cold and conniving that she was using what he'd done as an excuse to dispense with him? Or was this something he was going to produce in court, whether he believed it or not? He wasn't about to see reason, so she had to diffuse the argument. 'Let's talk on the phone later. When you're calm.'

'Or maybe you're further down the line with Sam than I thought. Maybe you'll be discussing it with him on the phone tonight. It *is* his area of expertise. Friends with benefits . . . and free legal advice.'

'Don't you dare.'

Something in her expression caused Ewan to falter. 'Everything's about *my* behaviour. If you carry on with this, yours is going to be under the spotlight as well remember.'

'So, all of a sudden, I'm a bad parent as well?'

Ewan looked briefly wounded. 'You think I'm a bad parent?'

'No, but lately there have been too many occasions when it looks like you are.'

'You know I'm not.' The ire was back in his glare. 'But you seem hellbent on convincing other people that I am. And I suppose me being here when I shouldn't, because I want to see my daughter, I suppose you can use that too.'

'Ewan,' she cautioned harshly, '. . . go now and I won't mention this. I promise.'

'But Maisie might in passing,' he countered acerbically.

'There's nothing more for us to say. Say goodbye to her.' Lily nodded towards the car.

'And that's really what I'm going to have to do, isn't it?' He turned before she could reply.

Lily watched him walk to the car and open the back door.

'Got to go now. Got your water wings? Good. Stay away from the deep end and stay in until your fingers wrinkle,' he said playfully, as if it were a normal family day.

She marvelled at how quickly he'd changed his demeanour. But he could always do that. They could be in the middle of an intense row and Ewan could switch out of it when Maisie walked into the room. Lily couldn't do it, not in the blink of an eye.

Maisie said something to him that Lily couldn't hear.

'Soon. It'll all be sorted out and then we can do something fun too. Take care.' He leaned in and kissed her.

Lily watched Maisie's arm go around his neck and felt a pang in her throat. Had things been this bad even six months ago? They were still going about their weekly routines as a family then and, outwardly, nobody would have believed that they would be on the cusp of this. How quickly it had all happened, but Lily knew that this was the culmination of something gradual, a build-up of corrosive moments that she could no longer ignore.

Sam Castle had been one of the catalysts. He'd certainly made her consider that she shouldn't be content to put up with behaviour that was only going to get worse. She couldn't honestly tell herself that he hadn't been instrumental in her reassessing her marriage, but she would have taken the action she had when Maisie had been hurt regardless.

Ewan leaned into the car further and said something that Lily couldn't hear. Then he extracted himself, shut the door and walked back across the road without looking back.

Chapter 29

Lily checked the time on her phone. It was just after midday. She scarcely noticed the pain in her buttocks from sitting on the hallway floor for so long. No other images had arrived. A cold sensation crept over her scalp and she freed her seized limbs, awkwardly got up and rushed to the bathroom.

She leaned over the sink and painfully retched, but nothing came out. Lily blinked away the moisture in her eyes, rocked on her socked feet and a cold sweat prickled her forehead.

Don't pass out.

She gripped the edge of the sink and waited for the nausea to pass. She thought about Sam Castle, his quietly intense features and pale green eyes that subtly darted while he briefly considered every response he made. She recalled his warnings to her about Ewan. He knew him of old. They'd been buddies since college, so she'd known Sam almost as long as her husband. When Ewan's drinking had started to get out of hand, she'd believed the best person to confide in was his closest friend.

She'd considered talking to Paulette, but knew she would have enjoyed learning that not all was rosy at home. Paulette had been interested in Ewan in the early days and Lily was sure she still harboured resentment. Julie Medlocke had suffered abuse at the hands of her alcoholic husband, so she'd been positive what her advice would have been. Besides, Paulette and Julie didn't know Ewan. Not many people did. He was always civil and courteous to her sister and best friend, but very rarely opened up to anyone but Lily.

Sam Castle was somebody who knew Ewan and had frequently made allowances for the moments when alcohol pushed out his witty, warm and generous character and he became about nothing more than the pursuit of that one last drink. And then the next last drink. It was something that Ewan recognised and that he allowed Lily to regulate, but drinking with his students was fatal. Nobody in that situation was mature enough or interested in curbing the behaviour he defaulted to.

Sam Castle had seen it all. Had cajoled, extricated and rescued Ewan from a variety of situations and seemed like the best person to speak to when the nights Ewan spent with his students suddenly increased and he came home in a cab more often than his car. When they'd finished at college Sam went on to become a lawyer and Ewan had opted for teaching, though they both remained in touch and Sam had been best man at their wedding.

There had been a girl on the scene for Sam around that time, Martine. And they looked like a great couple. Both of them had golden fair hair, his static and dishevelled and hers in a tight bob. She'd been at the wedding too, but their relationship had ended not long after and since then Lily hadn't been aware of any other women in his life. But Sam remained a firm friend and, in the early days of their marriage, had been a regular visitor to their table. When Maisie had come along and sleep deprivation had put paid to late dinners he'd disappeared for a while.

However, as Maisie had got older Sam had come back onto the scene, and it was one night when he'd called in to see Ewan, and he still hadn't got back from leaving drinks with his students, that Lily decided to broach the subject with him.

She'd expected Sam to defend Ewan, to dismiss his conduct and tell her she was overreacting. But Sam seemed more concerned than she'd expected. It transpired that his father had been an alcoholic and had died of liver cirrhosis in the spring of 2014. That was something that Ewan had never told her, but it was clear that Sam was recognising a lot of similar behaviour.

When she thought about that conversation now Lily wondered if Sam had seen an opportunity. What had happened only months later had been unexpected to her, but had Sam used her vulnerability? But she'd instigated their contact more than him. He'd told her to call if she needed someone to talk to, and it was Lily who had first picked up the phone.

As Ewan's drinking prompted him to make more excuses to be away from Lily and Maisie, she'd leaned on Sam even harder. At one point each evening seemed to consist of her on the phone to him after she'd put Maisie to bed and Ewan was still absent. Then Sam was calling in on his way home from work.

Alarm bells should have rung. When she told Sam he shouldn't have been coming out of his way to check on her and Maisie he said that, even if he did have any reason to go home, he was still concerned about their welfare. Lily told herself that Sam had made her and Maisie his cause. That he didn't want to see Ewan go down the same road as his father. They talked about confronting Ewan. But Sam said they had to wait for the right moment. That's when she should have seen what was coming. There was nothing that couldn't have been discussed over the phone, but Sam became a reassuring presence that she encouraged.

One Friday evening Sam called in when Maisie should have been in bed. But she'd had a chest infection and was unable to sleep. Lily had tried to call the doctor, but the surgery had just closed. She'd also been trying to contact Ewan. But she'd only been getting his answering service. She'd answered the door to Sam and explained the situation and he'd walked into the room to find Maisie curled up in a blanket on the armchair.

'Maisie-doats, you keeping cosy?'

Maisie smiled weakly and coughed chestily in reply.

'Wow.' Sam shot a glance at Lily and then smiled at Maisie. 'That came from your boots.'

'She hasn't got a temperature, but it came on so suddenly. I think someone should examine her. I was thinking of taking her to the hospital.'

'I want to stay here,' Maisie protested listlessly.

'Keep wrapped up tight. I can turn the heating on in my car, OK?'

'I can drive her,' Lily insisted. 'Kettle's just boiling for some lemon and honey.'

Sam nodded and followed her into the kitchen.

When she turned, he was closing the door so Maisie couldn't hear them. 'You can't raise him?'

'I think he's turned his phone off.' Lily almost made it sound like an excuse.

Sam closed his eyes and shook his head.

Lily sighed and sagged. She had a migraine; it was the end of a long week and Ewan had barely been home. Most nights she only knew he was in safe when he crawled into bed with her. He'd taken to undressing on the landing so he wouldn't wake her. Or so she wouldn't realise how unsteady on his feet he was. 'I really think I should take her to the hospital.'

'You sure you won't let me drive? I've honestly got nothing else to do on a Friday night.'

'I'm fine. I know how to drive.' But she'd been tempted by his offer.

Sam's eyes darted and he nodded, knowing it was pointless to push it. 'Go. I'll wait in for Ewan and let him know what's happening.'

'No, that's really not necessary.' But Lily knew what was coming next.

'Maybe it's time I spoke to him while neither of you are here.'

'Not now. It's not the right time.'

'I suppose it's never going to be the right time.'

'I'm more concerned about Maisie at the moment.' She absently rubbed her temple.

'You look absolutely exhausted.'

She nodded and went to the cupboard to get the honey.

The cupboard was behind Sam. Whenever she ran the moment back in her head, she tried to find the division between what she was actually doing and what ended up happening.

As she walked towards Sam, he opened his arms. It must have looked to him like she was looking for an embrace. They'd embraced before but always when they greeted or said goodbye and usually when Ewan was present, not when they were alone in a kitchen.

It was a split-second decision. Sam had been so supportive to her over those difficult weeks. She'd already rejected his offer to drive her and Maisie to the hospital. His arms opened and she put her chin onto his shoulder before he squeezed. It felt good and she tried to remember when Ewan had last done it. She remained there too long.

When he released her she opened her mouth to speak. But she really hadn't known what she was going to say. That's when he'd kissed her. She'd immediately pulled away, took a few paces back.

'I'm sorry.'

'That's OK.' But it wasn't. She looked beyond him to the closed door.

'That was stupid.' But he left the remark hanging, to gauge her reaction.

'Yes. It was.' She turned her back to him and poured water from the kettle into Maisie's mug.

'Please, don't be like that.'

Lily was relieved he hadn't come closer. 'Like what? How should I be?'

'That was my fault . . .'

Yes, it was. But she'd remained in the hug longer than she should.

'I just feel . . . protective of you.'

She nodded, couldn't find any words. Her mind was briefly blank.

'I can't stand to see you being treated like this.'

But he'd proved there was much more to it than that and Lily chided herself for ignoring the warning signs. In the last couple of months, she'd spoken more to Sam than her own husband.

'If you want me to, I'll go now.'

He was still giving himself an opening. Making it her choice.

'I don't want you to do anything . . . you don't want to do.'

Lily didn't want to look at him. 'Maisie's ill. I'm taking her to the hospital. You'd probably better leave.'

There was a short silence. 'I'm sorry. Let me know how you get on. Call me when you can.'

Lily stared down at the clear water in Maisie's yellow mug and heard him saying good night to Maisie before the front door clicked.

She didn't see him again after that. They spoke a few times on the phone and he did his best to skirt around what had happened, go back to the way they'd been during their conversations about Ewan before. But Lily said that she wanted to make it work with Ewan and he said he understood.

It was months later that Ewan had become suspicious. Sam hadn't been around and when Ewan called him to meet up, he always made an excuse. Ewan had asked Lily if she knew why this was. Had she given herself away when she said she didn't or had Maisie mentioned that Uncle Sam had been around the night she went into hospital? Whatever the reason, Lily was sure Ewan suspected that something had happened between them.

Chapter 30

Lily pulled the lid down on the toilet and sat on it. Queasiness still crashed over her. Ewan and Sam . . . they were the only men who had really been significant to her since she'd left college. But they both loved Maisie. Surely they wouldn't subject her to one moment of this. Maybe she was too focussed on who was in her life now. Perhaps there had always been someone standing on the periphery. She considered the photos in the album again.

Was there someone in work? Martin Pickton, the paunchy office bachelor? But although he was in his late thirties he seemed more interested in Bridget Holby, the young new intern. Julie said he gave her the creeps but then she did have a blanket downer on men.

She cast her mind further back. Tried to identify another face that united the occasions in the album. But she realised she couldn't distract herself any longer. Maisie could be anywhere, and she could only wait and imagine what was happening. She stood again and leaned over the sink, running the tap in readiness.

Her phone buzzed in her hand and she quickly checked the display.

Another image had arrived. Lily stabbed the screen with her finger and clenched herself in readiness as the picture opened.

For a few seconds, she struggled to work out what she was looking at, but as she focussed on the splayed adult hand in the middle of the photo, she realised, from the rear of her shoulders still clad in her banana yellow pyjamas, it was a close-up of the back of Maisie's head. The hand was resting lightly on her scalp, the fingers sunk into her fair hair. Those digits touching her daughter shrivelled Lily's stomach.

She was vaguely aware of a choked noise escaping her.

What was he doing? Patting her on the head, guiding her with his hand? There was nothing else visible in front of her, no other discernible details of her daughter's darkened location. Was that where she was actually being held? Maisie didn't like the dark. But he probably knew that and was deliberately using it against them both.

It was the first glimpse she'd had of the person, or one of the people, who had taken them but seeing the male hand didn't make them seem any more human. She examined it closely and there were no rings or distinguishing features, no hair on the knuckles. It gave no indication of the age of its owner.

She jumped as her phone rang.

Lily quickly answered. 'Tell me she's OK.'

'Of course she is,' the same male voice assured her.

'Put her on. Let me speak to her.'

'Not possible.'

'Why?'

'She's asleep.'

'Liar. Let me speak to her now. She'll be terrified.'

'I'm doing all I can to keep her calm. Hence the reason she's asleep.'

'Where is she?'

'In the next room. She's been such a good girl.'

Lily felt another nausea rush. 'Give her back to me. I promise I'll do whatever you want.'

'That's all well and good but can you promise me Maisie will be as obedient?'

'Yes. Of course. You have my word.'

'I think she's overcoming her shyness. Perhaps those trips to the child psychologist weren't in vain.'

How did he know about that? She thought of sitting in Doctor Hart's office while Maisie had sat in silence. Maisie had hated Doctor Hart. Didn't like the redness of his bald pate and the grey hairs in his nostrils. Lily had pulled the plug on the treatment three weeks in. It had only succeeded in making her even more gloomy and withdrawn. Had their kidnapper been watching them go in and out of his office during that time?

'She's really developing her own personality now.'

'Please, just let me speak to her.'

'I told you, I can't disturb her.'

'So why did you call?' Lily wanted to yell.

'I wanted to make sure you were OK. I appreciate it must have been something of a shock to find her gone.' He almost sounded apologetic.

'I'll only be OK when she's returned to me.'

He didn't respond.

'How long are you going to keep her?'

'She's only just got settled.'

Lily closed her eyes. 'Please, at least let me speak with her, to reassure her.'

'Of what?'

'That she won't come to any harm.'

Silence from the other end.

'Can I assure her of that?' Her voice tremored.

'When she wakes up, you can assure her of anything you like.'

'Please, wake her now.'

'We've already had this conversation.'

'Just give her back!' But Lily regretted the outburst before the words were out of her mouth.

'I'm hanging up now.'

'Please, don't. I'm sorry. Please, call me when she wakes—' Lily could hear the sound of crying in the background. It was definitely Maisie. A bubble of relief burst in her chest, but it was quickly replaced by a desperate need to comfort her. 'I can hear her. She's awake. Please, can I talk to her now?'

He hung up.

Chapter 31

Lily snapped awake on the toilet. Her jeans were still rolled down her legs. She'd obviously passed out exhausted. What time had she sat down to pee, around eleven in the evening? Her phone was lying face down on the tiles. It must have slipped out of her hand. She leaned forward and snatched it up.

23:27

Dread immediately took hold again. She checked for new messages, but there were none. Lily flinched as she stirred her muscles. The ones at the back of her legs felt dead where the edge of the seat had cut into them. Her neck ached as well. She'd been asleep with her chin on her chest. Her feet and buttocks felt cold. The temperature in the bathroom had definitely dropped. She started pulling up her pyjama bottoms and jeans.

Thump.

Lily froze. That had sounded like it was in the hallway. She held her breath and waited. Was that what had woken her? No other noise. She quickly finished dressing.

Another thud. Softer this time.

Lily took her weight on her numb feet.

The floor outside the bathroom creaked.

Lily did her zipper up but remained where she was. He had to know she was in the bathroom. She put her hand in her robe pocket, but the paring knife wasn't there. Had it dropped out when she'd lain on the floor? Her eyes flitted about the room for a weapon. There was nothing she could defend herself with, but as her attention settled on the mirrored bathroom cabinet beside the door, she wondered if she could depend on his faithful replication of everything in her home.

She took two painstaking paces to the cabinet and cringed as she opened the door and it squeaked. Inside was her clear plastic tooth mug with the spare toothbrushes in it. And her nail scissors.

Lily slid them out and held the handles dagger style, the small blades protruding only half an inch from her fist.

Creak.

That was right outside the door. He must have just walked in through the front. Lily gripped the cold metal of the scissors tighter and waited for the door handle to go down.

But the steps continued down the hallway. He'd passed her. She took one step to the hinge side of the door. If he came in, she could stab him in the back. She raised her fist in readiness.

The footsteps reached the kitchen.

He would soon gather exactly where she was. But surely he'd know that from watching her on the cameras. She dropped her fist. What was the point of attacking him? He had Maisie.

Whatever he was doing here, she had to comply. Every cell of her told her not to go into the hallway, but why bother hiding at all?

Lily slid the nail scissors into her robe pocket. They were there if the opportunity arose to use them, but again, she figured her captor had already anticipated it.

There was no point in delaying the moment. Lily breathed in through her nose and put her fingers on the cold handle.

Slam.

She hesitated. That came from the kitchen. Was that the fridge?

Lily pulled down on the handle hard. It made a noise and she wanted it to. She needed him to know she wasn't hiding, wasn't trying to be stealthy. She walked out into the hallway but couldn't see anyone through the kitchen doorway. Her gaze briefly tilted up to the camera. 'I'm coming into the kitchen,' she announced, and her voice sounded so loud.

There was no response.

She took a pace forward.

Creak.

And she hadn't made that noise. Sounded like someone was adjusting their footing as she approached. Lily stepped harder, wanted them to know she was near. 'I'm unarmed,' she added, even though it weren't strictly true. But there were no cameras in the bathroom. At least, none that she knew about. And if he was in here with her then he definitely didn't know she'd concealed the scissors.

Lily turned her head so she could see around the doorway as she reached it.

A rustling sound greeted her arrival.

She paused then entered the kitchen and as she moved past the jamb she could see who was standing by the fridge.

Maisie looked up. She had a packet of string cheese in her fist and was biting through it.

'Maisie . . . Maisie.' Lily checked if there was anybody else in the room, but it was only her daughter. She ran to her, fell to her knees and hugged her tight. 'Are you all right?' She held her by her shoulders then pushed her away so she could take her in.

Maisie didn't respond. Her eyes rolled to the food in her hand and she took a huge bite.

'Maisie?'

She chewed on the processed cheese, closed her eyes and breathed in, as if the food couldn't have come any later.

Lily examined her expression. 'Maisie, are you OK?'

She still didn't answer.

'Say something.'

Her daughter's expression was glazed. Had she been drugged? She wanted to examine her now. Take off her clothes and check her all over. She put her hand to her cheek. It was so cold. And so were her hands. She squeezed and rubbed them. 'What happened to you. Where did he take you?'

But Maisie didn't reply or even react to the fact that she'd been returned to her.

Lily hugged her again. Her yellow pyjamas felt freezing. Where had she been? She could feel her shivering against her. 'Come with me.' She took her by the hand and led her to the bathroom. 'Let's get the bath running. Wait.' She grabbed the purple hoodie blanket from her room and wrapped it tight around her. 'Come on.'

Maisie dropped the string cheese as if she'd forgotten she was holding it.

Lily sealed the bathroom door and then stood Maisie by the bath, turned on the hot tap and rubbed her through the blanket.

'Maisie, speak to me.'

But her daughter just stared blankly from the hood around her face.

Chapter 32

As the bath filled the thundering sound of the water barely drowned out the clamour of thoughts in Lily's head. Maisie had been gone for at least seventeen hours. It had felt like a week. But what had happened to her in that time? She turned off the tap. As she splashed water over her daughter's torso, she closely examined every inch of her skin. There was a faint yellow bruise at the top of her left arm. Had that been there previously? 'Where did he take you?'

Maisie didn't answer, just kept gripping the sponge Lily had handed her. The green one that was shaped like a turtle that was exactly like the one she had at home.

'Maisie.' Lily tried to meet her eye. 'You have to speak to me.' Ignoring Lily had often been Maisie's way of not answering questions or demands she didn't like, though she'd gradually learnt it never made them go away. 'What can you remember?'

Her daughter blinked but there was no other indication she'd heard.

Was she traumatised? Lily looked her over again and rubbed her arms to get her circulation going. Had she spent every hour abandoned and locked away in one of the freezing cold rooms above or below? But even though that thought made her furious, particularly as she'd only been wearing her pyjamas and could have caught her death of cold, Lily prayed that was all that had happened. 'Can you remember anything?'

Maisie shook her head slightly, the water droplets on the dark ends of her fair hair dripping into the bath.

'OK.' Lily knew she shouldn't push. 'We're going to get you warmed up, wash your hair, make you smell nice. Then we'll have some supper. That sound good?'

Maisie looked down at the sponge in her fingers.

Lily knew she had to be outwardly calm, for her daughter's sake. Should she push her to tell her what had happened, or would that make her withdraw further? 'Let me get your shampoo.' She stood to reach it down from the shelf of plastic bottles above them. Same selection as they had in their real bathroom. She squirted some into the palm of her hand and noticed how much it was shaking.

She gently massaged the coconut shampoo into her scalp. This was how she always relaxed Maisie when she was upset. She stopped when there was plenty of lather. 'Smells delicious. That feel good?'

Maisie's shoulders remained rigid, her head still.

Lily continued massaging. 'We'll dry it and I'll brush it the way you like.' She hadn't opened the drawers in Maisie's room but didn't doubt that the dryer would be present. 'Maybe do some plaits. Would you like that?'

Maisie was still motionless.

'That will never happen again.' Lily said the thought out loud.

But the words didn't cause any reaction.

Lily felt the tears building but fought them back. She told herself she'd have to deal with how she'd allowed Maisie to be taken another time; but her vision blurred, and a droplet ran down her face and into the bath.

Maisie let the turtle go and it glided away from her along the surface of the bath water.

'Never.' But Lily had already made her daughter one promise she'd broken. She blinked away the tears. She couldn't let her see them. 'You have to talk to me.'

Maisie's hands remained in her lap and her eyes were fixed on the cold tap.

It was slowly dripping into the bath.

'Maisie.' Lily turned it off.

But as she helped her out of the bath and dried her off she still didn't make eye contact. Lily wrapped her in the big white towel and turned to the door. 'I'm just going to grab you a fresh pair of pyjamas and your dressing gown. I'll be two seconds.'

Maisie's hand suddenly shot out and grabbed her wrist.

Lily kneeled down. 'Don't worry. I'll be back now. I don't want you to catch a chill in the hallway.'

Maisie shook her head emphatically.

'OK, OK.' She tried not to show the relief that her daughter was communicating. She clasped her to her breast and her cheek was warm, the smell of her coconut shampoo in Lily's nostrils. She hugged her tighter and felt the tears build again. 'I'm so sorry.'

Maisie remained still, trapped in the folds of the towel.

'Come on.' Lily lifted her, grabbed her hoodie and carried her out of the bathroom and across the hallway to her room. She closed the door with her foot and set Maisie down. She quickly got another pair of her pyjamas from the drawer, but she almost didn't want her to wear them. They were neatly folded and brand new, but he'd touched them. He'd touched everything.

They had no choice. 'Put these on and then your slippers and dressing gown.' Lily quickly composed herself while she watched her daughter. She looked exhausted. 'Do you want to eat now?' But she could tell from her drooping eyelids that Maisie was about to fall asleep. The bath always did that, but she still worried that she might have been medicated.

Maisie looked at the door and shook her head again.

Did she want to sleep with Lily but was afraid of what had happened happening a second time? 'I'm going to lie in here with you. It'll be so cosy.'

Maisie regarded her bed but still seemed reluctant.

'I'm not going to go to sleep. I'm not going to let anything happen to you. Come on, get under the covers.'

Maisie seemed too exhausted to argue and got onto the mattress.

Lily put the duvet over her and slipped in beside her little body. 'We'll soon warm up.'

Lily stroked her hair and Maisie was asleep in a matter of seconds. She was relieved to see that whatever her daughter had experienced that day drain from her face.

She decided she would make sure that Maisie was fast asleep first and then quickly grab the carving knife and hammer. If he tried the same she would kill him.

Chapter 33

Lily twitched awake, her fingers gripping Maisie's hand tight. She hadn't wanted to fall asleep, but the emotional fallout of the past day had caught up with her. Her face felt freezing. She relaxed her grip on her daughter, but it had woken her too. 'Sorry, go right back to sleep.'

But Maisie was looking around the room in alarm.

'It's OK. You're safe and I'm not letting go,' Lily assured her.

Maisie blinked a few times and kept scanning the room. When she'd fetched the knife and hammer Lily had turned the light off so only the globe bedside lamp was on. She'd tried to lodge the chair under the door again, but had to be content just to lean it there, so it fell over if anyone opened it. She glanced at her phone.

03:43

The last time she'd looked it had been 03:34. She hadn't been asleep long but chided herself for nodding off. At least Maisie had got a few sporadic hours. After what had happened to her Lily had to be alert to every sound. How long could she keep this up though? She had to rest. But was their food drugged anyway? Or maybe he could lace the water supply whenever he needed. She hoped their captor had made his point. Lying here thinking about how easily he'd taken Maisie, she'd decided that she had to make him believe they'd learnt their lesson. Only until a solid opportunity presented itself would she even consider breaking the rules again.

He couldn't really be watching them all the time, could he? Again, she speculated that there could be more than one of them though. That they took it in turns to monitor them. She shivered.

Maisie released her hand and sat up.

'What is it?'

'I thought I heard something.'

Lily sat up too but was more relieved that her daughter had spoken her first words since she'd returned.

They both listened for a few tense minutes, but there was no other sound.

Was Maisie just jumpy? 'I can't hear anything.'

Maisie shook her head. 'I'm too awake to go back to sleep.'

'OK but it's still very early. How about we go under the duvet to keep warm.'

Maisie eventually nodded. 'OK.'

Lily lay her head on the pillow and her daughter followed suit. She pulled the duvet over their heads and punched an indentation in the pillow between them so air could get under the edge. 'Let's whisper.' She still wasn't sure if there were microphones in every room. 'That way we can keep an ear out.'

Maisie nodded and her head hissed on the pillow.

Lily could just see her daughter's face in the weak light

from the lamp that trickled in the gap above them. 'Why don't you tell me a story.'

Maisie blinked a few times in confusion.

'About a little girl's adventures.'

'Me tell YOU a story?'

'Yes.' Lily smiled to encourage her. She hoped Maisie talking was a promising sign, but would she set her back again by making her relive the ordeal? 'Do you want to tell me about your adventures yesterday?'

'No,' she refused flatly.

'OK. How about you just tell me how you got back here then?'

'He let me in, I think.'

'Who did?'

'The scary man,' Maisie replied, as if it were a stupid question.

'And where did you come from?'

'Upstairs.'

'And what's upstairs?'

'Can I tell you a different story?'

'I really like this one. Even though it's a bit scary. Were you scared?'

Maisie didn't react.

'I know I would have been. I'm not sure I would have been as brave as you.'

'We were playing a game upstairs but I didn't like it.'

Lily's body tautened. 'What sort of a game?' She tried to keep her tone light.

'A guessing game.' Her response was emotionless. 'He put something on my head.'

Lily's mouth was dry. 'Do you know what it was?'

'It was made of cloth and it smelt funny.'

Anger mounted. 'Why didn't you take it off?'

Maisie's breathing quickened.

'Maisie, why didn't you take it off?'

'I . . . couldn't.'

'Why not?' Had he tied her hands? Lily hadn't seen any marks on her wrists or ankles.

'I wasn't allowed.'

Lily could hear her own circulation surge in the ear against the pillow. 'So you did everything he told you to?'

'I had to.'

What did that mean? Lily could see tears twinkle in her daughter's eyes. 'Why?'

'He said, if I took it off . . . horrible things would happen to you.'

Chapter 34

Lily tried to restrain the colliding emotions she felt and reached out to stroke Maisie's hair. What could she tell her? 'He was only saying that to make you do what he wanted.'

'But I thought . . . we *had* to do what he wanted.'

Lily nodded. 'Right now we do. And you did the right thing.' Lily wanted to scream at the camera. But she had to know. 'What else did you do?'

'He made me sit on a stool. It was tall. My feet couldn't touch the ground.'

Lily's face was hot, and it felt like she might suffocate. 'Did he . . . when he was nearby . . . did he put his hand on you?'

Maisie nodded once. 'He lifted me off the stool and stood me on the floor. He took the cloth off my head and I was looking at the wall. He put his hand on the back of my head.'

For the photo. 'And what happened after that?'

'He put the cloth back on me and lifted me onto the stool again. Told me not to move or . . .' Maisie started crying.

'OK, you don't have to go on.' But Lily wondered if she

should get it all out now, while it was still clear in her head. 'Let me get you a tissue.'

'He said he'd hurt you.' Maisie's chest pumped out the words. 'That I'd never . . . see you . . . again.'

Hatred for him burnt at Lily's core. She touched Maisie's cheek. 'But you can see now, he was making all that up. I'm here, he hasn't hurt me. And I'm not about to let him hurt either of us. He's like that horrible boy who picked on you your first day of school. They were just cruel words.'

'But he . . . took me.' Tears ran down Maisie's face. 'And . . . you couldn't . . . help me!'

'Ssshhh, ssshhh.' She didn't want him to hear this. Didn't want him to know how helpless it made her feel. 'He wouldn't dare hurt you.' She realised her voice had risen. She dropped it to a whisper again. 'Wouldn't dare. That's why he let you come back to me.' She gently wiped the tears from Maisie's eyes with her fingers. 'And now he knows how strong you are too.'

'I just want to go home.' The words barely grazed Maisie's throat.

'So do I. And we will. But sometimes nasty things happen. The sorts of things that make us realise how lucky we are to have each other.' Lily needed to know about the rest of the time her daughter had been away from her. 'Do you remember him taking you from here?'

Maisie shook her head.

'What was the very first thing you remember?'

'I woke up . . . and I was in a different room.'

'What then?' But what had happened when she'd been

asleep or drugged? How many hours did that account for?

'I called for you.' Even wrapped up in a whisper, Maisie's voice was suddenly small.

'What did the room look like?'

'It wasn't a bedroom. It was cold and . . . empty and dirty.' Maisie's sobs were dwindling now. 'And it wasn't even a proper bed.'

Lily imagined her waking alone on a mattress in one of the derelict rooms upstairs. 'What did you do?' She had to keep her focussed.

'I went to the door but it was locked.' She released a sigh from her chest. The tears had momentarily abated.

'OK . . .'

'I was cold, so I went back to bed and tried to keep warm. Then the scary man came in and turned off the lights.'

Lily closed her eyes. How could she broach the question she had to ask? 'Was he in the room with you long?'

'No. Just to put the cloth over my head. Then he gave me some socks and told me to sit on the high stool.'

'And apart from when he put his hand on your head, he didn't touch you?'

'No.'

'You're sure?'

Maisie nodded and sniffed.

'And you spent the rest of the time on the stool?'

'Yes. He wouldn't let me off it, even to pee.'

The son of a bitch. How could he have put her through that? But Lily was glad that, as far as Maisie was concerned, he'd barely touched her. However, any relief she felt was negated by the time before she'd woken that Maisie couldn't remember. 'Did he give you anything to eat?'

'No. Just some water . . . with a straw so I didn't have to take the cloth off my head.'

Lily wondered if he'd always known he was going to return her when he did.

'I don't want to go back to the stool.' There was palpable fear in Maisie's voice.

'You're not going to. I promise you.'

But Maisie was silent.

'Do you remember anything else he said to you?'

'No. He turned on a radio so I couldn't understand what he was saying to the lady.'

'What lady?'

'She was in another room but I could hear her talking to him.'

'You're sure it was a lady's voice?'

'Yes. They were arguing. I heard a door slam and then I didn't hear her again.'

So there *was* more than one person holding them. But how could a woman be involved in this, in mistreating and subjecting her little girl to such a terrifying and humiliating ordeal? Lily felt contempt for their captors burn even stronger. She needed fresh air. She pulled the duvet from her hot face and let the cool air settle on them. 'OK,' she rubbed Maisie's arm. 'That's enough hiding.'

Chapter 35

Even though it was the early hours of the morning, they were both fully awake and decided to get up. Daylight routine didn't seem important. Lily was just glad to have Maisie back and didn't want to let her out of her sight.

She led her to the bathroom to clean her teeth and, while her daughter squeezed the paste onto her duplicate tiger toothbrush, Lily closed the door and scanned the bathroom again. Were they really free to talk in here or were they being monitored at this hour? She now knew there was more than one person involved in their incarceration. Perhaps their male and female captors took it in turns to keep tabs on them. She couldn't identify anything that could be a camera but there was a grill above the cabinet. Lily wouldn't remove it as she had the one in the kitchen. She wasn't about to give their captors any further reason to punish them.

Maisie was watching her, the brush paused at her teeth. 'Can he see us in here too?'

Lily briefly put her finger to her lips to shush her. 'Come on and don't forget to do your gums.' She started running the tap and knelt down next to her. There was still something she needed to know. She whispered in her ear. 'When you came back, did he let you in through the front door?'

Maisie thought about it and whispered back. 'I had the cloth on my head. I know I came down some stairs. Then up a few. When he took it off, I was standing in the hallway.'

'Up a few?' Lily made a mental note of that. 'Did you see him leave?'

'No.'

'You didn't hear the door close behind him?'

Maisie shook her head.

Lily gestured for her to brush her teeth and she obeyed. Had they both been so drugged that he was able to just walk in and lift Maisie out of bed or was he using another entrance? It made sense that, as he'd built their prison, he'd give himself easy access to them. What about the locked front lounge door? Was there really a room behind there and, if so, why was it still sealed to them? Perhaps it led immediately to the place he was watching them from.

She had no concept of the geography of the floor they were on. Did freedom lie beyond the thickness of that door? But there was no light around it. Did it have a metal plate over it like the front door? Maybe they were both permanently sealed and he was getting in through a wall. 'Do you remember what the lady and the scary man were arguing about?' She'd envisioned the man with the hood stealing in while they slept, but perhaps it had been a woman.

The brush paused in her mouth. 'I couldn't really hear over the radio.'

'Anything at all?'

Maisie thought about it. 'Just before she left she said something about the storeroom.'

'The storeroom?'

Maisie nodded. 'I think that's what she said.'

'That was all you heard?'

'Something about opening it up.' But Maisie didn't look sure.

Lily nodded. 'And there was nothing else?'

'Sorry.'

'Don't apologise. You were so brave.' Another thought occurred to Lily. 'And the radio station he put on, what was that like?'

'All pop music.'

'But was it like the radio that I listen to?'

'What do you mean?'

'Were there people talking in between?'

'Yes.'

'Can you remember the names of the people talking?'

'No. It was a man and a woman.'

'And were they talking in English?'

Maisie nodded.

'Did you hear any news?'

Maisie thought about it. 'I think so.'

'Can you remember what they said?'

'I wasn't really listening.'

This was a partial relief. From the window Lily hadn't seen any indication that they were still in the UK. But wherever they were their captors could easily find an English-speaking radio station. If they'd been smuggled out of the country to be trafficked in some way what would be the reason to create the environment they were in? Lily leaned in close to Maisie's ear. 'Keep brushing. This is going to be our place for secret chats, only when this tap is running. So he can't listen in on us. If you remember anything more or have something you want to say to me that you don't want the scary man to hear, you say to me "Please can you take me to the bathroom".'

Maisie paused, froth about her lips. 'But I don't need you to take me to the bathroom.' She was mortified.

'I know that. But he doesn't.' But did he? Did he know them more intimately than even she realised? 'Only do it if you think you really need to tell me something. We'll talk here first thing in the morning or just before we go to bed. If we do it too often, he's going to guess we're fooling him, OK?'

'But what if I really need to tell you something quickly?'

'Then tell me you feel sick and we'll come here. Understand?'

'Yes.' Maisie spat some toothpaste into the sink.

'OK, finish your teeth now. And when I turn off the tap it means he's listening to us again.'

Maisie seemed thoughtful.

'What is it?'

'What if he finds out?'

Lily could see the fear begin to swell in her eyes. 'He hasn't told us we can't talk to each other. It's just that here we can talk in private.'

She whispered even lower. 'He won't take me away again?'

'No. I've told you. That's never going to happen again. I'm

turning the tap off now. We'll talk again here when you brush your teeth later.'

Maisie nodded and Lily switched off the tap. 'OK, good job. Let's go and find something to eat. You must be starving.'

But before Lily could open the door to the hallway, they heard a loud click from behind it.

Chapter 36

'Stay there.' Lily squeezed Maisie's shoulder and stepped to the closed door. She listened at the panel.

Maisie formed her fingers into a tube and whispered at Lily. 'Is it the scary man?'

Lily held her palm up to be quiet. Surely he hadn't been able to hear what they'd been saying. Maybe he didn't like them shutting themselves away to have a conversation. But how would he have known that that was what they were doing? They hadn't been in there longer than a few minutes. But Lily still suspected the bathroom was as wired up as the other rooms.

No other sound from outside.

Damn, she'd left the knife and hammer in the bedroom. But she still had the nail scissors in her robe pocket. She slipped them out but kept them concealed in her hand.

'What's that?'

She'd tried to do it sneakily because she didn't want to alarm Maisie. She shushed her and put her ear to the door.

After a few minutes she still couldn't hear any noise. Lily slowly pulled down the handle and peered out of the crack in the door.

From her position she couldn't see anyone in the hallway. But something seemed different. Lily opened the door wider and realised what it was – the illumination had changed. It was less dingy. She stepped cautiously out and found the light source. The lounge door was half open.

'Who is it?' Maisie asked from behind her.

'Just wait here.' Lily didn't take her eyes off the door and the light beyond it. Was this a trick? But she had to find out where it led. Maybe it was about to close again. 'Are you in there?' She directed the question towards it, but nobody responded.

'Let me see.'

She could feel Maisie at her waist and turned. 'Just wait here. I'll be back now. Not a peep. Do as I tell you.'

Maisie opened her mouth to protest, but Lily closed the door on her. She quickly returned her attention to the lounge and took a few paces towards it. A game, a test? Maybe the argument that Maisie had overheard had changed the situation. Perhaps the woman persuaded their captor to return Maisie or even release them. But Lily doubted their ordeal was about to end that easily.

Another two steps towards the door and she could hear a humming sound, like a low electrical motor. What the hell was that? She halted, reluctant to get any nearer. He'd opened this door, wanted her to walk over the threshold. Was he waiting for her the other side?

Lily waited to see if he, or she, would appear. She shot a glance to the camera to her right. There was no element of surprise for her. Sooner or later they knew she would look through the doorway. Even if she didn't enter, there was no point delaying the moment.

She took the four paces that would take her to the edge of the door and then leaned and looked inside. She took it in for a few seconds.

It was a room and not a corridor that led to freedom. The dimensions were about the same as her front lounge. But she couldn't tell if there were any windows. There was very little floor space left unoccupied. Boxes were stacked up almost to the ceiling.

Lily's eyes drifted to the right and she saw the source of the noise. It was a large, white industrial chest freezer that ran the length of the wall. Above that were metallic shelves with more boxes stacked on top. 'Hello?' But she guessed there was nobody inside. There was scarcely any room for her to squeeze in.

'What have you found?'

Lily turned to find Maisie standing behind her. 'Go back to the bathroom.'

'Is this food?'

Lily returned her attention to the room. It was. And she recognised some of Maisie's favourite brands printed on the cartons. Juices, cereals, boxes of baked beans, noodles, rice and crisps.

'Can I see?'

'No.' Lily held her back by the nape of her neck. She still wasn't sure if this was a booby trap. But if they'd wanted to take Maisie from her, they could have just kept her upstairs. She pulled the door open wider. 'Stay here.'

'No.' Maisie looked up the corridor towards the camera.

'Just let me check first and then you can come in. Count to twenty out loud.'

Maisie started doing so immediately.

'Too fast. Slow down. One and two and . . .' Maisie picked up the counting, and Lily stepped inside and pulled the door closed behind her. She examined the stack of boxes in front of her. They almost touched the far wall. She skirted them until she reached the gap there and peered up it. She could just squeeze through the dingy aperture there to the back wall. No windows where they should be. And certainly no TV. Looked like this room hadn't been completed. Or was it destined for this purpose? This had to be the storeroom that Maisie had heard the 'lady' talking about.

She took a breath and entered and when she reached the rear, she squeezed quickly along a wall of toilet rolls and down the other side, so she was at the door again. Lily noted the camera above it. She opened the door quickly and was relieved to find Maisie still there.

'Can I come in now?'

'No, wait.' Lily turned her attention to the chest freezer to her left. 'I'm going to close the door again just for two seconds.'

'Why?'

'Two seconds.' Lily did so and turned to the freezer. Why was it so big? Had they stockpiled as much in there as they had in dry storage?

Maisie knocked the door. 'Let me see.'

'Did you count to twenty properly?

'Nearly.'

'How many seconds did you have left?'

'I got to fourteen.'

'Then finish counting.' Lily gripped the handle of the freezer.

Chapter 37

When Maisie reached eighteen, Lily heaved up the heavy lid of the freezer and took a step back. The action wafted the cold mist and she peered through it at what was inside. As the cloud dispersed Lily was relieved to see that one half of it was stacked with bags of veg and meat and the other half contained large bottles of frozen milk.

'Coming!' Maisie entered through the door.

Lily didn't turn.

'Wow.' Maisie peered at the packed chest freezer.

How deep was it? How much milk was that and how many meals were contained within it and stored behind her?

'Is this all for us?'

Lily nodded grimly. There was enough food to survive here for months and months and that revelation made Lily's legs tremble beneath her.

'Choca-Pops!' Maisie pointed to the logo on one of the boxes. 'Can I get all the free toys?'

'No,' Lily answered absently.

'But there must be boxes and boxes here. Please can we get the toys out of each one?'

'No.'

'Please . . .' Maisie entreated.

Lily turned to her. 'I said no.' But she said it too sharply.

Maisie blanched.

'These are not ours. They belong to the scary man.' She still couldn't keep the harshness from her voice.

Maisie shook her head, not understanding. 'Aren't you glad we won't be hungry?'

'Yes, of course.' She couldn't tell Maisie what the room meant. That their captors intended them to be prisoners for a very long time to come. And what would happen when the food ran out? Would they simply lock the door again and restock?

'I thought you'd be happy.' Maisie's face prepared for tears.

'It's good we've got food.' She knelt and gave Maisie a hug. 'Come on now. It *is* good.' She put her hands on her shoulders. 'But it belongs to him.' Lily wanted to say that they wouldn't need the food because they weren't going to stay one second longer than they needed to. But they were probably listening. 'We only take what we need.'

Maisie breathed in unsteadily.

'We still have enough food in the kitchen for the moment, so we don't need to come in here.' How had they opened the door? She hadn't heard the front door close behind them. Was there a hidden door to this room and was that how they'd brought Maisie back?

'I want some Choca-Pops.'

'We've already got another box of cereal open.'

'But they're there.' Maisie pointed, as if Lily hadn't seen them.

'Finish the first box of cereal.'

'But there's so many here. Just one, so I can have the toy.'

After all that Maisie had been through Lily almost felt tempted to rip open the box and pull out all the toys she wanted. But she wasn't about to accept anything from the people who had taken her. 'You're not to come back in here without me, OK?'

Maisie lifted her shoulders and sighed, her eyes on the navy blue carpet.

'OK? I need a promise.'

She nodded. 'I promise.'

'We don't know if the scary man might be hiding amongst these boxes.'

Maisie looked suddenly alarmed.

Lily felt a pang of guilt. But if it meant Maisie wouldn't be tempted to go in there the tactic was justified.

'I want to go now.' Maisie wriggled on the spot.

'Come on then.' Lily stood and let Maisie slip around the door first.

Maisie waited for her in the hallway. 'We should close it.'

'Good idea.' Lily pushed the door shut.

'And lock it.'

'I can't.' Lily pointed at the keyhole. 'No key.'

Maisie seemed troubled. 'How did *they* lock it?'

She didn't want Maisie to have the same thought process as she had about hidden access. 'We'll look for the key. It must be here somewhere. Then we can lock it ourselves. Breakfast first though.'

Maisie turned over what she'd been told and knew she'd been fobbed off. 'Shall we try to break the window again?'

'No, we can't do that. We have to behave. I've promised,' Lily said for the benefit of the camera over the kitchen doorway.

'If we're not going to do anything . . . how are we going to get out of here?'

'By behaving ourselves.' She turned her back to the camera and winked at Maisie.

Maisie smiled briefly, pleased to be part of Lily's subterfuge. 'Yes, we'll be on our very best behaviour,' she said a little too affectedly.

Lily widened her eyes at Maisie. 'Breakfast then.' She turned and walked to the kitchen, deciding to look briefly up at the camera. It would be unnatural for her to stop doing so and she didn't want to give the impression that they really had been performing for the camera's sake.

She would speak to Maisie tonight about being natural when they were back at the tap. But she realised that planning to do so meant she'd already accepted that they were spending another night there.

Chapter 38

Maisie ate little of her cereal, and Lily just made herself a cup of coffee. She completely filled the kettle and left the remaining water to cool to give to Maisie to drink later. They had no choice but to use the tap and Lily acknowledged that their captors could put whatever they wanted into the supply. Although seeing the storeroom had been a shocking illustration of just how long it looked like she and Maisie were going to be captives, it was also reassuring. The amount of supplies indicated their captors' obvious desire for them to remain alive.

Lily drank a large mug of black instant Colombian. Maybe she should do a cup every couple of hours. She'd be buzzing but it would keep her awake and she was determined to change her sleeping patterns. Some people she knew managed on only a few hours a night. But would it make any difference? If the man or woman wanted to enter they only had to wait for Lily to fall asleep, at whatever time and however briefly it was. She would learn to sleep light but she was still convinced she'd been drugged the night Maisie had been taken.

'What shall we do now?' Maisie was staring into her full cereal bowl.

Lily glanced at her cracked phone on the table. It wasn't even five in the morning. 'How about some crafts?'

Maisie frowned deeply.

'Come on. There's no TV. Let's make something.'

'OK.' She didn't sound very enthused.

But Lily was considering another idea. Something that would tell them for sure if the storeroom was definitely the way they were getting in. 'Let's use these old magazines.' She picked up a stack from inside the recycle container and flicked through them. An identical selection to the old glossy supplements at home.

Maisie came around to her side of the table. 'What shall we make then?'

'Have you heard of a mood board?'

Maisie shook her head.

'It's a collection of images that sum up an idea or the way you're feeling about something.'

Maisie seemed to like the idea. 'I get it.'

'Why don't you go through these and find the pictures you like. Then we'll cut out the ones that best fit your mood.'

Maisie accepted them from her and started leafing through them.

'You do that, and I'll find the scissors and Sellotape.'

Maisie nodded, already distracted by the task at hand.

Lily rose from the table, went to the drawer and rummaged around until she'd found both. Then she sat back down with Maisie and helped her select the images.

'I like this one.'

It was a photo of a chimpanzee screaming.

'Yes, I'd pick that too. Cut it out then.' She handed Maisie the scissors. 'We'll use this as a board.' Lily pulled the bag of cereal out of its box and handed it to her.

After Maisie had found enough images Lily got her to cut up the box and they used the front panel to stick the pictures on. As well as the chimp there was a mushroom cloud, a man from an indigestion pill ad with arrows in his stomach, a frightening enlargement of a bedbug, a window from a double glazing ad, Bela Lugosi as Dracula with his black cape around a female victim and a cupid angel with a bow and arrow surrounded by hearts.

Lily pulled strips of Sellotape, bit them off and stuck them to the leg of the kitchen table. 'So, tell me what they mean. How about the man with the bad tummy?'

'That's how I feel. Like it's all full of butterflies.'

Lily nodded. 'Good. And we know what that window is.' She made sure she pulled off a couple of strips more than they had pictures. 'What's that?' She pointed to the bedbug.

'That's how I feel too. Icky.'

Lily had expected it to be the scary man.

'The chimp too. The chimp's screaming.'

'Do you feel like screaming?'

Maisie nodded.

'And what about him?' She pointed to Bela Lugosi.

'That's you.'

Lily was taken aback. 'Me?'

Maisie registered her reaction. 'You're protecting me, like he's protecting her.' She indicated the female victim.

Of course, Maisie had no real idea who Dracula was. 'Is that not me?' Lily pointed at cupid.

'That's the lady.'

Now she really didn't understand. 'The lady upstairs?'

'Yes.'

'But you didn't see her.'

'That's what I think she looks like.'

'You think she's a nice lady?'

'I think she is,' Maisie declared earnestly.

'Did you think that when you heard her voice?'

Maisie considered that and then pouted. 'Not really.'

Lily thought about it. Maisie hadn't even found a picture to represent the scary man. He was obviously somebody she didn't want to contemplate and, after her ordeal, Lily could see why she was so desperate to believe that one of the people holding them was the polar opposite.

'But I don't think she'll let the scary man harm us. She wanted him to show us the storeroom.'

Lily nodded. Indeed, she wanted the scary man to show them and leave them in no doubt that they weren't going anywhere else now or even in the distant future. Was that honesty or sadism?

Chapter 39

As Maisie finished sticking her cut-outs to the mood board with the Sellotape lengths Lily unrolled more, bit them off and stuck them to the leg of the table. By the time they were finished she had plenty left there for what she needed to do. She leaned forward and furtively pulled four of the lengths off and fixed them to the back of her hand. Moments later the last picture was attached to the cardboard. 'That looks great. Think of where you'd like to hang it. I'm just going to the bathroom.'

Maisie nodded distractedly and took in her handiwork.

When Lily got in there, she went to the bathroom cabinet and pretended to be looking for something. She glanced up at the grill in the wall above. If there was a camera there, she was in a blind spot below.

She quickly pulled a hair from her head, unpeeled a piece of Sellotape from the back of her hand and stuck it to one end of it. She ripped off another and fixed it to the other end. She pulled another hair out and repeated the process. She stuck the hairs to the palm of her right hand, took the canister of painkillers out of the cabinet and closed the door.

Lily left the bathroom and returned to the door of the storeroom.

'What are you doing?' Maisie called out from the kitchen.

'Just making sure this door is closed properly.' Lily pushed on the handle for the sake of the camera in the hallway and then leaned against the panel as if listening. As she did so, she fixed the hair across the edge of the door with the Sellotape. It was something she'd seen in an old detective movie. If the hair was broken she'd know they'd opened the storeroom door to get in.

Lily went to the front door and repeated the process. If neither hairs got broken and they still got inside, she'd know there was another entrance.

'What are you doing now?' Maisie had wandered into the hallway.

Lily didn't want her asking questions about the Sellotape. 'Don't come near these doors. Back to the kitchen.'

Maisie regarded her suspiciously but turned on her heel and walked back.

Lily paused outside the storeroom door and listened again for effect before following her there.

'Can we put it on that wall?' Maisie was holding the mood board and pointed to the area beside the sink.

'Sure.' Lily pulled another piece of Sellotape off the leg of the table and fixed the mood board to the plaster. 'How's that look?'

Maisie nodded, as if she were satisfied.

Lily took in the board with its collection of disparate images. It was a unique addition. Now the kitchen had something that didn't tally with their real one. How else would their surroundings change in comparison to their real home before they were freed? If they were ever freed.

'You've gone very quiet.' Maisie sounded worried.

Lily shook away the thought. 'Just admiring it.' She unstuck the Sellotape and hung it straighter to sell the lie. 'There.'

'Can we open the blind now?'

'It's still dark outside.'

'But it'll be light soon.'

'Just leave it for now.'

'Are you scared if we open it the scary man will take me again?'

'There's just no point at the moment.' But that's exactly what she was afraid of. Would she deprive them of their only source of natural light because of what had happened?

'As long as we close it again . . .'

'But it's still dark.'

'But it's morning, not night.'

'Somebody could still see the light. And that's what we're not allowed to do.' Lily hoped he or she was listening. 'You're not to touch it. Under any circumstances.'

'I get it.' Maisie sounded despondent.

'Why don't we make our own window?' Lily suggested.

'What do you mean?'

'We've got more cardboard. Why don't you draw one so we can stick it to the wall? You can put whatever you want as a view.'

'Like our garden?'

'Yes.'

'That's a silly idea.'

'Why?

'We won't get any light through it.'

'You can draw a beautiful day, with all the flowers blooming. That'll brighten us up.'

Maisie returned to the kitchen table but started tidying up all the paper.

'Have a think about it. You're so good at drawing.'

'Maybe another day,' Maisie replied, like Lily often did when she wanted to let Maisie down gently.

'I'd really like to see what you'd come up with.' She needed to distract Maisie. What were they going to do next? The day hadn't even started.

But Maisie suddenly clutched her stomach and bent over.

'What's wrong?' Lily rushed to her.

'It hurts.' Maisie let out a sigh of pain. 'Really hurts.'

'Sit down a moment.' Lily lifted her onto her chair.

Maisie shook her head. 'I don't feel very well.'

'Where's the pain, high up or low down here?' Lily pointed to her stomach.

But Maisie doubled over again.

Chapter 40

Lily knew they couldn't call an ambulance or doctor. Would their captors help them? 'OK, try to be calm,' she said to herself as well as Maisie.

'It's getting worse.' Maisie wriggled in the chair.

'When did this start?'

'Only just now.'

Was it the cereal? But it seemed odd that they would try to poison Maisie. Lily still didn't know what the motives of their captors were, however. Did they just delight in torturing them?

'I feel sick.'

'OK, let's get you to the bathroom.' But it was then it occurred to her that it could be Maisie play-acting. That was what they'd agreed she should say if she wanted to have a private conversation. 'You really do feel sick?' She met Maisie's eye and she nodded, but there was also mischief in her glance.

'Yes.' Maisie got down from the chair and headed out of the kitchen.

Lily felt anger at Maisie having alarmed her. She'd never feigned illness like this before, but she realised that this was probably a deceit game she hadn't wanted to miss out on. 'I'm right behind you.'

Maisie ran the tap as Lily walked into the bathroom.

'Lean over the sink.' Lily knelt beside her.

Maisie did as she was told.

Lily pulled her hair from her face. 'OK?' She dropped her voice to a whisper. 'Are you pretending?'

Maisie turned to her and smiled.

Lily's relief escaped in a breath. 'I said you were only to use that fib if you really needed to talk, in an emergency.'

'This is an emergency.' Maisie sucked on the column of water from the tap and spat it out.

'What do you need to talk about?'

'I think that if we hear someone outside again and need to look out of the blind, you should pretend you want to talk to the scary man in one of the other rooms while I have a look.'

'No,' Lily said as firmly but as quietly as she could.

'But if they're too busy watching you I'll be able to peep.'

Lily tried not to be too annoyed with her. 'I know you're trying to help but we can't risk that.'

'Why not?'

'You said you heard two of them. They're probably both watching us and can see what we're doing, even if we're in different rooms.'

'But I could be really quick.'

'No. OK? You know what happened the last time we looked out of the window.'

'That's because you tried to smash it.'

'Do you really want to go upstairs again?'

Maisie shook her head once.

'Do you want to sit on that stool again?' She didn't want to remind her of what she'd been through, but Lily had to make sure she understood.

Maisie's expression became stern and suddenly she seemed much older than her five years. 'You said you wouldn't let that happen.'

'I won't. But we mustn't make them angry.'

'I was just trying to help.'

'I know you were. But only bring me here if you've got something really important to tell me.'

'I thought that was important.'

Lily leaned in closer to her. 'It was good that you wanted to ask first. Always do that. But only I'll decide what we're going to do and, for now, we behave and do as we're told.'

'How long though?'

'I don't know. But you have to believe that I'm going to do everything I can to get us out of here.'

'I'm sorry.'

'Don't be. But you are going to have to pretend to be ill now. Otherwise they'll think it's suspicious if you suddenly don't have tummy ache anymore. I'll put you to bed for an hour or two and then get up and say you're feeling better.'

Maisie flinched. 'I don't want to be sent to bed.'

'That's what you'll have to do now.'

Maisie glowered at her, affronted.

Lily could see why Maisie thought it might be a punishment. But now she'd got her back she doubted she could ever punish her for anything again. 'I don't think you're going to be sick,' she said louder.

Maisie nodded. Play-acting again. 'No. I feel much better now.'

Lily cringed. It was perfectly obvious that they'd been having a confab.

Maisie switched off the tap. 'I'm still feeling funny though.'

'Oh dear.' She felt Maisie's head. 'You don't have a temperature.' Lily considered it would seem more plausible if she didn't.

'I think I'll go to bed for a while.' Maisie pulled an afflicted face.

'Go and hop into bed. I'll be in now.'

She turned about and headed for her room.

Lily rose slowly and watched her go. If they were going to fool the people watching them, they were going to have to get much better at it than this.

Chapter 41

While Maisie pretended to sleep Lily tried to busy herself tidying up the kitchen table. Cat brushed by her legs and nosed at the empty bowl. He'd been keeping a low profile and she'd almost forgotten about him. She refilled the bowl and watched him noisily eat. She knew her daughter would probably get bored in ten minutes and that it would be difficult to persuade her to stay in bed. What would they do then? With no TV or laptop it was going to be a challenge to keep her occupied.

Her phone buzzed in her robe pocket and she quickly answered.

'You can lift the blind when it's light,' the male voice said.

They had been discussing drawing a window in the kitchen or had he overheard their conversation in the bathroom? 'We're terrified of doing what we're not supposed to.'

'Is Maisie OK?'

Did Lily detect a note of concern in his voice or was he aping it? 'She's still traumatised from being taken from me.'

'She's resilient,' he dismissed offhandedly.

'How could you let her soil herself?'

'I'm sorry but, as you'll appreciate, the working facilities here are limited. You have the best ones. The only ones, in fact. Perhaps, in future, you should do all you can to ensure that Maisie isn't deprived of them.'

'I will.' Lily restrained the aggression in her reply. 'Please don't take her away from me like that again.'

'I doubt it'll be necessary but that'll be up to you.'

'I still don't know how deeply what you did affected her. She's just a child.'

'That's not something I need to be reminded of.'

She changed tack. Still wondered if he'd eavesdropped on their sink conversation. 'I'll do my best, but I can't always control her.'

'Are you happy with what's in the storeroom?'

She didn't respond.

'Lily?'

'How long do you intend to keep us here?'

'Three hundred and fourteen days.'

His immediate answer was like a blow to her stomach.

'Are you OK?'

She sucked in a breath and shook her head. Until then he'd given away nothing about his plans for them.

'But having seen the storeroom I'm sure you've already guessed that you're in for the long haul.'

'You can't keep us here that long.'

He was silent.

She had to prevent him from hanging up. 'Why . . . why that specific amount of days?' Her voice cracked.

'I've answered your question. Be grateful I have. That's something that wasn't done in the past.'

'What happened in the past?'

'Is there anything else you need?'

'No. Please, tell me why you're doing this to us.'

'Have you checked all the supplies?'

'No.'

'Then how do you know that you don't need anything else?'

'What happens after three hundred and fourteen days?'

'It's over,' he answered eventually.

'You mean, you'll let us go?' But there had been nothing in his tone that indicated that.

'You'll be released.' He didn't elaborate further.

'Both of us walk free?'

'Is there any specific medication you need?'

Lily tried to absorb the question.

'I know Maisie needed antihistamine last year. Anything else I might have missed? Lily?' He prompted.

How did he know about the antihistamines? 'Maisie said you have a lady friend.'

The line was silent.

'Please, may I speak with her?'

'No. That's the very last thing you want to do. Now, this might be your last opportunity. Is there anything else you need?'

'I don't know. I haven't checked what's in the storeroom.'

'Make it priority then. The medical supplies are on the shelf above the freezer.'

'I haven't had chance.'

'While Maisie is . . . convalescing . . . you should have plenty of time.'

She registered his sceptical tone. 'And what if there *are* things I need?'

'Make a list on your phone. I'll call once you've done it. Be thorough.'

'How do I know you're not tampering with these supplies?'

'You don't. But they're all you've got. Use them sparingly and they should last you.'

'What about fresh fruit, fresh vegetables?'

'What about them?'

'You can't expect us to live without those.'

'It's amazing what you can adapt to.' He hung up.

Chapter 42

After Lily had been in the storeroom for just under an hour, Maisie wandered in, still wearing her pyjamas over her clothes.

'What are you doing?'

'You feeling better now?' Lily asked, for the benefit of the camera over the door.

Maisie frowned but quickly cottoned on. 'Yes. Much better.'

'So, you actually slept?'

'Just woken up.' She rubbed her eyes.

Lily knew it was for real. That was good. And the fact she'd managed to do so alone in her own bed was even better.

'Is that food?' Maisie indicated the three large cardboard boxes that were lined up on top of the freezer lid.

'No. First aid.'

'Oh.' Maisie's gaze shifted back to the stack of Choca-Pops to her left.

Lily's mind had been blank as she'd sorted through the contents – bandages, tampons, pads, plasters, cotton wool, antiseptic, cough and cold medicines and tablets, the antihistamines as well as pills for indigestion and headaches. Every eventuality covered? There was bound to be something that had been missed. How often would she be able to ask for specific medication or was this her only chance of boosting the supplies? Again, she considered what would happen if they had a real emergency and Maisie needed urgent medical care she couldn't give her.

'You look worried.' So did Maisie.

'Just thinking.' She put her hands on her hips. What potential conditions could she foresee? Maisie still hadn't had chicken pox. She sorted through the box in front of her and found a bottle of calamine lotion.

'Were you talking to the scary man earlier?'

Lily turned to her and gave her a warning look. 'Yes.'

'What did he say?' Maisie asked with apprehension.

She wasn't going to tell her about the number of days he'd mentioned. 'That I have to make sure we've got everything we need.'

Maisie looked about her. 'Doesn't he think we have?'

'He wants to know if there's anything specific we want.'

'We can ask for anything?' Maisie's eyes widened.

'This isn't about what we wish for. It's about what we need,' Lily said sternly. 'We have to think carefully about what might happen while we're here.'

'Happen?'

'Yes.' Lily didn't want to alarm her though. She held up the plasters. 'Like do we have enough of these if you cut your finger?'

'How many are there?'

Lily counted. 'Twelve boxes.'

'That must be enough. If I'm careful, we shouldn't need any.'

Lily couldn't help but smile. 'He says we're allowed to lift the blind when it's daylight.'

'Can I open it now? The sun will be coming out soon.'

'We'll do it together. Let me finish in here first.'

'Can I explore in here?'

Lily preferred her to be where she could see her. 'Yes, but you can't open anything, understand?'

Maisie looked dejected.

'Even if there are free toys inside.'

'OK,' she agreed and walked by Lily towards the back of the room.

Lily returned her attention to the interior of the box in front of her but, as much as she tried to concentrate, the phone conversation she'd had about the length of their incarceration and their fate beyond it was all she could focus on. Was that really the truth or just another way of torturing her?

A few minutes seemed to pass as she distractedly rummaged but then a noise interrupted her thoughts. It was the low metallic tapping sound that had drawn them to the kitchen window before. When she looked at her phone, she realised another half an hour had gone by. 'Maisie?' She turned to the stacked boxes behind her.

No reply.

Tap, tap.

That was definitely the same sound. 'Maisie?' She called louder and walked to the back of the room. Lily peered down the tight passage between the wall and the boxes. No sign of her there. She moved quickly down it and emerged the other side. No Maisie.

Tap, tap, tap.

Panic ballooned and she rushed to the door and pushed her way through it. 'Maisie!' She yelled.

'I'm out here!' Maisie's voice came from the kitchen. That was exactly where she didn't want her to be. As Lily approached she could see that the room was lighter and knew why. She entered and saw Maisie sitting at the kitchen window. She'd pulled up the blind.

'Look, he's out there again.' Maisie turned back to the window and waved.

'No!' Lily darted to where she was sitting and looked out.

'He's seen me!' Maisie said excitedly.

Lily could see the man from before. He was standing by the freezer again, sledgehammer in hand. And he was looking up at the window.

Maisie waved harder. 'Help us! Please help us!'

He saw them both and Lily froze.

Chapter 43

Lily's first instinct was to consider the camera behind them. 'Get away from the window!' She kept her focus on the man below.

He put his hand to his brow so he could block the sun from his eyes.

'He's definitely seen us!' Maisie exclaimed. 'We're saved!'

'No. Down, now!' Lily gesticulated but didn't move from her position at the pane.

'Help us!' Maisie mouthed at him.

Lily took hold of her daughter's arm.

But she resisted. 'Ow, you're hurting.'

Lily guided her down but didn't shift her attention from the trespasser.

He was still gazing up.

Lily reached for the string of the blind and started unwinding it from the prongs to drop it. She took as much time to do it as she dared.

'No!' Maisie stood on tiptoes and grabbed her hand with both of hers. 'We have to signal him!'

But he'd obviously seen them, and Lily knew that if she

closed the blind on a distressed child that would look even more suspicious. Would he come to investigate?

But Maisie had hold of the string and was holding it tight in place.

'Maisie, we've spoken about this, let go!'

'Don't close it!'

Struggling with Maisie looked good for the camera. It sold the idea that Lily was doing everything to obey instructions and control her daughter. Maisie didn't realise that. And Lily couldn't explain that to her if their captors were listening. 'Maisie, this is my last warning.' She glanced briefly at the string, and when she looked up again the figure had stepped down from his position on the rubble.

'I'm not letting go.' Maisie's knuckles were white as she held onto the string so Lily couldn't loosen it.

'Let it go!' Lily bellowed.

Maisie just gritted her teeth and held on.

Lily straightened each of Maisie's fingers, pulled her hand away and secured it in hers. 'Don't.' She swiftly undid the string securing the blind with her other then let it go so it dropped down hard.

Maisie screamed in exasperation.

Just before the view from the window was obscured Lily saw that the bearded man was walking towards their building, his head still angled up at them and a frown on his face.

'He was going to help us.'

'I had to. We have to do as we're told.'

Maisie's attention returned to the blind.

'Maisie . . .'

Lily beat her to the edge as she tried to lift it. This was good. If the trespasser saw a further struggle, he might want to find out exactly what a small child was doing inside a derelict building. Particularly if someone was trying to conceal her. But she also had to make it look like she was desperately trying to restrain Maisie as well. She had much stronger arms than her daughter, but as she held the edge, she made sure it was lifted and yanked a few times so the man below would be in no doubt. 'That's enough!' she shouted, when she was sure it had been.

Maisie folded her arms petulantly.

'You know what we were told.'

'You said we were allowed to open the blind.' Tears glistened in Maisie's eyes.

Lily felt sickened by the struggle she'd just had with her daughter, but kept up the façade for their watchers. 'Yes. We were allowed. But if you see anyone out of the window you must call me.'

'I did.' Maisie sniffed and her bottom lip trembled.

'We have to keep quiet.'

'But we might not ever see anyone else.'

'It doesn't matter. What does is us doing all we can to keep ourselves safe in here.'

'He could've let us out,' she protested and wiped away a tear.

'No. Nobody is getting through the front door.' But she prayed that wasn't the case. That whoever had been outside would find the steel plate over it and realise they were prisoners.

'You don't even want us to leave!' Maisie bawled and tightened her arms to her chest.

'That's enough of *that*,' Lily cautioned her, until they had chance to talk in private.

'If Daddy was here, he wouldn't want us to stay.'

That took her by surprise. 'But Daddy isn't here.' Was he? Did she still believe he could be part of this or was that just a slender hope she couldn't let go?

Maisie rubbed her eye. 'He'd know what to do.' She lowered her voice, like she knew how much it would hurt Lily.

'You're right. He wouldn't want to stay. Like he didn't want to stay with us.' She immediately regretted saying it.

Maisie turned her head away from Lily and stared at the blind.

'But that was because he didn't want to stay with me,' she mitigated. It was too late though.

Another tear ran down Maisie's face but she let it fall from her chin.

Lily put her hand to her cheek, but she jerked away. 'That was all our fault, Maisie. Nothing to do with you. But I know that if Daddy were here, he would want to do everything to protect you. Like I'm doing.'

'If Daddy had been home nobody could have taken us away.'

Lily had momentarily forgotten the camera. But now she wondered how significant this conversation was for whomever was watching them. 'We'll talk about this when you've calmed down.' She tried to suppress her own reaction to what Maisie had said. Was she right? 'We'll leave the blind closed and you're not to touch it, OK?'

Maisie eventually nodded but then froze.

Somewhere nearby, a door had slammed.

Chapter 44

They both remained stock-still. It was the first time Lily had heard any indication of other people moving about the building.

Maisie gulped. 'That was right by us.'

'Ssshhh.' Lily held up her palm.

They both listened.

Slow, tentative footsteps echoing.

'Is it the man from outside?' Maisie whispered.

Lily held her finger to her lips.

The footfalls slowed and halted.

'Or is it the scary man?'

Lily shook her head and crept across the tiles to the wall over the sink. From what Maisie had said, their captors were at least one floor above them.

Maisie started to follow.

Lily gestured for her to stay where she was, but her daughter crossed the kitchen to join her.

A few more footsteps.

They sounded to Lily like they were just the other side of

the wall. Should she cry out for help? She felt the presence of the camera tingle on her back. Perhaps this was a test.

The feet moved from right to left. Lily moved with them. This was too much of a coincidence. It had to be the man they'd just seen from the window.

Maisie was close behind her. 'They're going that way,' she hissed.

Was there a corridor adjacent to the kitchen? Lily shuffled a few paces forward. But how could she react when their every move was being monitored?

Maisie thumped her little fist on the solid kitchen wall.

Lily took hold of it and shook her head. Not because she didn't want to signal to whoever was there but because she doubted they'd have heard it from the other side. And because she had to be seen to prevent Maisie from giving them away.

'He's walking away from us! Help!' Maisie wrestled herself from Lily's grip and ran out into the hallway.

'Maisie, come back here,' she whispered sharply. But she let her go, gave her a head start.

Maisie trotted down the hallway.

Lily waited a few seconds in the blind spot below the kitchen and hallway cameras before jogging to catch up with her.

Maisie beat the wall with both hands. 'Hello! Hello! We're in here! Help us, please!'

Lily reached her and put her hand over her mouth.

Maisie wriggled and yelled hard into her palm.

Lily could feel the heat of her breath and the intensity vibrating through her fingers. She hated doing it for the camera but hoped that Maisie had shouted hard enough for the trespasser to hear.

Maisie dug her nails into the back of Lily's hand and screamed hard so he could.

Lily ignored the pain and held her daughter tight.

'Hello?' A man's voice.

They both went rigid.

'Hello, who is that?' He had an Irish accent.

Lily barely resisted the reflex to respond. Maisie still struggled, so she briefly let her fingers slip from her mouth.

'In here. Help!'

Lily covered her daughter's lips again. 'Ssshhh.'

'I saw you in the window.' There was fear in his voice. 'Are you OK?'

Lily made sure Maisie couldn't answer. She wouldn't either. If neither of them did now then it would be clear to him that something was wrong.

'Just knock on the wall if you need help.'

Lily held Maisie fast. It was what their captors would want her to do. But their silence also telegraphed the fact that he'd found something he shouldn't.

'Can you hear me?'

Lily shook her head at Maisie.

The man's footsteps went back and forth on the other side of the wall.

'I can't find a way in here. I'm going to try the other side.'

The footsteps went left and then another door slammed.

Rustling at the front door

Maisie looked longingly towards it, but Lily shook her head.

'I can't get in here.'

Lily wondered how long it would take one of their captors to come down the stairs from where they were watching the situation. Should she warn the man? But if she did and he didn't escape what punishment would be meted out?

'Please, say something if you're in trouble. I know there's a child in there.'

Lily clamped her fingers tighter on Maisie's mouth and felt the breath coming hard down her nostrils. She'd said enough. Too much for their captors? Would it be better to take her chances on the stranger outside now or would that just endanger them both?

'There's no lock. Is there another way in?'

Lily remained motionless.

'Please, answer!'

Chapter 45

Maisie squirmed in Lily's grip, but she frantically shook her head at her daughter.

'I know someone's in there. I'm going to see if I can get in the other side. OK?'

Maisie screamed into Lily's hand.

Lily stifled her for the camera.

'I heard that!'

The footsteps trotted past the front door, and Lily turned her head to the open door of the bathroom.

A few moments later they heard knocking on the wall in there.

'If you don't let me in, I'm calling the police!'

Slam!

Lily knew it came from the direction of the door they'd heard earlier. Somebody else had just walked through it. Was the bearded man aware of their approach? He was the other side of their prison now.

Lily turned back to Maisie and met her eye. She'd heard it as well and her body had stiffened. 'Not a sound.'

But Maisie couldn't comprehend why she wasn't being

allowed to reply to their rescuer and regarded her with bewilderment.

More banging on the bathroom wall.

Footsteps quickly followed the path of the trespasser, and Lily heard them pass the front door.

Maisie's eyes opened wider as she realised who it probably was.

The trespasser had been alone. One of their captors was about to intercept him. Should they shout a warning?

'OK. Police it is.'

Lily made a split-second decision. 'Get out of here! Leave us alone!'

The knocking stopped.

Lily couldn't hear the second set of footsteps either.

'I saw a child! What are you doing in there?'

'Believe me, you must leave. Now!'

'No, tell me what the hell is going on in there! Why isn't there a door?'

'We're fine in here. Go now, quickly!'

'I can't do that. Not until I know the child is safe.'

How could she warn him, and would that be as punishable as trying to escape? If he couldn't find a way in, there was little chance of him rescuing them. She had to persuade him to leave. Maybe then he would call the police.

'I'm not getting any reception on my phone.'

Of course not. She wondered what the radius of whatever was jamming her phone was. 'Please!' There was hysteria in her voice. 'Get away from here!'

No response.

Lily briefly relaxed her grip on Maisie.

'Come back!' Maisie tried to get to her feet.

Lily dragged her down and covered her mouth again.

Silence.

Maisie tried to shout something else, but Lily held her fingers tightly over her wet lips. She could feel the circulation pounding in her daughter's body.

Footsteps, not as loud as the trespasser's, moved slowly then sped up as they crossed the area behind the bathroom wall. A few moments later they stopped.

Lily knew what the sound meant but she waited, muscles tensed, as she held onto Maisie. Her daughter's breaths squealed in and out of her nose. A few minutes later the trespasser still hadn't spoken. Lily released Maisie's mouth.

She took in a few breaths and regarded Lily as if she were demented. 'Hello!' She stood and entered the bathroom.

Lily held her breath. Wanted to hear his voice again.

Maisie went right up to the wall. 'Hello! I'm in here!'

'Maisie.' Lily didn't want to remonstrate with her again. Not when her daughter was about to find out they weren't about to be saved. What had happened to the bearded man? Had he just been dragged away?

'Come back!'

'He's not going to reply.'

Maisie turned on her, as if it were her fault. 'Where has he gone? Why didn't you tell him about the scary man?'

'He couldn't get to us.' How could she tell her that their saviour had probably been knocked out or worse? 'I think . . . the scary man has taken him away.'

Maisie shook her head as the realization of that soaked in.

'That's why we've been told not to bring attention to ourselves. They see everything. They would have known he was coming here.'

'Where have they taken him?'

'I don't know.'

'Will they harm him?'

Lily shrugged and saw the horror setting on her daughter's face. She got to her feet and joined her in the bathroom. 'We weren't allowed to help him. That's why I tried to send him away. We've done nothing wrong.' But Lily wasn't convinced of that.

'Hello!' There was desperation in Maisie's cry.

Still nothing.

Lily gave Maisie a hug from behind but she remained rooted to the spot.

They both waited, but there were no further sounds from the other side of the wall.

Chapter 46

An hour later Maisie was sitting quietly at the kitchen table still refusing any food or drink.

'Come on. You've got to eat something.'

'I'm going back to the bathroom.' She started to get up from her chair.

'Stay put. I've told you. You won't hear anything else.'

Maisie remained on her feet. 'Please, just let me wait there.'

Lily shook her head.

'Just a bit longer.' She tried to negotiate.

'We waited there long enough. I want you to stay where I can see you.'

'I promise I won't get us into trouble again.'

'And what would you do if you heard him again?' But that was the wrong thing to say. 'Or what would happen if you saw somebody else from the window?'

Maisie sat down and fixed her eyes on the duplicate salt and pepper set.

Lily didn't want her to feel any worse than she did, but now was the time to hit home the message. 'You must never react in the way you did. Always come to me.'

Maisie chewed her lip.

Lily didn't want her to withdraw into guilt. 'We just have to hope that the man is OK.'

'If he was, he would have answered us,' Maisie said dejectedly.

'We don't know what happened. Perhaps he went outside because his phone wasn't working.'

But neither of them believed that.

On cue, Lily's phone buzzed in her back pocket. She answered quickly.

'Did you have any other requirements?' he asked officiously.

Was he really not going to talk about what had just happened? 'Yes. I want some LiClean.'

'What's that?'

'For head lice. Maisie had a bout of it recently and I hadn't finished the treatment.'

'LiClean . . .'

It sounded like he was writing it down. 'And some Sevrol eye drops. For her allergies. She needs them but they're prescription.'

'Good. Anything else?'

'What happened to him?'

'Who?'

'Please don't. I did everything I could to keep him away from us.'

'Well . . . you appeared to.'

Lily didn't like the suspicion in his tone. 'You *did* tell us that we could open the blind.'

'I did.'

'As soon as I realised what was happening, I tried to close it.'

'Yes. I saw that. I saw everything.'

'What is he saying about the man?'

Lily realised Maisie was listening intently to the conversation. She silently shushed her. 'I've talked to Maisie about this. It won't happen again.' She kept eye contact with her daughter.

'You said that last time.'

Lily gestured into her bedroom, but Maisie wouldn't leave. She covered the mouthpiece. 'Go to your room.'

Maisie scraped her chair out and reluctantly obeyed.

Lily waited for her to walk slowly to her bedroom and knew she was taking her time so she could eavesdrop. She turned her back and moved to the sink. 'Please tell me he's OK.'

'He's OK.'

Lily sighed. 'Where is he now?'

'He won't be coming back to the site.'

Lily felt a spike of anger. 'And what does that mean?'

'Exactly that. Maisie shouldn't look for him now.'

'She's in the other room. You can tell me.'

'I know she's in the other room. But she's standing at the door listening to one side of this conversation.'

Lily didn't turn. Didn't doubt he was watching them both. 'I just need an assurance that there won't be another punishment,' she whispered.

'Why would there be a punishment? D'you think you've done something wrong?'

'No,' she retorted abruptly.

'And what about Maisie?'

'No.'

'But you said she won't do it again. That implies she has done something wrong.'

'Don't take her. If you think we've done something wrong, punish me.'

'You were the last time. But don't worry. Punishment has already been handed out.'

'What do you mean? To the man who came here? The one I tried to send away?'

'Yes,' he sighed '. . . you've made it clear that that's what you tried to do.'

'I just need to know he's OK.'

'You asked me to tell you he's OK and I did. If you really want to know what happened to him though . . . I slit his throat and buried him in the rubble.'

Chapter 47

Lily felt as if the room were folding in, his words slipping coldly through her.

'I was left with no choice,' he declared impassively.

She was breathless, as if her chest were being crushed. 'If you're trying to scare me . . .'

'I know. You're scared enough already.'

'Then tell me you're lying.'

'I'm lying. Again, I can tell you anything you want me to.'

Was that a bluff? Another psychological strategy to keep her in line? 'We didn't hear a struggle.'

'No. He didn't.'

But there had been no sound of the trespasser leaving. No two sets of footsteps as he was escorted out.

'It's not my fault. You brought him here.'

'We didn't. I tried to hide us.'

'So that's something you have to live with now.'

'No . . . don't do that.'

'If taking Maisie away from you didn't persuade you sufficiently that you have to toe the line then maybe this has.'

'I don't need any more persuasion!' Lily erupted.

'That's good to hear.' His voice remained level. 'Because I really can't have any outsiders interfering with what we're doing here. Careful . . .' he added, 'Maisie's coming back.'

Lily turned and found her daughter at the kitchen doorway. 'Go back to the bedroom.'

'Why are you shouting at him?'

'Just do as you're told.'

But Maisie had picked up on Lily's expression and her own registered anxiety before she turned on her heel.

Lily waited for her to walk back into her bedroom. 'And what exactly are we doing here?'

'I've already given you more information than is necessary.'

'If you did what you say you did . . . to that man . . .'

'"If?"'

'If you did what you say you did . . . why wouldn't I think you'd do it to us?'

'There is no reason for you not to think that.'

Lily's mouth was dry. Should she be pushing him like this? 'If that's what's going to happen, why don't we spend every minute trying to escape?'

He exhaled, as if he were already bored with the conversation. 'Because you know what I'll have to do. If you behave, there's always a possibility the two of you will come through this.'

Lily closed her eyes. 'I need to know Maisie will be all right.'

'I've told you how many days you have.'

Lily didn't like his evasion. 'But not why. And what about afterwards?'

'That's a long way away. Concentrate on you and Maisie getting there first.'

'I'll do as you say but I need some—'

'Will you though?' he interjected. 'I'm not seeing much evidence of that so far.'

'We'll do as you say. I promise. But I need some assurances.'

'So you keep saying. They were a luxury that was never offered in the past.'

'You mentioned that before. Talk to me about that.'

There was a pause, as if he were considering it. 'So you want assurances *and* a story? Choose one.'

'Please . . . just tell me.'

'One or the other,' he enunciated.

'Are you going to kill us?'

'You want me to say no?'

She was going to reply 'yes'. But she turned to the camera and nodded.

'No.'

Lily kept her gaze on the lens and tried not to let her hatred burn through it. 'Put her on.'

'She's not here.'

'I don't believe you. Is she a mother too?'

Silence.

'She probably isn't. If she was, she could never be part of this.' She went to the wall and tugged down the mood board. 'This is what my daughter thinks she looks like.' She showed it to the lens, pointed at the image of cupid. 'But you already know that. Maisie used this picture because she needs to believe it. I need to believe. Give me something.'

'You get nothing.' It was a woman . . .

Lily's vague hope shrivelled. The emotionless voice was hoarse; the three words grated into her ear. 'Please, let me talk.'

'You can talk all you like. I'm hanging up.'

'Don't! Please!' Was that her natural voice? Sounded like it was only hanging on by a thread.

'You don't give the orders, bitch,' she rasped then ended the call.

Lily noticed Maisie standing back in the doorway.

'What did the scary man say?'

Lily looked down at the mood board and the image of the angel with hearts around it.

Chapter 48

Lily tucked Maisie into her double bed and realised she hadn't made her wash or brush her teeth. She'd been on autopilot since she'd taken the phone call. All Lily could think of was the man who had been killed trying to help them. That was if their captor was to be believed.

'Maybe he might come back tonight,' Maisie said after Lily had kissed her forehead.

'Maybe.' She hadn't even intimated what she'd been told on the phone. Nor would she. It could have been a lie. That was still a scant possibility to cling to.

'I'll stay awake when you come to bed. That way, we won't miss him if he does.'

Lily nodded. Despite her attempts to misdirect her, Maisie had spent most of the day in the bathroom listening at the wall. 'We shouldn't get our hopes up. I've told you, it would be better for him if he didn't come back.'

Maisie frowned. 'I still don't understand.'

She sat on the bed. 'The people who want us here will do anything to make sure we stay. If people come, it doesn't mean we're going to be rescued. It might just mean they're putting themselves in danger.' That was the most succinct explanation she could think of.

'So nobody can save us?'

'Yes, *we* can save us.'

That didn't seem to convince Maisie. 'But we haven't done that yet.'

'We're doing as we're told. That's the best way.'

Maisie's expression said she thought otherwise.

'Try to sleep now.'

'I will. But wake me when *you* come to bed.'

Lily could see how frazzled Maisie was. She glanced at her phone.

'What time is it?' Maisie yawned.

'Nearly eight o'clock,' she lied. It was only six fifteen in the evening. It was still light outside but then it usually was when Maisie went to bed. They'd still been up nearly fifteen hours, however, and that wasn't healthy for Maisie. Lily felt like she was going to burn out too.

'When are you coming to bed?' Maisie rolled onto her side.

'Just going to make a coffee and then I'll be in. Want anything?'

Maisie was already asleep.

Lily padded from the room, scarcely glancing at the camera, and wondered if they were already getting too used to living under surveillance. She'd hidden the carving knife and hammer under her pillow. They'd know that. Would have seen her do it but she hoped they took it as a warning.

She made herself a big mug of instant and examined the drinking vessel. She realised it was Ewan's Looney Tunes mug, that Maisie had bought him, with Wile E. Coyote on the side. At least, it was a mug that looked exactly like it. This one was more pristine though. She thought about what Maisie had said about him knowing what to do if he'd been locked away with them and then recalled what he'd said when Lily suggested they get a mortgage on a place. Ironically, Ewan insisted he preferred to rent because he didn't want a house to take him prisoner and hold him to ransom for the rest of his life.

Truth was he probably would have handled what had happened with the bearded man much differently. But however he had, it would have been the same outcome. They were trapped inside their prison with no way out and certainly no way to let anyone in. And if Ewan had encouraged the trespasser, what sort of punishment would he have brought on them? Lily was still unsure if their visitor had escaped or if the man on the phone had been lying to her. She was determined to stay awake the whole night though. She took a big slug of hot coffee. Maybe she'd catch some sleep tomorrow when Maisie was wide awake and could alert her if anyone tried to get in.

She waited a few minutes for Maisie to fall asleep properly and then crept into the bedroom, positioned the chair in front of the door, got under the duvet fully clothed and then propped herself up on some pillows beside her daughter.

Lily kept quietly sipping the mug of coffee. After an hour she went and made herself another and settled back into place. She'd get another if necessary. As she slowly drained it, she considered everything she'd learnt about the people holding them. There were at least two of them. And appealing to the woman's maternal instincts wasn't going to work. What else? Wherever they were watching from was above them. They knew that she knew that, so maybe it didn't matter. What was the significance of three hundred and fourteen days? It appeared to reference an episode in the past that he'd hinted at on two occasions. Would he reveal more or was it just further deception?

She shivered as she contemplated the notion that she'd never find out the reason they'd been imprisoned. Would that be the ultimate torture?

Just before two in the morning she was woken by a sliding sound.

Lily sat bolt upright and strained her ears. Where had that come from?

Maisie stirred beside her. 'What is it?'

But Lily didn't need to tell her to be quiet.

Maisie sat up and they both waited for further noise.

A soft thump.

Maisie pointed at the door and mouthed 'That was in the hallway,' as soon as Lily turned to her.

Lily nodded, swung her socked feet out of bed and quickly grabbed the carving knife from under the pillow.

Maisie was open-mouthed as Lily brandished it.

'Wait here.'

A creak.

Somebody was definitely out there. But the difference now was that Lily was only going to use the blade if they tried to take Maisie. Even if she injured one, there was still at least one other to deal with.

'I don't want to do this anymore.' Maisie was clutching her hands but her whole body was quaking.

Lily went silently to the door and quickly took her robe off. She tossed it over the camera so it was covering the lens. They would have seen the knife. But she wanted them to. Wanted to signal exactly what they'd be walking into.

She held the blade high and waited for the door to open.

Chapter 49

Lily waited until her arm started to ache. After several minutes more the only sound was their breathing. She deftly shifted the chair from in front of the door.

'Stay with me.' Maisie clutched the duvet tightly to her.

Lily shook her head. Despite the camera being obscured their captors knew she had a weapon and was poised to use it. Would the intruder just wait for her to open the door? But there had been no noise since she'd taken her position there. She strained her ears. Could it have come from outside their walls?

Lily gave it another few minutes before opening the door. But she hesitated with it cracked and listened. A cold draught blew around her feet. 'Hello?'

Nobody answered.

Lily leaned around the edge of the door and quickly took in the hallway. Just opposite the storeroom a small cardboard box had been positioned on the black and orange carpet. She looked towards the kitchen. The room was in darkness. Was somebody hiding there waiting to pounce as soon as she examined it?

'Wait there.' Lily stepped into the hallway.

'Come back!'

She closed the door against Maisie's protest, strode to the kitchen, quickly flicked the light on and simultaneously jumped backwards. Nobody in there.

Lily stole down the hallway and halted at the box. She pushed on the storeroom and front doors and they were still sealed. The hairs taped across both were unbroken.

They were using a different entrance.

Lily tried not to react in front of the camera and knelt to the box and quickly opened it. Inside were several boxes of the treatment she'd asked for. Even the Sevrol. How had they got that if it was prescription only? She took the bottle out of the box and saw that it was only two thirds full. Had they fetched it from Fallstaff Gardens?

'Is it safe to come out?' Maisie had partially opened the door and had her face at the crack.

'Stay there.' Lily finished examining the contents and glanced up at the camera over the kitchen doorway. She lifted the box and stood. How had they accessed the hallway to leave it? It was either through Maisie's bedroom, the bathroom, the kitchen or the hallway itself.

'What's inside?' Maisie asked as she walked back into the bedroom.

'Just some things I asked for.' She closed the door behind her and slid the chair back in place.

'Can I see?'

'There isn't anything interesting for you in here.'

'But I want to see.'

'In the morning. Back to bed now.' She swivelled her away from the box.

'But what if they come back?'

'I don't think they will. They just wanted to leave us the box. I'll stay awake. You need to get your sleep though.'

Maisie climbed back onto the mattress. 'I won't be able to sleep now.'

'Close your eyes and see what happens.'

Maisie put her head on the pillow and Lily dumped the box on the carpet and removed her robe from the camera. She didn't want there to be a punishment for that. She climbed in with Maisie and pulled the duvet over them.

'Where are you going to put the knife?' Maisie asked with her eyes shut tight.

Lily had tried to conceal it behind the box as she'd re-entered the room, but that had been pointless. Maisie now knew where it had been hidden. 'Back in its place.' She slid it under her pillow.

'You'll keep it close to you tonight?' Maisie kept her eyelids sealed.

'Yes.' But Lily didn't want Maisie to think it was normal. 'You're never to touch it, OK?'

Maisie thought about it. 'Not even if the scary man comes into the room?'

'No. I'll protect you.'

'What if something happens to you?'

Lily was dismayed by Maisie's matter-of-factness. 'Nothing's going to happen to me.'

'Something happened to the man who tried to rescue us.'

'We don't know what happened to him,' Lily lied.

'What did the scary man say on the phone?'

'He didn't say anything.' But Lily could tell from Maisie's silence that she still didn't believe her.

'But I heard you ask him,' she eventually said.

'He wouldn't tell me.'

Maisie exhaled.

'Sleep. I'll be watching over you.'

Maisie opened her eyes. 'Where should I stick it?'

'What do you mean?'

'If something happens to you and he attacks me, where should I stick the knife in him?'

'That's enough of that.' But should she tell her? Perhaps preparing for that was exactly the right thing to do. Was Lily fooling herself that she could shield Maisie from their captors? Shouldn't she put aside that notion and be as pragmatic as Maisie? She'd been effortlessly taken from her once already.

'Should I put it in his stomach?'

A cold current passed through Lily. Is that what it would come down to? If their captors could use a hidden entrance to get to them anytime they wanted, it was likely that, at some point, they might both need to physically defend themselves.

'Or in his heart? If he was standing up, I'm not sure I could reach that.'

'Shush. We'll talk about it in the morning.' But would that be too late? There were still plenty of hours left before daylight and did that matter anyway? They could walk in whenever they wanted. But Lily hoped that the box was a good sign. They wanted them to remain healthy, wanted them to see out the time ahead. Or was all of it just a bluff?

Chapter 50

The next day they both rose at five. Mercifully, Maisie had dozed off but Lily hadn't slept at all and knew she couldn't sustain it.

While Maisie ate her cereal, Lily walked into the hallway and switched on the light there. She'd already examined the kitchen over the course of breakfast and hoped she'd done it subtly enough for anyone watching. She hadn't found any slits in the wallpaper or lino. Besides, they hadn't heard any noise in the kitchen.

'Where are you going?'

'Just to the bathroom. Empty your bowl before you get down from the table.'

'But I'm not hungry.'

'I don't care. You need to eat. Empty bowl.' Lily made for the bathroom, opened the door but padded past it to the storeroom. She slowed her pace and, without moving her head, cast her eyes around the walls and the ceiling above. She didn't want to make it obvious to the camera behind her that she was examining them.

Did they access their prison from upstairs? But she couldn't see any sign of joins in the ceiling wallpaper that could conceal a door.

Her attention shifted to the black and orange carpet beneath her green socked feet. Maybe the area below it was hollow and there was a tunnel there. But again, she couldn't see any outline around the large tiles that could hide an entrance.

She stopped at the storeroom door and confirmed that the hair was still held in place by the tape. It was the same story at the front door. So how the hell had they left the cardboard box? Lily didn't acknowledge the camera and put her ear to the storeroom door panel as if she might be listening for movement inside. Her face was turned away from the lens, so she surreptitiously examined the carpet more carefully.

She scanned the black and orange squares below her all the way to the front door and then clocked something she hadn't noticed before. The edge of the carpet was slightly lifted and overlapping the bottom of the skirting at the base of the wall on the right-hand side of the front door. Had it been like that before?

Perhaps it was just the way the carpet had been laid and it hadn't been cut properly; she was sure she would have noticed that before though. The carpet was raised about a quarter of an inch over the skirting base.

'Is there somebody in there?'

Lily turned to where Maisie was standing in the kitchen doorway. 'You finished?'

Maisie nodded. 'Is there?'

'No. Thought I heard something fall over in here.'

'Why don't you check?'

'I think I was mistaken.'

'I'll go and look if . . .' she trailed off.

'If I'm too scared?'

Maisie considered how to answer.

'We need to go in later anyway. Have to get some frozen milk. I just need the bathroom first.' Lily walked to it.

'Will you teach me then?'

Lily paused at the bathroom doorway. 'Teach you what?'

'Where I need to put the knife.'

'No more talk like that.' But should she tell Maisie exactly what to do when they were next brushing their teeth?

'I want my own.'

'No,' Lily refused flatly. 'You're not sleeping with a knife.'

'I do already.'

'I keep it under the pillow. My pillow.'

'Lots of kids carry knives.'

Lily couldn't believe she was having this conversation with her five-year-old, even under their circumstances. 'You're not having a knife.'

Maisie pouted and plodded back into the kitchen.

She sighed and quickly went into the bathroom. She needed a pee but as she sat down she was devising a way of getting at the skirting. She could cover the hallway camera, as she had in her room, but wondered if there was going to be a penalty for that.

Could they block its view another way while Lily pulled up the carpet? She had to be so careful about this. If there was a hidden way in it was also an exit and she couldn't afford to let them know she'd spotted it. She wouldn't tell Maisie. Had to sit on what she'd found until she'd decided what was the best way to use it and when. *If* there was a door there.

She quickly washed her hands and looked at herself in the mirror over the sink.

Stay calm.

But she'd already thought of a way to find out if she was right.

Chapter 51

'I'd like to try something tomorrow,' Lily whispered over the running tap as they brushed their teeth that night.

Maisie's eyes lit up. 'What?'

'We're going to move a big stack of boxes from the store-room into the kitchen.'

Her gaze dimmed again. 'What for?'

Lily turned the cold water on harder, so the flow was noisier. 'I can't tell you just yet.'

'Why not?'

'You'll soon find out. Just trust me. We'll move the boxes after breakfast.' It would look suspicious if they started shifting stuff when they were meant to be going to bed. And Lily needed to psyche herself up.

'Which ones?'

'It doesn't really matter.'

'Choca-Pops?'

'OK. We'll move some of those but we're going to have to do it in a particular way.' Lily sucked some water from the tap and spat. 'Get right to the back with that brush,' she said louder then leaned in closer to Maisie and told her exactly what she wanted her to do when they rose the next day.

Lily didn't sleep again that night and watched over Maisie while she did. The plan she'd outlined would hopefully conceal her search for an entrance at the skirting at the end of the hallway. If it wasn't there, they would carry on with their stock up and leave their captors none the wiser. She hoped.

Maisie woke just after seven and Lily told her to get dressed.

'Why do I need to? I'm not going out.'

She still hadn't told Maisie about the skirting. She knew her daughter wouldn't be able to resist looking at it and Lily couldn't have her doing that while their captors were watching. 'I don't want you to catch a chill.'

Maisie harrumphed while she slipped on jeans and a sweat-shirt that looked like they'd just been taken out of a packet.

Lily pointed at Maisie's socked feet. 'Slippers as well. Your toes were freezing last night,' she lied and didn't look up at the camera.

Maisie obeyed. 'You have to get dressed too then.'

'OK. Fair enough.' She was glad Maisie had insisted. Now it looked natural. But Lily wanted them to be properly clothed. Was there really a chance they'd end up outside? She'd laid out jeans and a bottle green sweater the night before, on top of the carving knife. She picked up the blade the same time and, blocking the activity from the lens with her body, furtively slipped it into the back of her jeans while she dressed. 'Let's eat then.'

Lily mechanically chewed cereal with a dry mouth and only managed to swallow it by taking big glugs of coffee.

'Are you OK?'

Lily focussed on Maisie. 'Yes, why?'

Maisie examined her uncertainly. 'Looked like you just fell asleep.'

She blinked and sat up straight. 'No, I'm fine.' Lily took another swig of coffee. When *had* she last slept? She was sure she'd nodded off a few times in bed but her ears had been straining for noises in the hallway.

'Why don't you lie down. I'll keep watch over you.'

Lily smiled at her daughter. 'Thanks but I'll be fine.' She could feel the cold blade against her buttock. 'We're running low on a few things. Let's get a few boxes out of the storeroom.'

Maisie tensed. 'OK.'

Lily finished her coffee and made brief eye contact with her daughter to reassure her. 'Come on then. We'll get you some Choca-Pops.' She stood and headed into the hallway and heard Maisie behind her.

Just act naturally. Ninety-five per cent of what they were about to do was anyway.

But Lily's heart pumped faster. Was she risking punishment? Their captors had allowed them to test all the doors before. But that was when they were sure they couldn't get out and this was one they weren't meant to know about. If it did exist. Lily had examined the bathroom and Maisie's bedroom. There was nowhere else they could have got in. It had to be there.

Lily halted at the storeroom door. The hair was still fixed across the door and the jamb. She went to the front door and pretended to listen there and confirmed the hair was still stuck there too.

'What are you doing?'

Lily returned to the storeroom door where Maisie was waiting. Still nobody had entered using either door. She'd initially assumed that when the storeroom door had been opened for them it had been from the inside. Now she thought otherwise. And when they'd brought Maisie back to her she'd figured they'd come in through the front door. Was it permanently sealed? She'd said she had something over her head, had no memory of how she'd got back in, only of walking down then up some stairs.

Maisie folded her arms, as if becoming impatient.

Lily couldn't blame her. She'd told her what she had to do but not why. 'Let's see how heavy these boxes are then.' She pulled on the handle of the storeroom door and it opened outwards. She swung it so it was almost flat to the hallway wall.

Inside the freezer was still buzzing and Lily stepped into the room and put her hands on her hips. She ignored the camera that was positioned over the door inside. 'OK, Choca-Pops first.' She reached up to the highest box and slid it from the stack.

Maisie stood where Lily had told her, on the threshold of the room so she wasn't in sight of the storeroom camera or the one at the far end of the hallway.

The Choca-Pops box was light and she easily swung it from its place to Maisie. 'Both hands.'

Maisie took it and set it on the floor in the hallway exactly where Lily had told her.

Lily handed her another Choca-Pops box and she stacked that on top of the first.

So far, so good.

Was this really going to work? Lily's circulation thudded in her temple as she lifted out the third box.

Chapter 52

'This one's heavier. Pasta shapes.'

Maisie grunted as she took the weight.

'You OK?'

Maisie nodded and hefted the box on top of the first two.

Lily glanced at the stack and calculated they'd need another four or five boxes. She selected a more lightweight one. Instant noodles next.

After Maisie had placed the fourth box she couldn't reach any higher.

'I've got the last few.' Lily only needed to stack another three boxes on top to get the height she wanted and quickly completed the task.

They were both now standing inside the storeroom on the threshold and out of sight of both cameras. The stack of boxes was exactly against the left of the threshold and was about six feet high. The stack was about five feet from the front door end of the hallway where the skirting was and effectively blocked the view of the camera at the opposite end of it. It would conceal her movement to the skirting but she had to stay rigidly in line with the boxes. 'Anything else you can think of that we need?'

'Um . . .'

As planned, it was down to Maisie to keep talking now. If somebody was listening, they had to convince them that they were holding a conversation about their supplies.

'. . . maybe crackers.'

'I can't see any of those on this side.' Lily nodded at Maisie to keep chatting and slid around the right side of the stack so the boxes were blocking her presence there. She kept her head low.

'I can't see any either,' Maisie continued.

'Maybe they're round the back,' Lily said from her hiding place. She bent low and took a pace forward.

'I don't want to go round there. It's too dark,' Maisie improvised.

'Don't be scared,' Lily replied and crept the three paces she needed to get to the skirting and crouched down on one knee.

'If I have to get them from there, I don't want crackers.'

Lily quickly ran her fingers along the carpet that rested against the skirting. Gripping the tight edge she lifted it up two inches and revealed the wooden floor below.

'I can see Cheez-its up there. They're like crackers,' Maisie kept going.

Lily let the carpet drop back into place and frantically scrabbled her hands around the edges of the black and orange squares. There was no concealed slit. Nothing that could be lifted. Was she in the wrong area? She squinted at the carpet to the left of her. But if she reached out to it her arm would be visible to the camera. But it looked the same as the area within her reach. Maybe there was no trap door at all.

'A bit like crackers anyway. I don't like the cheese dust though. It makes me feel sick.'

She could return to the storeroom now, rejoin the conversation before it started to sound too one-sided. But how else could they have got in? There had to be a door here somewhere.

She dragged up the carpet from the skirting again, yanked it back further. Her arm trembled.

'Why are you looking at me like that. I don't like the dust.'

Maisie was likely to give away their deceit at any moment. Lily's eyes darted back and forth along the skirting.

'It makes me cough.'

She had to get back to the storeroom. They could do this another day. Same method. Now she was out of time. But she kept the carpet pulled up and used her other hand to hold it firm.

'And make my fingers smell funny too.'

Lily got up off her knee and took a step backwards. She had to remember to keep in line with the boxes. She was about to release the carpet when she spotted something below the left of the skirting.

'I think we've got what we need.'

She turned to Maisie who was standing in the same position but gesturing her to come back. She held her hand up to her and returned her attention to the vertical line extending from under the skirting a foot away from her. She tugged the carpet back further and scanned the wood closely. There was another vertical line extending from under the right-hand side of the skirting.

'We've got enough for today.'

Lily could hear the concern in Maisie's voice. But this was something significant. What were those? They were about four feet apart. Lily put her hand dead in the middle of the floor between them and pushed. The wood bowed.

'I want to go back to the kitchen.'

She pushed harder and the floor between the two lines dropped down below the edge of the skirting. There was now a two-foot aperture below the bottom edge of the wall. Her knees wobbled on the edge of it. She reversed a foot and pulled the carpet from the opening.

She could see wooden steps below and weak daylight beyond those. Should she cover it back up? Lily turned to Maisie and there was panic in her daughter's eyes. They had a way out. Had their captors got suspicious though?

'I want a drink now.'

Something brushed Lily's arm and she jumped.

Cat. He darted past her and disappeared down the steps.

Shit. Even if she closed it up and aborted their escape anyone watching would now wonder what had happened to the animal.

'Let's go back to the kitchen.' Maisie's voice rose.

Lily shook her head at her and extended her arm. They had to go now.

Maisie shook her head.

Lily beckoned her emphatically.

Maisie still wouldn't budge.

Lily mouthed, 'We're going. Now,' and gestured for Maisie to join her again.

Maisie reluctantly slid around the boxes and hurried in a straight line to where Lily was. She looked agog at the opening.

Lily gripped Maisie's arm firmly and whispered, 'I'm going through first and I'll tell you if you should follow.'

Maisie shook her head.

'No time for this. I'm going now.' Lily put her feet into the opening and put the sole of her right deck shoe onto the top step.

Chapter 53

'Don't leave me here,' Maisie hissed.

Lily turned to her. 'I'm just going to check it out. Count to twenty in your head.'

Maisie closed her eyes and mouthed, 'one.'

Lily took her weight on both her shoes and slid through the gap under the wall. She crouched there so her shoulders slipped through and found herself looking down another seven steps. The bottom one was bathed in daylight.

She listened for signs of movement below, but could only hear her heartbeat thudding in her throat. There was no time to hesitate. If they were being watched then it wouldn't be long before their captors realised what had happened.

Gripping the untreated wooden bannister to her right she cautiously descended the steps, ducking her head below the wooden beams above. Her hand slid against the rough rail and she felt a splinter prick her palm.

Lily reached the bottom step and took in her surroundings. She was in a vast and derelict empty office space and there was nobody around. There were no tables or chairs but a maze of walled booths stretched away from her. Wires hung down in knotted bunches from panels in the ceiling and there were pools of water on the dirty grey carpet. A few of the windows were broken and a harsh breeze blew noisily in through the empty panes. That was the sound they'd heard from inside.

She turned to where she'd emerged and was looking at a structure on low wooden stilts. It was their prison and its exterior consisted of panels of pulpwood reinforced by struts made of the same material. She took a few paces back and walked around the right-hand side. It was positioned in one corner of the office space against one wall and tight against most of the window wall. That was why the only daylight they'd had was in the kitchen end.

Lily listened for any signs of footsteps above the wind. Nothing. But she was sure that wouldn't be the case for long. She crouched and quickly ascended the wooden steps again.

Maisie was crouching looking through the opening, her nervous expression rigid.

'Quickly, slide yourself through,' Lily whispered.

Maisie stayed where she was. 'What's down there?'

'Just a big office space. Come on.'

Maisie still didn't move. 'The scary man might be down there.'

'He's not. Not at the moment.' Lily went up another two steps and put her hands through the opening. 'I've got you.'

Maisie took a pace back. 'We might be safer here.'

'I don't have time to argue.'

Lily took hold of her.

Maisie yelped.

'Be quiet. They'll hear you.' Lily guided her through the gap. Maisie's hot cheek was against hers and, as she walked backwards down the stairs, she anticipated turning to find him standing right behind her.

Once she was clear she swivelled on her heel, Maisie still tight in her grip. Still nobody around.

Maisie surveyed the gutted open-plan office. 'You can put me down.'

Lily did but was already looking for an exit. There were double doors to their right, where the box of their apartment finished. That must lead to the corridor the trespasser had walked down before he'd accessed the other side. He'd obviously found a way up from ground level. But their captors had quickly accosted him, and she wondered if there was another way out. There had to be in a building this size.

She squinted to the dingy end of the office floor. There were more doors there. 'Follow me.' She took Maisie's hand and they headed into the rat run that cut through the maze of partitioned booths.

Slam!

They both stopped and turned back. That was the door in the corridor.

'Somebody's coming.' Maisie's hand tightened.

'Hurry.' Lily spun them back the other way and she walked them briskly down the saturated carpet. 'Don't turn back.' But the doors looked to be over a hundred yards away.

Rapid footsteps echoed

'We won't make it.'

Maisie was right. It sounded like whoever was coming was approaching fast.

A door squealed.

Lily dragged Maisie left and into the maze of partitions that covered most of the office floor space. She ducked down, turned them right, then right again then took a left. They were now somewhere towards the middle of the maze and she jerked them into one of the booths. There was no desk, only empty plug sockets.

Lily put her back against the partition and put her hand over Maisie's mouth.

A door squealed shut and all was silent.

Was whoever had come down standing in the doorway listening for them? Lily slightly repositioned herself and held Maisie still. The floor around them was littered with rodent droppings. They waited but they couldn't hear any movement.

Then a heel scuffed carpet.

The sound was still far over the other side but they were obviously searching the office floor. Lily wondered if there were cameras positioned in this room too. Could they see exactly where they were hiding?

A creak and that was much nearer. Were they entering the maze?

She could feel Maisie's body pump as they worked their way closer.

Chapter 54

Lily looked down at Maisie and saw her eyes were clenched shut.

Squelch.

That was loud. Inside the maze. They'd obviously walked through one of the puddles on the carpet.

Maisie released a tiny sob.

Lily tightened her hand over her lips.

Silence.

Either they'd heard Maisie or they'd paused to get their bearings. Should she and Maisie stay put or would that mean they were just waiting to be discovered? They were still some way from the doors and maybe those were locked. She slipped the metal carving blade out of the back of her jeans and firmly gripped the handle.

Maisie opened her eyes and then wider when she saw it in Lily's hand.

Then Cat trotted into their hiding place.

Had it followed them after they'd emerged?

The cat's ginger back arched and it hissed at them.

Lily frantically waved it away with her hand, but it stood

its ground, its head tightening to its scrawny body and its mouth snarling louder.

It was going to give them away. Lily maintained eye contact with it. It was the sure way to get Mr Gingerbread to back down, but it wasn't having the same effect.

Another creak even nearer.

The cat buzzed and growled, its green stare unblinking.

This was payback for them ignoring him. She had no choice. She had to shift the animal. Lily extended her leg and attempted to kick Cat, but the movement was enough and he slunk away.

Should they do the same? Perhaps they should double back. Aim for the doors their captor had entered through. But without standing straight she had no idea where in the maze they were. There had to be an exit the other side. If they could just get clear she could make the decision about which direction to go.

She shook Maisie's shoulder gently and pointed back out the way they'd come.

Maisie shook her head.

But an idea occurred to Lily. She put the knife carefully on the grey carpet and pulled out her phone. She found the timer. How long should she set it for?

Material swishing.

They were close. Lily set if for one minute, placed it on the floor and picked up the knife. She squeezed Maisie's arm and, gesturing her to follow, leaned around the edge of the partition they were behind.

Nobody in the walkway in either direction but they could

easily run into them as soon as they took a left or right. She looked down at the screen of her phone. It was already on forty-eight seconds. Taking Maisie's warm hand, she led her out of their hiding place.

Footfalls. Quickening.

Lily froze. She couldn't work out which side of them they were coming from. Should they just go back to their hiding place? But they were probably working their way through. Plus, they were standing up as well, so they could see exactly which areas they had to cover.

Maisie tugged on her hand. She wanted to go back.

Lily shook her head at her. They had to move soon. Otherwise the alarm would go off and give away their location. Lily led Maisie forwards. There was a left turning about twenty feet ahead.

The footsteps suddenly stopped.

Lily turned but the walkway behind them was empty. She tugged Maisie forward but froze. She could hear breathing. It was coming from the other side of the walkway wall directly to their right. She put her finger to her lips, and they waited.

The person caught their breath. Swallowed.

They had to get clear of the phone. It seemed like a couple of minutes had passed already. Lily gingerly pulled Maisie towards the left turning.

The alarm sounded. Shrill and loud.

Lily and Maisie scuttled around the turning. At least the sound would give them some cover. Behind them she could hear hurried footsteps, could feel the vibrations through the floor. Lily brandished the knife.

She led them right at the next turning then left again and hoped she was leading them in the general direction of the far doors. She paused them at the next right corner and they both listened.

The alarm was still sounding. Had they not found it yet? If they had they'd know it was a decoy. She and Maisie had to get out of the maze and decide if they should hide or try to make it out of the building.

The beeping stopped.

Somebody had turned it off. They had to keep low, not be tempted to take a look over the wall, however briefly. Lily pulled Maisie to the next left turning and, when they reached it, they were looking at the windows that ran down the left-hand side of the office.

They'd made it to the other side. Lily poked her head out quickly and looked in both directions. Nobody. To her right was a forty-yard space between them and some grey swing doors.

The footsteps were hurrying now. Working their way in their direction.

There was no time for second thoughts. Lily dragged Maisie out of the maze and indicated she should keep down. They dashed for the doors. If they stood, they would immediately be seen.

The footfalls sounded close now. They had to know where they'd be headed. Should they have turned left and headed back to the first doors? It was too late. They scrambled for the ones in front and Lily was searching for signs of them being locked. If they were, they were trapped.

The footsteps changed pitch. They were behind them now. Out in the open as well.

Lily stood straight and jerked Maisie up so they could pick up speed. They were only about ten feet from the doors. There was daylight through the circular portals.

Maisie's legs couldn't keep up.

'Come on, sweetheart.' Her hand was out to the doors.

'I can't.'

Lily gathered her daughter up and launched herself at them.

Chapter 55

Lily found herself at the top of a dingy stairwell and, without looking back, quickly descended the dirty concrete steps. Before she was halfway down, she heard somebody hit the swing doors.

'Behind us!' Maisie shrieked.

Because she was holding Maisie, she couldn't see her feet on the steps and prayed she didn't lose her rhythm before she reached the bottom.

Footfalls resounded close behind them.

Lily barrelled through another set of doors on the next level. There was a service elevator in front of them, but it took her a split second to decide that there wasn't time to open the next fire exit door let alone punch the button.

As the doors continued to swing open, she rammed her back against them and gritted her teeth in readiness.

A second later the person chasing them butted the panels, and Lily turned her body sideways and put her shoulder forcibly against the middle of the doors. Before they could batter it again, she slipped her left arm through the two handles and clenched against the next impact.

It jarred her hard and the edge of the door caught her cheekbone, but she slid her arm further through the handles, so her shoulder was lodged against the metal. She gripped one hand tightly in the other.

'You're crushing me.'

'Drop to the floor!'

But Maisie put her hands tighter around Lily's neck.

Another severe jolt. She cried out in pain but pedalled her feet against the door so they couldn't bust through.

The doors relaxed but Lily knew they were probably taking a run at it. She looked frantically around and saw the fire hose on the wall. 'Maisie, get that for me.'

Maisie opened her eyes and followed Lily's gaze.

Bang!

The blow parted the doors wider and the handles bit acutely into her arm. Lily screamed, water filled her vision and she choked back the agony. 'Get it!'

Maisie slid from between her arms and dashed to the hose.

'Grab the end and uncoil it!'

Maisie grunted as she tugged on the nozzle, but it wouldn't release from its rusty red spool.

'Pull it harder!'

Maisie crouched as she attempted to yank it out.

The wood struck Lily's body and she bounced off it, her feet sliding a few inches back. They shouldered it again, pressing their weight firmly against her. Maisie gritted her jaw and pushed back, grimly interlinking her fingers. They'd have to break her arm before she let them through.

Maisie's body jerked as she hauled repeatedly on the end of the hose, but it still wasn't going to come free.

Sharper, faster bashing from the other side. They were booting the door.

Lily yelped as the metal cut repeatedly into her forearm. 'As hard as you can!'

Maisie yelled and leaned back and the hose coil squeaked and turned. She staggered backwards and fell over, but quickly got to her feet and ran with the nozzle end to Lily.

Lily grabbed it from her just as their pursuer stamped the doors with even more force. But Lily couldn't afford to shift her arm for even a few seconds so she could feed the hose through.

'Get away from us!' Maisie thrust her bulk to the door.

But the next strike threw her a pace from it.

Lily swallowed the shock and waited for the next one, but it didn't immediately come. She squinted through the gap.

She could see a shadow the other side. They were reversing to take a run. Lily seized her chance. She tugged her arm clear and tried to swiftly feed the metal nozzle through before they broke in. But the nozzle wouldn't fit. The neck of it was too wide to go behind the handles.

'Quickly!' Maisie screeched.

Lily swiftly took hold of the hose a foot below the nozzle, made a loop and fed that through the handles. She wound it once around them before they slammed into the door again.

The doors bowed and opened inwards an inch, but the hose held.

Lily drove herself back against them and, ignoring the throbbing in her left arm, wrapped the hose repeatedly around the handles and then fed it over and under the circle to secure it in place. She jumped back from it.

The yellowing canvas hose creaked as it resisted the efforts from the other side. It was holding but Lily didn't know for how long. She turned to the service elevator, jabbed the button repeatedly and listened.

No sound from inside the shaft.

Lily's eyes shifted to the fire exit door. Should they wait or take their chances on the stairs?

The hose complained as the doors were buffeted again.

'It's not working.' Maisie dragged Lily's hand towards the fire exit doors.

But Lily resisted and remained where she was. 'Wait . . .'

Maisie wrenched on her hand. 'We've got to go!'

'Hang on.' She bent her ear closer to the elevator doors.

Maisie released her palm and made for the fire exit.

Smash!

That was glass breaking. Then they were using something heavy to strike the doors.

Maisie opened the door of the fire exit.

'Maisie!'

Her daughter halted and heard the noise too.

A whirring from inside the shaft. The elevator was on its way up.

Chapter 56

The elevator was quickly with them but even after it had settled into place the doors didn't open.

Thunk!

They swivelled to the swing doors again and saw they'd been lodged nearly a foot open. The hose was still holding but its jaundiced canvas was stretched tight.

Lily could see that the end of a red fire extinguisher canister had been jammed below the door handles.

The blade of a fire axe appeared through the gap above the hose coil and slid down harshly against it, bouncing off.

'They're getting in!' Maisie recoiled and put her hand on the fire exit door handle again.

'Wait! Two more seconds!'

The elevator doors still hadn't opened.

The axe chopped downwards a second time, and the edge lodged in the canvas hose. They waggled it, pulled it out and raised it for a third attempt.

Maisie opened the door wide.

Lily could see the darkened stairwell beyond. But if the doors gave how quickly would their pursuer catch up with them on the stairs? They could always go back up and try to hide on the upper floors, but getting out of the building was their best option.

The axe scraped down the wooden edges of the door harder and one coil severed and pinged away from the handles.

'OK, let's go.' Lily joined Maisie at the door and looked back.

The axe hacked away quickly at the hose and another coil dropped from the handles.

Then the elevator doors slowly parted.

Lily hesitated. How long would it take them to close again? But if they rode in there it meant they would be on ground level in seconds.

'Come on!' Maisie tugged at her sleeve.

Lily calculated there were still a few more coils of the hose to cut through before the swing doors opened. 'In here!' She grabbed Maisie's hand and ran for the elevator.

Once they were inside Lily repeatedly punched the G button and they both waited breathlessly for the doors to shut.

The swing doors were being forced and they were moving more easily now half of the coil had been hacked away.

'It's opening!' Maisie pressed herself against the back of the elevator.

They were nearly through and if they broke in now there would be no time to get out of the elevator. They'd be trapped. Where was her knife? It was no longer in her hand. Had she dropped it on the way down the stairs? Her eyes darted around the stairwell floor, but she couldn't see it there. She had nothing to defend them with.

The axe bounced repeatedly up and down in the widening gap of the door, the action becoming increasingly frenzied as the hose was reduced to shredded threads.

The doors of the elevator hummed and started to judder closed.

'Come on!' Lily screamed.

As if it were a shout of encouragement to their pursuer, the axe finally cut the last coils.

Just as their doors sealed shut.

'We did it!' Maisie sobbed.

But Lily kept hitting G. If he got through and pressed the button in time the doors might open again.

'Why aren't we going?' Maisie jumped on the spot.

Lily wanted to do the same. Willed them to drop. Her finger kept stabbing the button. 'Go, go, go!'

Outside the elevator they heard footsteps.

Seconds passed like minutes. Only Lily's finger continued to move.

The elevator made a series of clicking sounds and they both waited for the doors to open again.

Lily felt her stomach gently bounce.

They were dropping.

But still neither of them released a breath.

What floor had they been on? From their view out of the kitchen window she'd estimated them to be about ten floors up. And they'd already come down one flight. That meant there wasn't a long climb down for their pursuer.

'Will they come down after us?' Maisie was still frozen.

'Be ready to run as soon as the doors open.' They wouldn't

have a huge head start and she had no idea what they'd find at ground level. The smell of stale urine suddenly stung her nose, and she took in the interior of their clattering box. There was graffiti on the walls and the digital floor display over the doors was broken.

'I don't want to run anymore.' Maisie tugged in a lungful of air.

'You're fine. We'll be fine,' Lily said to them both. 'We've got this far. We'll be safe soon.' Was the building locked up? It was likely, so they wouldn't have much time to find a way out before he caught up with them.

Their capsule juddered and squeaked and began to slow.

'Just do as I say . . . and if we get separated . . .'

Maisie shook her head. 'Why would we get separated?'

'Listen . . . if we get separated, you have to run and hide. OK?'

She nodded, as if she were terrified to verbally agree to it.

Lily wondered if they shouldn't stop a floor above ground. They would be expected to go all the way down. Maybe they could hide there and find a different way out. But what if they bumped into them coming down? Which floor were they both on now? She stared at the cracked and lifeless display.

They jerked to a standstill. Ground. The elevator had made the decision for them.

Lily took Maisie's hand. 'Ready?'

Chapter 57

The doors rattled apart and Lily held Maisie back as a dingy and derelict foyer revealed itself to them. There was a long, grubby marble effect reception desk directly in front of them and, to their left, a floor-to-ceiling window with a revolving door in it.

Maisie started to move forward.

Lily restrained her. 'Wait.' She scanned the shadowy corners of the area but there wasn't anybody in evidence. But that probably wouldn't be the case for long. 'OK, stay close.' She walked her through the doors.

Silence. Only their feet crunched on the fragments of plaster that lay about the black tiled floor. Adrenaline supressed the pulsing of Lily's injured left arm.

The doors closed unsteadily behind them. Lily turned and punched the button on the wall to open them again. She picked up a large lump of the plaster and put it on the right-hand side of the door runners. They tried to close again but repeatedly bounced off it. Now, nobody could summon the elevator from above and they could still get back in it if the need arose. There was another, larger, elevator beside reception, but it had an 'out of order' sign on the doors. Lily prayed it couldn't be used.

Maisie tugged Lily towards the revolving door, but she suspected they wouldn't be able to get out there. Sure enough they found the mechanism locked and the situation was the same with the one door beside it. Lily pulled hard on the handles and the door rattled in its frame.

Maisie gazed at the heaped rubble that lay beyond the glass illuminated by the blue morning light. 'Can we smash it?'

Lily looked around for something heavy but guessed it was probably reinforced glass. Was there a way out the other side of the foyer? There were two wooden doors there just beside some scaffolding that supported the wall. 'Try over here.'

Maisie allowed herself to be led there.

The elevator door continued to bounce off the plaster and they both eyed the door to the stairs beside it as they crossed the tiles. No sound of feet on steps . . . yet.

The first door handle was tight and couldn't be depressed, but the second one opened. They stepped into what looked like a security area. A bank of empty screens filled one side and there was a small office through an open door to the rear.

'Let's take a quick look.' Lily ushered Maisie through.

In the poky office there was a couch and a desk with plastic chairs inverted on it. Beside that was a blue wooden door. Lily opened it. It led down a flight of concrete steps. 'Just stay here for two seconds.'

Maisie didn't protest as Lily released her hand and quickly scuttled down them. Before she reached the bottom, she realised she was in an underground parking zone. She could see daylight filtering down a ramp on the far side but there was a shutter pulled down there. It looked like the only exit.

'Come back!' Maisie hissed down.

Lily looked up at her. 'What is it?'

'Somebody's coming.'

Lily climbed the steps again and listened. 'I can't hear anything.' But then she could.

Feet echoing as they thudded down steps.

'OK. We'll hide down here.' She quickly slipped back to the first door and pulled it quietly closed. As soon as she did Lily heard the stairs door open. She froze and put her finger to her lips.

Slow footsteps crunching in the foyer.

Lily pointed to the door leading to the steps, and Maisie crept there. Lily closed the middle door. There was no way to lock it. She followed her daughter down. They'd have to find a way out or they'd be cornered. When she got back down Maisie was already heading for the ramp and her feet were echoing off the ceiling. 'Ssshhh!'

Maisie slowed down and trod lighter.

Lily noted the support pillars at intervals around them. At least they'd be able to hide behind them. Once their pursuer knew they hadn't gone out of the main door they'd be heading straight down here.

Maisie reached the metallic shutter and tried to lift it.

Lily could see the two padlocks holding it in place by loops in the concrete.

Maisie rattled the shutter with her hands and the noise reverberated around the parking zone.

'Quiet.' Lily turned back the way they'd come. Shit. Were the keys for the shutter in the office? She should have looked when they were up there. It looked like the place had been cleared out though. But Lily knew she had to go back. 'Come with me.'

'Where are we going?'

'You're going to hide behind that pillar over there.' She pointed to the one nearest the steps. 'I'll go quickly back upstairs and see if I can find the keys.'

Maisie looked out through the shutter and shook her head once. 'We can't go back now.'

'There's no time to argue. Wait down here and if you see anyone but me go by then sneak upstairs and get back in the elevator.'

Maisie shrank back against the shutter.

'Now.' She pointed.

Maisie avoided her glare but indicated the pillar nearest. 'I'll hide there.'

'No. That'll be the first place they'll look.'

'That one by the steps will be the first place they'll look.'

'Not if he thinks you're trying to open the shutter. Now move.'

Maisie folded her arms around herself but started to run back. Lily kept up with her and then gestured her to the pillar near the bottom of the steps. 'I'll be back as quick as I can,' she whispered after her.

Maisie disappeared behind the pillar, but then peeped out.

'Don't do that. Not until you hear me say it's all clear.'

Her head ducked back round.

Lily hesitated briefly at the bottom of the steps. How long would it take them to work out where they'd gone, and would they be in the office already? Lily quickly scaled the steps and listened at the top.

No activity in the office.

Lily leaned in and clocked the drawers in the desk with the chairs on. Would the keys be in there, if they were here at all, or was there more chance they'd be in the room where the screens were?

Still no noise.

Lily covered the few feet between her and the table. Didn't sound like anyone had entered the security area yet but there was every chance they'd heard Maisie rattle the shutter. Perhaps they were on their way around to the ramp. She flinched as she slid the first drawer out.

Empty.

She opened the next and found that one was too.

Should she try the security room, even though they might just be about to walk into it?

Lily opened the door to it just as someone entered from the foyer.

Chapter 58

Lily pulled the door shut again and reversed through the rear office. She didn't hesitate to find out if she'd been seen or heard but slipped silently back down the concrete steps. She trotted over to where Maisie's pillar was. But Maisie wasn't there. Lily stuck out her head so she could take in the others. There were twenty or so. Where the hell had she gone?

Footsteps cautiously descending.

Her eyes flitted about the space for a sign of Maisie. But Lily had to dart her head in as the feet reached the bottom and halted. Had Maisie returned to the pillar beside the shutter?

Shoes started moving again. Slowly.

Lily pressed her back against the pillar, used it as a brace to keep every one of her muscles taut around her trapped breath.

They stopped, nearby.

Lily wouldn't move until she was discovered. Then she would fight. But for now she had to stay hidden. If they found Maisie first, Lily would attack.

The footfalls continued, moving so softly that Lily could

barely hear them. Had they paused again? Lily weighed up if it was worth looking and risking giving away her hiding place. She regretted leaving her phone in the maze. Now was the time they could really have done with a decoy.

Lily made a decision. If their pursuer had walked by her then it was likely they would find Maisie first. But not if she led them away. She breathed out and stepped from behind her pillar. The others obscured her view all the way to the shutter. Nobody was in sight. Were they working their way around the edge? No matter. She needed to lure them back upstairs before they found Maisie. She'd consider how to get back to her daughter once she'd lost them.

Lily loudly ran to the steps again and looked right to see if she was being followed.

'Wait!' Maisie streaked from behind a pillar just beyond the one that Lily had just emerged from.

Lily stopped dead. Waited for another figure to emerge behind Maisie. 'Run!' What would they do now? She'd figured on scaling the steps in double-quick time, but Maisie wouldn't be able to move as fast.

She ran to Maisie and scooped her up.

As she put her foot on the bottom step, Lily could hear rapid pursuit. 'Don't look back,' she panted and propelled Maisie up to the office.

They reached the top step and the sound of the feet changed. They were coming up too.

Lily turned and slammed herself against the door. There was no lock. 'Quick!' she yelled at herself. Lily released Maisie and grabbed the edge of the desk she'd been searching only minutes before. Plastic chairs toppled and it grated noisily against the floor as she dragged its weight to the door, which immediately tried to open against it.

Lily grunted and rammed the table against the panel, holding it in place with her bodyweight.

Banging the other side.

There was another, smaller, longer table against the wall. Lily gripped its edge and heaved it across the floor. She positioned it at a right angle to the first. If they shoved against the one blocking the door it would get lodged against this one and the wall.

The edge of the door pounded at the first one but there was scarcely an inch gap. They weren't slipping through there. Lily grabbed Maisie by the hand and they exited the back office. She pulled the door closed and then lugged an empty cupboard in front of that one. She picked up Maisie again and ran into the foyer.

The elevator door was still bouncing against the chunk of plaster. Should they get back in it and try to find another way out on the first floor?

Behind them the door butted against the desk.

They couldn't get out. But there were at least two kidnappers in the building. Lily knew the most direct route out was the best. They had to smash the window. Was there something heavy enough she could use? She carried Maisie to the reception and looked behind it. Nothing. Just plaster and balls of dust on the floor. What about the scaffolding?

Lily returned to the wall it was holding up and examined the steel poles.

'What are you doing?'

They were held in place by metal clips, but she managed to release one and slide out a heavy length of tubing. 'Stand over there.' Hefting it, she staggered back to the door beside the revolving one and launched the tube at the glass.

It bounced off and back at her and she had to sidestep it as it clanged onto the tiles. But there was a snowflake effect where it had impacted.

'Do it again.'

Lily panted as she picked up the weighty pipe again and drove it against the same place.

The snowflake turned into a cobweb.

She kept hold of the pipe and repeatedly thrust it at the pane.

'Keep going!'

Her bashing at the window sounded just out of time with the thudding on the door in the office. She was letting anyone nearby know exactly where they were.

A huge crack opened up in the glass from the middle of the web to the top of the door, but as she kept striking the pane it still wouldn't break. 'Come on!' She wrenched some extra energy from within herself and intensified her attack on the window, but it remained intact.

The banging in the office stopped.

Lily paused and they both turned. Had they given up or had they got through?

A crash behind them made them swivel back to the door.

The plate glass had collapsed from the frame and lay in shards on the tiles. A cool wind blew in.

Lily blinked as the fresh air gusted against them. 'Careful. Let me go first.' Lily stepped gingerly through them until she was standing outside. There was nobody around. 'All clear.'

Chapter 59

'Come on . . .' Lily extended her hands. Maisie reached out and Lily seized her under the armpits and swung her over the main fragments. Their feet crunched and ground splinters as they headed for the rubble before them.

Lily glanced over her shoulder. She still couldn't hear any sound from the office. Had they given up and gone to try and escape through the shutter? But that was securely locked. Maybe they had the keys though. They might if they'd been regularly in and out of the place. In which case, they could be on their way from the rear of the building.

Maisie halted. 'Which way?'

They'd reached the edge of the debris. On the far side they could see the top of the other collapsed block.

Lily wanted to get them out of the area as quickly as possible. Could they go around the rubble? It seemed to make sense to do that for as long as they could. 'Be careful where you step. You go in front of me.' She indicated Maisie right, steadying her under her elbow as she traversed the odd bricks that had rolled down from the heap. Again, Lily looked back, but nobody was following them through the shattered door.

'Do you know where we're going?'

'As far away as we can get.' The area was clearly condemned, and she didn't know if they were about to run into a fence they couldn't climb. They'd have to tackle that as and when.

A hundred yards along they came across some more stacked up rusty industrial freezers and cookers. They hadn't been able to see these from the kitchen window, so it at least meant they were making progress, getting away from the block and out of sight of anyone who might be watching them from the front windows.

'Shall we go around?' Maisie pointed to the right edge of the stack, but there were a lot of broken bottles lying about on the ground that side.

'Go up onto the rubble and round.' Lily gestured to the left side. 'Just be careful where you're putting your feet.'

Maisie nodded and extended her arms like she was a balancing act as she started to climb.

Lily went up after her, but the bricks and powdered concrete felt unsteady beneath her deck shoes.

Maisie bent forwards as she clambered the steep slope and used her hands to support herself.

Lily did the same, her fingers grabbing shattered cinder blocks. She spotted broken glass glinting amongst the broken hardcore. It was the last place a little girl should be. 'Take your time and don't cut yourself.'

'I'm fine.' Maisie scrambled ahead.

'Slow down. We don't need to go much higher.' Lily stopped and squinted behind them again. Nobody in pursuit.

When she turned back, Maisie had vanished.

'Maisie.' She wanted to yell harder but knew she shouldn't give away their location.

No reply.

'Maisie!' Now she couldn't restrain her alarm. Lily picked her way towards where her daughter had been standing and was looking down a tight crevice between a ten-foot square of a collapsed red brick wall and some misshapen concrete with gnarled reinforcing wires sticking dangerously out from it. Maisie was lying on her back eight to ten feet away at the bottom and the dim morning daylight only just illuminated her. She leaned in and shouted down. 'Maisie, can you hear me?'

She was motionless.

Were her eyes closed? There wasn't enough light to tell. 'Maisie, answer me!'

Still no movement.

Lily darted her eyes around the rubble. Nobody moving across it who had been alerted by her shouts. 'Maisie?' Had she been knocked out cold, or worse? She felt panic surge. Maybe she'd struck some of the rusty cables on the way down.

Maisie's head rolled.

'Maisie.' She could see a faint frown of pain on her features. Thank God. But she could have concussion or broken bones. 'Are you hurt?'

'I don't think so.' She rubbed her face, got dirt all over it.

Lily leaned in further. 'See if you can sit up.'

'My back,' she grunted groggily before she could do it.

Had she sustained a serious injury in the fall? 'Can you

move your legs and arms OK?' She tried to keep her tone calm.

Maisie stirred her legs and wiggled her fingers. 'Yes.'

'OK, just try and sit slowly up.'

'Watch out that nobody's coming.' Maisie's voice sounded suddenly terrified.

'I will.' Lily cast her eyes about the uneven terrain around her. 'Nobody up here. Just concentrate on sitting up. Do it slowly and stop if it hurts.'

'OK.' Maisie seemed to gather her strength and jerkily sat up.

'That's good. How do you feel?'

'My head's aching.'

'See if you can stand . . . but take your time.'

Maisie struggled to her feet.

Lily could now only see her daughter's grubby face staring up at her from the dinginess below. 'Try and grab one of the cables sticking out.'

Her daughter regarded the bent wires.

'But be very careful. They're embedded in the concrete, so they should be able to take your weight.'

Maisie tested one, pulled on it. Damp concrete immediately crumbled, and the wire bent down towards her.

'Try another. If you can pull yourself halfway up, I should be able to lean in and lift you out the rest of the way.'

Maisie nodded uncertainly and tugged another wire. That bent in her hand too. 'It won't work.'

'Just keep trying,' Lily encouraged her. 'You only need to get out by a few feet . . .'

A noise. Rubble sliding.

Lily turned in the direction of the sound, which came from right behind her. Somebody was coming up the stack, displacing bricks with their sluggish steps.

Chapter 60

In seconds the eyeline of whoever was climbing up would connect with hers. Lily had no choice. 'Move to one side,' she warned Maisie. 'I'm coming down.' There was no time to turn around. She had to go face first.

Maisie squeezed herself to the side of her pit, her expression wide-eyed as her mother descended.

Lily's body teetered and then her weight carried her forward. She attempted to slide down to the left of the rusty cables, but as she dropped, the shape of the crevice directed her at them and her side was grazed deeply by their sharp ends, the metal dragging at her skin as she plummeted. She saw Maisie's alarmed features fill her vision and then her nose was butting her daughter's shoulder and arm before she halted abruptly.

'Are you OK?'

'Ssshhh.' Lily gritted her teeth against the raw pain in her ribs.

They both waited, frozen in their positions.

Lily's ears pounded as blood rushed into her head. Above them she could hear the footsteps getting nearer. Had they already seen her at the hole? Why else would they have climbed the stack? But perhaps they didn't know exactly where she and Maisie were and had hauled themselves up there to get a view from the top.

The feet paused.

Sounded like they were nearby. Lily had to take a short breath in and flinched as the injury to her side smarted. Her left arm joined in and she gritted her teeth against crying out.

Bricks scraped above, as if the person up there was readjusting his footing.

The interior of the crevice smelt of damp soil, and she could feel Maisie's chest rising and falling as they waited.

The footfalls slogged nearer.

What would happen if they grabbed her legs? Could she reposition herself or was she stuck like this? If so, she was powerless. At least she could hold onto the cables and shield her daughter. But she was vulnerable. They could injure her and soon get to Maisie.

The crunching above ceased.

Were they peering into the hole? Lily didn't want to shift her position to try and look in case her body slid further down and she made any more noise. She could feel her forehead throbbing and prayed Maisie wouldn't move.

Seconds passed.

Were they looking at the soles of her feet, considering exactly when to reveal the fact that they'd found them?

They tramped away a few paces and stopped.

Maybe they hadn't seen the hole. Maisie hadn't spotted the trap until she'd been right on top of it. Lily awkwardly tried to swallow upside down.

The feet kept on moving erratically away, trudging and then dodging over obstacles.

Lily gripped Maisie's shoulders to support herself. 'Just stand still, sweetheart.' She used her daughter to push herself back up again so she could address her face-to-face. 'I'm going to try—' Agony shot up her side.

'You're hurt.'

'Ssshhh, just a scrape.' But Lily knew there was blood. She could feel its warmth oozing down towards her bra. She tensed, gripped the edges of the cables above Maisie's head and pulled herself further against the back of the crevice so she could drop her feet down. But she couldn't support her weight and felt her body conform to gravity. 'Crouch down, put your hands over your head.'

Maisie quickly obeyed.

Lily tried to hold herself back but plummeted, the bottom half of her body landing on Maisie. 'Are you all right?' She could feel her daughter below her and her head nod. Quickly repositioning herself, Lily managed to find footholds and straightened up. She shot a glance up at the diagonal opening above them. There was nobody standing there.

Maisie still had her hands over her head and peeped out. 'Are you OK?'

Lily nodded and whispered. 'How about you? Head still hurting?'

Maisie rubbed the back of it for good measure.

'Let me take a look.' Lily lifted her fair hair at the back and saw a red mark at the roots. 'Think you banged it when you landed.'

'Is it bleeding?' Maisie asked fearfully.

'No. No blood.' But Lily could feel her own running down to her waist now. She would check it later. She didn't want to send Maisie into a panic.

Maisie seemed to read her mind. 'How did you hurt yourself?'

'Think I just pulled a muscle.' She hissed in air for effect, but it actually helped stem the pain. 'At least we can get out of here now. You climb up onto the wires and I'll push the soles of your feet so you can crawl out.'

Maisie nodded with determination.

'Right, I'll lift you up as high as I can then I'll come up after you. Quick.'

Maisie turned her back to Lily and raised her hands to be lifted.

Lily flinched as she tried to take her weight.

Maisie regarded her over her shoulder. 'You sure you're OK?'

'Just concentrate on not cutting yourself on these things.' Lily studied the twisted wires. They were dangerous but, if they were careful, they might serve as a ladder at least some of the way out. 'Ready?'

Maisie nodded and Lily hefted her. Hot pain gushed through her side and arm and she grunted hard to cover an exclamation.

Maisie carefully rested her feet on a length of wire.

'Is it taking your weight?' Lily released her slightly and she was held in place there. 'Good. I'm behind you. See if you can climb higher and then I'll come up too.'

Maisie began to scale the wires, but froze.

The footfalls were coming back.

They both looked up to the aperture above them.

The steps halted nearby. Then somebody appeared at the top and looked in.

Chapter 61

Maisie screamed and climbed back down but even with the dingy light behind him, Lily immediately recognised the man.

'Are you all right?'

It was the bearded guy with the baseball cap and Irish accent who'd come up to their floor.

Lily blinked a few times to make sure she was correct.

'No. We need help.' Maisie responded first.

He knelt at the side of the hole. 'Either of you hurt?'

'Yes,' Maisie answered.

'We're fine.' Lily didn't want him to know that. She couldn't trust him.

'I should call you an ambulance.' The man took out his phone.

'Call the police first. Tell them where we are.' Lily held Maisie to her. 'Where are we?'

The man's finger poised on the keypad. 'You don't know?'

'Just tell me.'

'Fernham.'

'Where's that?'

'You're not joking, are you?' He took in her expression and it confirmed she wasn't. 'Kent.'

She was relieved they were still in the UK, but they were miles from South London. 'And what is this place?'

'Seaton Gardens. What's left of it.'

'My daughter and I have been held here against our will.'

'Whoa – what?'

'Call them now. Tell them that we're Lily and Maisie Russell and that we were kidnapped and brought here.'

'Kidnapped?' he repeated incredulously.

'We've only just managed to escape.'

The man gazed down at them, open-mouthed.

'Call them!' Lily snapped him out of it.

He dialled. 'Police. Yes, I'd like to report . . . a kidnapping. Yes, you heard right.'

Were they outside the signal jamming area? It sounded like a genuine conversation.

As he relayed the situation and location to the police, Maisie tugged at Lily's sleeve. 'Tell him to be careful.'

She was right. Their captors could be watching them right now.

The man hung up. 'On their way. Shit, I should have told them you need an ambulance.'

'Don't worry.' Lily was more concerned about who else might be about. 'Listen, take a look around. Is there anybody nearby?'

He scanned his surroundings and shot a nervous glance behind him. 'Not that I can see.'

'We need to get out of here as quickly as possible. Help us up but keep an eye out.'

He seemed spooked. 'For the people who kidnapped you . . .'

'They could be looking for us.' She didn't want to frighten him away. 'Maisie will try to climb up to you and I'll push her out. Can you grab her?'

He nodded and leaned into the hole.

'OK, like you did before.' Lily supported Maisie as she ascended the cables again.

The man shuffled forward and extended his arms. 'That's good. A little higher.'

Maisie's weight bent the rusted cables as she clambered up but she was soon in touching distance of the man.

Lily kept one eye on her daughter and the other on the space above him.

'OK. Reach out to me now.' He wriggled forward an inch more and took hold of Maisie's hands. 'Can you boost her from down there?'

'Yeah.' Lily climbed the cables but each one immediately buckled under her heavier weight. 'Just . . .' She slid her deck shoes as near the cement as she could but each one still bent immediately she went higher. She quickly seized Maisie. 'I'm not going to be able to hold her long.'

'Just elevate her a few more inches . . .'

The injuries in Lily's side and arm ached and needled as she lifted her She heard bricks being disturbed at the top. 'What was that?'

'It's OK. That was my feet moving them,' he reassured Lily.

She hesitated to push Maisie forward. 'Are you sure?'

'Yes, quickly. I can't hold this position for long.'

But Lily didn't comply. 'Wait.'

'There's nobody up here but me. Just push.'

But Lily cursed herself for not thinking of it sooner. 'What happened upstairs?'

'When?' He grunted.

'When you came inside to investigate, and we spoke to you through the wall.'

'What about it?'

But Lily didn't like the hesitation before his reply.

'If you couldn't get to us, why didn't you call the police?'

But at that moment, Maisie was tugged clean out of her hands.

Chapter 62

Lily reached out for her daughter, but she disappeared over the lip of the hole. 'Maisie.' She wanted to scream her name but was still mindful of who could be close by.

No reply from above.

'Maisie, answer,' she whispered.

Nothing.

She heard bricks being disturbed around the edge and climbed frantically, her soles slipping down the gnarled cables as she got closer to the opening. 'Maisie?' She stretched out with both hands from her perch and the pain of the wounds to her side snatched the breath from her. She couldn't quite bridge the gap.

The man's face appeared above her again, his forehead wrinkled with concern. 'You OK?'

'Where's Maisie?'

'I got her to hide by some white goods down below.'

Lily didn't believe him. 'You've left her on her own?'

'She's safe. Just give me your hand.' He offered his.

But she didn't take it. 'What happened upstairs?'

'Come on. Let's get you out first.'

'Tell me.'

He shook his head and looked shamefaced. 'Some guy . . . he gave me some money, told me to keep quiet about what I'd heard.'

Lily still didn't extend her arms to him. 'He paid you?' That didn't sound plausible.

He briefly closed his eyes. 'Just let me help you now.'

'You walked away, didn't think of calling the police?'

'Look, why d'you think I came back?' He opened his fingers. 'Quick now. Maisie's waiting.' He squirmed forward. 'Take my hand.'

Lily opened her mouth to respond but suddenly she was dropping, the cables underfoot giving under her weight.

The man lunged and grabbed her wrists and, as she lost her foothold, her body tautened.

Lily groaned as her arms took her weight.

'Use your feet!' he gasped, his face suddenly red.

Lily pedalled her legs and her right deck shoe found the surface of the collapsed brick wall. She took the pressure off her shoulders and tried to heave herself up.

'I can't hold on for long.' His whole frame trembled.

She felt his body slide forward. Whoever this man was, he was her only lifeline. She had to get out and protect Maisie. She zoned out the agony, clenched her stomach muscles and pushed herself off the wall and up towards him.

'I'm going to let your right hand go. Use it to grab my shoulder.'

She obeyed and clutched the cold brown leather of his jacket and repeated the action with her left hand. She crawled over him and collapsed at the side of the hole.

He rolled back from his position there and caught his breath.

As they both panted Lily was already looking for Maisie. 'Where is she?'

'I told you . . . she's safe.' He sat up. 'I'll take you to her now.'

But he hadn't stepped away from the hole with Maisie for long. 'Where?' Lily got to her feet.

He stood and pointed downwards to the stack of freezers and cookers they'd tried to circumvent. 'There.'

Lily squinted. 'I don't see her.'

'Just follow me.' He started off down the side of the stack.

Lily frantically scanned their surroundings for anyone else, but it was just the two of them. Why couldn't she see Maisie? She reached between some of the bricks at her feet, pulled out a shard of glass and concealed it in her hand.

'This way.' He trudged rapidly, picking up momentum.

She tried to keep up with him. 'Don't make so much noise.' She could feel the edge of the glass sharp in the joints of her fingers.

'The road is on the southside. That's where the police will arrive.' He didn't look back as he spoke.

Lily picked up half a brick in her other hand and prepared herself to strike him with it.

'I'll take you there, but I don't want to hang around and answer any questions.'

'Why not?'

'I've been trespassing here.' He staggered onto the flat concrete, his pace slowing to a standstill.

Lily stepped off the rubble and followed him to the wall of junk.

'Once they've arrived, I'll make myself scarce.' He turned to her and his gaze settled on the brick in her hand that she was trying to conceal at her side. He halted. 'Thinking of using that on me?'

'Just tell me where Maisie is.' But hearing his reaction to her weapon had made Lily realize something about her escort.

'Right here.' He gestured behind him.

'Where? And why have you suddenly stopped using your Irish accent?'

But at that moment Maisie started yelling.

Chapter 63

Maisie's voice was muffled.

Lily hefted the brick and clenched the glass in her palm.

The man's dark eyes darted then slid right to one of the freezers. He moved to the rusted door and pulled on the metal handle.

Maisie was crouching inside, clutching her arms around herself. Her petrified gaze switched from him to Lily.

But as she shot out of her prison, the man grabbed her by her hair.

Her head jerked back, and she screamed.

Lily lunged forward, but the man turned, swinging Maisie with him.

He had a serrated knife at her throat. 'Not another inch.' He tightened his grip on Maisie.

The blade was hard against Maisie's jugular. Lily froze a few paces from them.

'Step back.'

She complied. Acknowledged his real voice was the one that had spoken to her on the phone. 'Take that away from her neck.'

'Further.'

Lily reversed another few feet.

'Now drop that and whatever else you've got in your other hand.'

What choice did she have?

The brick thudded to the ground and the glass shattered beside it.

'Let her go now.' She cursed herself for being duped by him again.

'He told me he'd hurt you if I cried out for help.' Maisie was on the brink of tears.

'It's OK. Just do as he says.' Lily fixed her daughter and then him.

There was relief on his expression. He took a long breath, so his chest filled and his shoulders raised. 'OK. Back on track.'

'Please . . .' She held out her palms to Maisie. 'Just stay still.'

'Listen to your mother.'

'I'm not going to move.' Lily's voice tremored. 'Just . . . please, loosen your grip.'

He looked down at Maisie, but her eyes were fixed on Lily. 'Why not?' He flicked his wrist, so the knife was at a right angle to Maisie's neck.

Lily took half a breath. 'I'm not going to try anything . . .'

He nodded, like that was a given.

'*You've* been holding us?' She had to distract him.

'Trying to. That was a great trick with the boxes.'

'So that whole routine – you pretending to be a trespasser and seeing us at the window . . .'

'You could at least look relieved I'm not dead. But I did convince you I might be.'

A piece of theatre to keep them in line? 'We did everything you asked.'

'Except escape.' His brown eyes briefly narrowed.

Lily took in the features under his baseball cap properly. His straggly dark beard covered half of them and his thick eyebrows converged on a narrow, slightly freckled pale nose. When he finished speaking the overgrown bristles of his lips sealed leaving only his eyes to express any emotion.

'I needn't remind you what happened the last time you disobeyed.'

But although his expression appeared calm, she detected panic in his body language. He clearly didn't want them to be in the open like this. But nobody was coming to help. The only person who had was their captor.

'But I'll be prepared to overlook it if you behave when you walk home with me.' He jerked his head back to the building behind them.

Did he really expect to put them back in their prison? But with a knife to Maisie, Lily realised he could do anything.

He studied her and nodded, as if he could hear her thoughts. 'You can walk in front. I'll follow with Maisie.'

Lily's mind raced. This was the closest they'd got to freedom. Once he sealed them back inside, he would make sure they never got out again.

'Let's move quickly then.' He darted his pupils around and nodded she should proceed.

Lily walked past them and made eye contact with Maisie

again. 'Just do everything he asks.' She strode unsteadily to the smashed door and every cell of her screamed not to go back inside.

'Pick up the pace. We're right behind you.'

Lily pinpointed the pieces of rubble and twisted metal around her that she could use against him, but there was no way she could risk endangering Maisie.

'All right, sweetie. Just pick your feet up.'

Lily thought of his hands restraining her daughter and how tightly he'd held the knife to her throat. Was he really capable of killing a child? Capable of killing at all? He'd fooled them into believing he'd murdered a trespasser, but that had been nothing but a charade. Should she allow him to return them to their prison when he might not even be a threat?

'I can hear your brain whirring, Lily. Just focus on getting back to the elevator.'

Chapter 64

Lily dodged the shards as she walked back into the foyer. The elevator was still bouncing against the piece of plaster in the door. She heard glass being compressed as she was followed inside and stopped halfway across the tiles.

The splinters crunching behind her ceased.

'Keep walking,' he ordered tersely.

Lily shot her eyes about. The only alternative exits were the doors to the stairs and the office. But she didn't want to go back up to another floor where he could trap them or get cornered in the parking zone again. Her options were rapidly running out.

'Step inside the elevator and put both your hands against the wall.'

Then he'd kick away the piece of plaster, walk in behind her, the capsule would close, and they'd be on their way back to imprisonment. Lily continued forward, the clattering door only twenty or so feet away.

'Ow, you little bitch!'

'Run!' Maisie exclaimed.

Lily spun around and saw that Maisie had broken free. She was heading towards the door to the stairs.

The man shook his head and sighed as he watched her scuttle

away, as if her escape bid was nothing more than a tiresome inconvenience. He examined the bite on the back of his knife hand and looked at Lily. 'Do you file her teeth or something?'

But in that moment Lily knew she had to seize her chance and buy her daughter time. She ran at the man, not considering what she would do when she reached him.

His expression sharpened and his knife hand came up. But he didn't see her as a threat.

Lily knew she had to exploit that and, as her eyes focussed on the blade in his fingers, she bent her body forward and aimed herself at his waist, like Ewan had shown Julie Medlocke's boys how to when he'd taught them rugby tackles in their walled garden. She closed her eyes, waited for the metal to pierce her face, but instead felt the buckle of his belt as her scalp slammed against it.

She heard the breath punched from him, but he seized her hair. 'Run, Maisie!'

She couldn't see her daughter. He was gripping her red locks with both hands now, her face looking down at the floor.

'There's no point in this.' But the irritation was gone from his voice.

'Let her go!' Maisie bawled.

'Run upstairs and hide!' If he was holding her with both hands, then he was unable to use the knife, but as soon as he released her, Lily knew she'd have to attack him again.

'Don't go through that door!' he yelled to Maisie. 'If you do, I'll hurt your mother like I said I would.'

'Don't listen to him!' Again Lily attempted to turn her head to see Maisie, but he held her fast. She gasped as his fingers tightened and pulled on the roots of her hair. 'Do as I say! Run and hide, now!'

No reply.

Had she gone? Lily prayed she had. 'Maisie?'

'Just stay right there or I'll hurt both of you!' There was definite panic in his voice now.

'Leave her alone!' Maisie screeched.

'Maisie, go!' Lily tore the words from her throat.

'She doesn't want to leave you here with me. And she's right not to. Just walk back over here, Maisie, and I'll let you both go.'

'He's lying!' Lily knew she had to act, even if his retaliation was swift. 'Run!' She interlinked the fingers of both hands into one big fist and brought it up as forcefully as she could between his legs. She felt them connect with the soft bulk between them.

The man howled and his grip loosened.

Lily jerked her head from side to side and freed her hair from his fingers. As she straightened, he was doubled over, so she immediately took off towards Maisie who was still standing by the door to the stairs. 'Go!'

Heavy footsteps staggered close behind her.

Maisie's eyes were wide.

'Open the door!' Lily shouted and anticipated being wrestled to the ground.

Maisie turned, pulled on the handle and quickly darted through it.

Lily knew there could only be a few feet between her and her pursuer. What could they do even if they reached the stairs? He was going to be on them as soon as they'd started climbing.

Maisie had started up the stairwell but her short legs meant she had to put both feet on each step.

Lily tensed herself and halted, crouching and balling herself as footfalls fast approached. There was a split second in which she thought he'd stopped the same time as her, but then she felt him strike her shoulders and his body landed hard on the floor in front of her and rolled left.

She was immediately on her feet again and rocketed through the doorway. Lily launched herself at the stairs and grabbed Maisie. She could move her faster that way, but her daughter's weight would slow them both down.

She heard the door bang against the wall behind them as he entered the stairwell.

'Quickly, Mamma!' Maisie screamed in her ear.

Lily pumped her feet. She was almost at the top of the flight. But she couldn't maintain this pace. Maybe she could repeat what she'd done upstairs and try to bind the doors shut again. But there was going to be only seconds to do that.

Heavy breathing echoed off the wall beside her. It was his. He was probably taking the stairs two at a time.

A set of double doors hove into view and as she reached the landing, she decided they were a better option than trying to climb further.

But they both swung outwards and a woman stepped through them. Her arm extended and she was holding something in her hand.

Lily recognised it was a Taser just before she dropped to the tiles with Maisie.

Chapter 65

Lily opened her eyes and focussed on a dried-out earwig curled up in the tufts of dust on the grey carpet. Momentarily she didn't know who she was let alone where she was lying. Then it all came back like she'd been jabbed with the Taster again and she suddenly drew breath and her body spasmed.

Maisie.

As her body tensed, she realised her wrists were tightly bound behind her back. Her ankles were as well. Her eyes darted around looking for her daughter. She was facing a panel of pulpwood. Her heart accelerated and the blood pumped around her restraints. Looked like she was back outside the shell of their prison.

She rolled away from the panel, grunting as she rocked her body and landed on her injured side. Now she could see along the damp carpet to the office's maze. There was nobody else around. No sign of the man or woman. She recalled her repeatedly jabbing Lily with her Taser until she'd passed out. Where was Maisie?

She struggled in vain against her bonds, but the ropes bit

into her flesh as she tried to free herself. 'Maisie?' she croaked. How long had she been unconscious? 'Maisie!' her voice escaped this time and echoed around the office. Now they would know she was awake. She didn't care. 'Maisie!'

Soft footfalls.

But Lily couldn't tell which direction they were coming from. She attempted to sit up, but her limbs felt sluggish. How many times had she been shocked? She remembered how the woman had knelt and held the Taser hard against her chest.

Now she could feel the footsteps vibrating through the side of her face. She had to get up. But Lily couldn't rally herself.

'If I piss blood next time I go to the bathroom, Maisie will be the first to know about it.'

The man's whispered voice came from behind her, and as she tried to turn, she felt his hand heavy on the side of her head. It jammed her face hard against the damp carpet, so her teeth were cutting into the side of her cheek. 'Where is she?' But her words were misshapen by the pressure.

'Ssshhh. You've got to keep quiet now. Looks like your little walkabout has attracted some unwanted attention. Somebody's paying us a visit. For real this time.' He increased the pressure on her face.

Lily could feel her pulse surging through the ear he was flattening. 'I want to see Maisie.' She growled through her gritted teeth.

'What did I just say? Another word and you'll never see her again.'

A door slammed but it sounded far away.

But Lily felt the man's arm go rigid.

'Not a peep,' he whispered close to her ear.

They both listened for further noise.

Lily wondered how near the door had been. Same floor?

Nothing.

But someone else was in the building. Somebody who had been able to get in because of the smashed front entrance, or had someone seen what had happened on the rubble and called the police?

'Ssshhh.'

Lily felt his hand lift away and then something solid take its place. As it crushed her she realised it was his kneecap. He was kneeling on her head.

'I'll break your skull and then Maisie's.'

Was this the last chance she thought she'd never have? Should she cry for help? But if the woman who had tasered her was with Maisie she couldn't risk it. But what would happen as soon as this person left, another punishment? Would she find herself sealed back inside the prison and never see Maisie again?

Footsteps hastening along a corridor and then slowing.

The man put more of his weight on his knee and Lily's skull as a warning.

The footfalls stopped.

All Lily could hear was the clamour of her own circulation.

After several minutes of silence, the man eased the pressure. 'They're still nearby.' He kept his voice low. 'Best to stay put.'

Lily thought he'd been talking to her, but a dull click after he'd spoken told her he was on a walkie-talkie. If they were jamming phone signals in the immediate vicinity, she figured that was why.

He stood, his boots creaking, and she lifted her mouth from the filthy carpet and took a breath.

'I don't like this.' His walkie-talkie clicked again. 'I'm going to take a look. They might have entered the stairwell.'

'Be careful,' came the woman's dried-out reply.

'I'll keep you posted. Just keep the girl quiet.'

Lily felt a surge of relief. It sounded like Maisie was OK.

'Lily's not going to make a sound because she knows what'll happen to Maisie if she does,' he said slightly louder for her benefit. 'I don't see any police cars down there, so it could just be private security keeping up appearances. If—'

Lily tried to turn in his direction as his sentence was cut off by a soft slap. She could hear his boots creaking.

Thud.

Sounded like he'd fallen to the floor.

Another thump behind her.

'Lily.' A familiar voice said.

A hand was on her shoulder, pulling her towards the voice.

The man squinting down at her in concern was the last face she expected to see.

It was Ewan.

Chapter 66

'Jesus, Lil.' Ewan's expression was horrified.

But Lily was too stunned to respond.

'Is there anyone else around?' he whispered and started untying the ropes binding her hands.

She nodded quickly.

'Where?' His eyes flitted about them.

'There's a woman.' She turned her head to where the man was lying motionless.

'He's out cold.' Ewan assured her. 'Where's Maisie?'

A hundred questions begged to be asked but, right now, that was the only important one. 'With her. I think they're somewhere upstairs.'

His fingers dug into her wrist as he tried to free the knots. 'Are you OK?'

She nodded again. 'Are you alone?'

'I tried to call the police, but I can't get any reception.'

'They jam the phone signal when they need to.'

'Who are *they*?'

'I don't know.' Lily attempted to sit up, but her muscles still felt weak.

'Is Maisie OK?'

Lily felt the rope loosen slightly and tensed her arms, but she still couldn't release them.

'Just hold still.' He picked at the knots.

'How did you find us?' She had to ask.

'Paulette called me. Told me you'd both vanished. I drove down but the police seemed to think you were both hiding from me. I watched the house. Saw a woman let herself in.'

Lily wondered if that was the occasion that they'd picked up Maisie's prescription medication.

'I thought it might be a neighbour watering your plants, but then she took off in a car. I followed her but I lost her a few streets from here. I told the police, but they seemed more suspicious of me. I've been scouring the area since and spotted this guy threatening you and Maisie before he took you both in here.'

'Hurry.' Again, Lily tried to part her hands, but they were still held tight. Ewan's sudden appearance seemed too good to be true. 'Try your phone again.'

Ewan took it out and dialled. 'Still the same.' He dumped the phone on the carpet and Lily could see 'No Signal' in the display. 'Just . . . keep still.' He yanked on another knot.

'Come back,' a gruff female voice said.

Ewan and Lily froze. They both turned to where the man lay.

His walkie-talkie briefly hissed and clicked.

'That's how they're communicating.'

Ewan stood and approached the prostrate figure.

Even though the ropes felt looser, Lily's wrists were still tied. 'Wait.'

'It's OK. I hit him with half a house brick. The one he made you drop.' Ewan picked the weapon up from the floor.

Lily could see dark blood on one edge of it.

Ewan took a few paces towards the man and then knelt beside him.

Lily continued to squirm against the ropes. 'Stay away from him. Get me free first.'

But Ewan reached inside the man's brown leather jacket and pulled the squat walkie-talkie from an inside pocket.

'Come back,' the woman repeated.

Ewan looked pensively at the walkie-talkie. 'What should we do?'

Lily managed to sit up and felt dizzy. 'If he doesn't respond soon, she'll know something's wrong.'

'Gabriel?' There was a trace of concern in the woman's voice.

Lily and Ewan both fixed on the man. So now they had a name.

'Move away from him,' Lily cautioned.

Ewan got to his feet.

'You might need to find something to cut these.'

But Ewan walked by her and pointed to the door. 'Is that the way up?'

'You're not going up there without me.'

'There's no time.' He brandished the walkie-talkie. 'If we delay any longer, we won't be able to take her by surprise.'

Lily felt a fresh surge of panic. She couldn't be left helpless. Couldn't suddenly allow Ewan to be responsible for the situation. 'Finish untying me.'

He briefly hesitated but shook his head. 'Maisie needs me.'

Lily wanted to yell at him, but realised he was right.

His attention returned to Gabriel. 'I could move you somewhere. Hide you.'

'No. Go,' she immediately replied.

He nodded and headed for the swing doors.

Lily watched him cautiously and quietly open one of them and slip through. Her gaze shot back to Gabriel, but his eyes were firmly closed. She twisted her wrists against her restraints, but with her hands and feet still secured she realised that Maisie's safety now depended entirely on Ewan.

When the door banged open again, she turned in time to see Ewan stagger back through it. He loped towards Lily, dropped to one knee then pitched flat on his face.

The woman entered swiftly behind him and jabbed the Taser repeatedly into his back.

Chapter 67

'Enough!'

The woman looked up at Lily as if surprised by her presence. She'd shocked Ewan for the fifth time and his body had stopped convulsing.

'He's unconscious now! You'll kill him!'

The woman jolted him with the Taser again and he didn't respond.

'Please!' Lily begged.

She narrowed her eyes at Lily and then swung her gaze to Gabriel. 'What did you do?'

Lily shook her head. 'I couldn't *do* anything.'

The woman stood. She was wearing grey sweatpants and a matching top that was flecked with white paint and a pair of boots that looked a couple of sizes too big for her. Her shoulder-length grey hair was lank and dishevelled, and her pinched features seemed stranded in the middle of her straight-jawed face. Dark pinhole eyes swivelled back to Lily. 'What did your *husband* do?' she dryly asked, as if she resented being made to again.

'Just knocked him out.'

The woman glowered at Lily and then pulled a length of rope out of her sweatpants pocket. She firmly bound Ewan's hands.

'Where's Maisie?'

The woman ignored her as she efficiently stuck to her task and then tied his ankles.

'Please.' As Lily watched her, she guessed she'd been responsible for her bonds.

The woman crossed the carpet and knelt by Gabriel. 'What about my son?' She examined the wound to his head. 'Gabriel?' She put her hand to his shoulder and gently shook him, but he didn't stir.

'Your son? Is he OK?'

The woman briefly regarded her with scorn. 'Your concern isn't going to score you any brownie points. Or Maisie.'

'Ewan's called the police. This is over. Just tell me where she is. The three of us will walk out of here. Give you time to leave with Gabriel. We can send the police elsewhere.'

The woman's expression didn't alter.

'I mean it. Just tell me where Maisie is.'

The woman put her fingers to Gabriel's neck. 'You were warned. Knew what your punishment would be. Just like I was.'

'What are you talking about?'

'My punishments . . .' Suddenly the woman's eyes seemed to be fixed on whatever time she'd been subjected to them. 'There was no leniency for me like there has been for you.' She raised an eyebrow at Lily.

Lily knew she had to tread carefully. 'I don't know what it is you've been through.' She tried to flex her wrists behind her back again, but they still cut into her skin. 'What led you to do this. But it's not too late. Nobody's been harmed yet.'

The woman snorted and gestured at Gabriel. 'Nobody?'

Lily's gaze flitted to Ewan. He still hadn't moved and, even if he did, he was now incapable of helping her. 'I give you my word.'

'Little girls shouldn't be subjected to such things.' The woman stood and folded her arms.

Lily was sure the comment was loaded. 'Yes . . . and I need to take Maisie away from this place right now. She's already been traumatised enough.'

'It's only been a handful of days,' the woman said with disdain. 'You have no concept of trauma.'

'I'm a mother like you.' But Lily was sure appealing to that part of her was going to be futile.

The woman's contemptuous reaction confirmed it.

'So the one thing you'll understand is that I don't care about any of this. Of what you've done. All that's vital to me is getting Maisie to a safe place.'

'You didn't feel safe in there?' The woman gestured to the shell of the prison.

'Of course not.' Lily felt the ropes burn her wrists as she stealthily worked them behind her back.

'Try three hundred and fourteen days.'

Lily had known the number was significant. 'You endured what we did for that long?' That had to be it.

The woman shook her head. '"Endured".' She briefly glanced at Ewan and made sure he was still out. 'You haven't even begun to endure.'

Cold rippled through Lily. These weren't the words of someone who believed the police were coming. She intended to put Lily and Maisie back inside the prison to exact whatever punishment she felt they deserved.

'You're to have your full term, like I did.'

'Why are you doing this?'

'Exactly the same question I asked myself for all that time. Over and over, wondering what wrong I'd done. I never had that answered. Not when I was held or when I was released. Only much later when I found out for myself.'

'If it's not money—'

'You know it isn't that. It certainly wasn't for him when he locked me away. I was only a teenager. Still a child.'

'Who locked you away?' Lily had to keep her engaged, keep her talking while she tried to get loose.

'And I was alone. To begin with anyway. Alone but not.'

Lily shook her head. She had to humour her.

'And even though the roles have been reversed, nothing's changed. I still feel alone, even with Gabriel beside me instead of inside me.'

Even though she'd managed to slip her thumb under the rope, and they felt suddenly slacker, Lily's hands halted. 'Who locked you away?'

'Your father. And not once in those three hundred and fourteen days, did he ever have the balls to show himself.'

Chapter 68

The woman only briefly allowed Lily's confusion to register. 'I was his pet subject. Although for all that time I didn't know I was. I actually met him a whole two years before I was imprisoned. I was fourteen then.' She paused.

Lily blinked, her words struggling to register.

'He'd helped me then. Called me Jack because he knew I hated Jacqueline. I scarcely spoke to him in those early sessions, but he made me trust him. As a teenager I was an extreme agoraphobic. Left an abusive upbringing and been shunted from care home to care home. That's what kick-started my condition. When I found a safe place, I was scared of leaving, terrified of what lay outside it and the thought of never being able to get back inside. Your father became my therapist.'

'You were treated by my father?' But Lily knew her incredulity wasn't about to change the answer.

'Doctor Samuel Croft. He told me I was making progress. That was before I woke up imprisoned in my bedroom. The small living quarters I had at the care home had no windows. He'd insisted on that. So initially I believed I was still there.

That the people looking after me had locked me in and it was them piping gas into the vents and entering the room when I was knocked out and harming me.'

Lily opened her mouth, but no words came.

'But anything seemed better than the alternative, being outside of it. Even when I'd worked out that I was living in a replica room as part of an experiment, I still didn't want to leave. I was given opportunities to escape and I never took them. Whatever happened to me when I was unconscious, whatever punishments were dispensed, I still didn't want to go outside.'

'Lies.' Lily was focussed on her lips, as if doing so would betray her deceit.

'He wanted to push me, to see what I would endure to avoid walking out of the door. I don't know at what point he lost sight of that.'

'You say you never saw him,' Lily challenged.

'No. I never did.'

'Then, if this actually happened to you . . .'

Jack's shoulders rose as her chest filled. She nodded, as if reassuring herself that Lily's denial was to be expected. 'I still have the scars. The physical ones . . . they've always been the easiest to deal with. But it was your father's confession that came out of the blue. It was only five years ago that I received it. I'd given up on seeking the identity of the man who had held me. Because whatever had happened to me . . .' she gulped, 'had worked. That was nothing to do with the twenty-two years after that I spent in hospitals and rehabilitation units. Nobody believed my story. I was a piece of trash. Your father's experiment was truly what had allowed me to open the door and walk out. The day he released me was the very first day I begged to go. I'd learnt that even when I was in my safest place, the place I didn't want to leave, terrible things could still happen to me there . . .'

Lily shook her head.

'Even during the pain, I convinced myself that I was still safe. That was my irrational conviction and the day I confronted it your father must have been so proud of me.'

Lily refused to process what she was being told. 'And why would he suddenly confess to you?'

'Because he was dying. I went to visit him at the hospice. I remembered that he'd been the only man who had truly showed me kindness. When I heard of his Parkinson's diagnosis, I wanted to see him and show him how I was living my life without fear. I didn't tell him of my ordeal. I wanted to spare him that. I just wanted him to know he'd made a difference. When I walked onto his ward, I didn't know just how much he *had* done. I was shocked at how his face had got so small.'

That image was one Lily still tried to repel. That this woman had hijacked it seemed repugnant.

'He didn't need to confess. He could have just let me touch the back of his hand and walk out.'

'When did you visit him?' Lily was still waiting for her to trip up. To convey some detail that would negate everything she'd said.

'It was three days before he died because, although I went back to the hospice the same night with a gag and ball pein hammer and the express intention of breaking every bone in his body, I realised that leaving him to drown in his own un-swallowed saliva was a better way for him to die. I did make him a promise before I left though. I whispered it in his ear.'

Lily imagined Jack at his bedside. Had she really been there?

'I told him that I was going to watch his daughter. Watch over her closely particularly because she had a baby. I told him I was making my preparations and that, when I was ready, I would subject not only his daughter but his granddaughter to exactly what he'd put me through. This time, though, it would be in reverse. That my two subjects would beg me for freedom on the first day but, by the time I'd finished, be so dependent on my mercy that they'd be terrified to ever leave.'

Anger burnt at Lily's face

'So he never warned you?' Jack raised an eyebrow.

It could all be lies. All of it. But why would she have put them through what she had? Lily recalled her father choking as he tried to speak to her the last day she ever saw him. Had he really been trying to warn her, or would that have meant he'd have to confess to what he'd done?

'You're paying for his crimes, Lily. And so's Maisie. And he's the biggest crime of all.' Jack pointed at Gabriel.

Lily felt something rushing through her, trying to find exit. Fury, disgust and the desperate need to escape. But her gaze followed Jack's to the bearded man still lying unconscious on the floor.

'Your father admitted everything before he died. That nobody else knew what he'd done or where he'd held me. That he was the one who came into my room when I was sedated.'

Lily closed her eyes. She had to focus on saving Maisie. Nothing else mattered.

'The punishments, the mornings I awoke not knowing what had happened while I'd been drugged. They became more and more frequent.'

'It's not true.' Lily mouthed to herself.

'It wasn't an experiment anymore. No matter how he might have justified it to himself. When he let me go, he was just disposing of his own guilt.'

'That's enough.'

'He probably knew I was pregnant before I did. I was sixteen.'

Lily could still hear his last incoherent words in her ear.

'I had Gabriel alone. After I begged to leave. Your father cut me loose just before I gave birth to his son.'

She didn't want to listen. She had to get free and find Maisie.

'That's your half-brother lying there bleeding.'

Chapter 69

As if in response, Gabriel stirred. His lips unsealed and he sucked in an urgent breath.

'Gabriel.' Jack knelt to him again.

He didn't open his eyes, but his head lolled and chest rose.

Lily knew she had to banish what she'd just been told and concentrate on getting to her daughter. Jack's eyes were on Gabriel. She pulled her right hand clear of the rope.

'Gabriel.' Jack gently touched his brow.

Attempting to slide her one hand down her right side to the knots at her ankles didn't work. It would only move an inch. It was still connected to her left wrist.

Jack darted her eyes to Lily and then back to Gabriel again. 'Gabriel, can you hear me?'

His foot twitched but he didn't respond.

'Gabriel.' Jack looked down into his face. 'Answer me.'

Lily guessed there was only one way to get free, but she had to choose her moment.

Gabriel hissed in air through his mouth and his torso spasmed. He turned his head to the right.

'Wake up, Gabriel!' Jack leaned in further to his ear.

Lily slid the loose rope to the edge of her buttocks and waited. There was enough slack to slip them under and down her legs, but was there enough to put her feet through, so her hands were in front of her body? Once she started, she would have little time to finish.

Gabriel snorted and his throat pumped.

Lily lifted her buttocks and frantically pulled the rope under her legs and bent them up. Her wrists were still bound and connected by a foot length of rope. She got the rope as far down as the back of her bound ankles, but couldn't pull it under and over.

'Gabriel!' Jack shook him.

Tensing her stomach muscles Lily pulled her knees as far against her chest as she could. She strained and quaked and held her grunt inside. The rope was held fast on the back of her ankles. She pulled hard and tautened her body even more and it slipped under the soles of her deck shoes. Her hands were clear. Dispensing with relief her eyes bounced between Jack and the rope knots at her ankles as her fingers picked at them.

Gabriel groaned.

Lily concentrated on the two knots and shakily undid them. She could feel the ropes loosen. But when she looked up she met Jack's eyes.

Jack immediately got to her feet and looked in Ewan's direction. She'd left the Taser beside him.

There was a split second when neither of them moved. And then both of them did.

As Jack dashed to the Taser Lily focussed on the ropes. Her

fingers worked furiously, and the knots fell away. She parted her feet and the ropes gave but she could hear Jack's footsteps towards her. Even though her legs were still held together she used one hand to push herself to her feet.

'Stay down.' Jack was only a few paces away.

Lily was half upright as Jack reached her and, with her hands still connected, she butted the top of her head into Jack's face. The impact was agony and both women yelped.

Jack stumbled back and the Taser dropped from her hand and slid along the floor towards Ewan.

Lily could feel the impact resonating in her head and tottered dizzily. She needed to stagger but her bound feet threatened to topple her.

Jack's nose trickled blood and she put her fingers to it and looked at them in surprise.

Lily bent and yanked the ropes, parting her feet in time to reel sideways.

Jack was already making for the Taser.

Lurching after her Lily reached her just as she bent to retrieve it. She kicked it hard out of her grasp, and it slid towards the double doors. Lily rammed her weight against Jack before she could straighten, and she pitched sideways.

Lily barrelled after the Taser, but her legs were numb from their bonds. She heard Jack thunder after her. Just as she reached the doors, Jack slammed into her from behind and they both burst through them into the stairwell.

Lily felt a fist smash into her ear and the sound of their echoing breaths in the stairwell was suddenly deadened. She lashed out, but her hand couldn't take a swing because it was still tied to the other. Where was the Taser? Had it been kicked through the door with them? Her eyes darted about the floor.

Jack was heading back to the swing doors.

It had to be in the office and whoever got it first would immediately be able to disable the other.

Lily pursued Jack as she pushed open the doors and hooked the rope tied between her wrists hard around her throat.

Jack howled incoherently as Lily dragged her back to the stairwell.

Lily told herself to hang on, at any cost. She tightened her fingers around the rope and the length against Jack's Adam's apple.

But Jack propelled her backwards and Lily's spine connected harshly with the rail over the stairwell. She was winded and briefly released her grip.

Jack started to struggle out from under her, but Lily caught her chin. Jack swivelled her head from side to side, so Lily slotted the rope back against her throat and dragged her rigidly against her chest.

Jack tried to turn sideways, and her elbow jabbed once then again into Lily's stomach.

If she let her get free, she wouldn't see Maisie again. She had to withstand whatever pain was inflicted. Withstand it and throttle her as hard as she could.

Jack's elbow assaulted her repeatedly.

Lily screamed as she pulled on the rope and it burnt her palms.

Jack choked and gurgled and kept squirming.

But Lily could feel the resistance start to wane.

Just hold on.

Jack's body started to go limp in her grip.

Hold on.

A bubbling, incoherent protest found its way clear of the rope.

Still Lily held on.

The elbow was back, hard in her stomach and Lily released the rope.

Jack flexed her body and ducked her head to get free.

Lily caught her throat with the rope again and dragged her up. But Jack still had so much fight in her. She wasn't going to be able to hold her much longer.

Another elbow in her stomach. And again.

Lily knew there was only one option left. She hooked her right leg over the metal rail.

Jack used the movement to try and get loose.

Lily started to slip over the drop. She could see the hard tiles ten floors below her. Gravity would give her the tension she needed. She let her body hang back.

Jack's waist was pressed harshly against the rail and her protest was cut short.

Lily still had one leg left on the other side. She hooked it over, so her entire weight was hanging on the rope. She could see the back of Jack's head trembling.

Sudden silence in the stairwell.

As she hung from Jack's throat, Lily lifted her legs up to put extra pressure on the rope.

Jack's body went limp.

And Lily knew what that meant.

Jack's legs relaxed and she hinged back and over the rail. They both plummeted.

It seemed to Lily like they were falling for some time, but it was the adrenaline accelerating her thoughts for the four seconds they fell.

Lily's scream was deadened as Jack landed on top of her.

She lay there, the echo of their impact ringing through her bones and for a few seconds she didn't move. Jack was motionless on top of her and all she could hear was her own breathing locked inside her skull.

Maisie.

She pushed Jack's body off her and when the weight was shifted the pain really kicked in. She knew she'd broken bones but that wasn't important. Lily pushed herself up and ignored the shooting sensation that bounced up and down her left leg and tightened like a vice on her injured left arm.

She climbed. One flight at a time. Going back up felt like it took an hour.

But it was six minutes later when she got back to the office where the shell of her prison was, and Gabriel had half sat up.

She picked up the Taser where it lay inside the doors and, zigzagging over, shocked him with it repeatedly until he was curled motionless at her feet.

Chapter 70

'Are you OK in there?' Maisie knocked on the bathroom door.

'I just need a minute,' Lily replied. But she didn't hear her daughter move away. 'Be out soon.' She was sitting on the toilet and turned to push the flush to underline her promise. Her left arm was still in a sling.

But Maisie remained outside. 'Dinner's nearly ready.'

'Be right there.' Lily heard another set of footsteps approach.

'What's going on?' Ewan asked. 'Come on, I asked you to set the table.'

'OK,' Maisie said eventually.

Their footsteps headed back to the kitchen.

Since their ordeal Maisie had been reluctant to leave Lily's side. There was a new closeness between them, but Lily now found it very difficult to get any moments alone. She'd taken her chance when Maisie had been helping Ewan with the casserole.

Ewan was living with them again in their new place. Maisie hadn't wanted to return to Fallstaff Gardens and nor had Lily, so they'd lived out of a suitcase in a hotel for a week while Ewan had helped them find a rental. A ground floor property with plenty of windows.

Lily had seen how much Maisie wanted Ewan's presence, so making her feel secure was her first priority. As for picking up the pieces of their relationship, that remained to be seen. They were at least beginning to talk about it when they persuaded Maisie to go to bed. She was having nightmares, still thought she might wake up in their prison again. So did Lily.

But Maisie had immediately wanted to go back to school. Lily assumed because she wanted to be surrounded by people again. She hadn't mentioned the bullies to Lily since. Was she just hiding that from her? Lily hoped that her ordeal meant that nothing she encountered in the playground could scare her now.

Jacqueline Heath was still alive when the paramedics had arrived at Seaton Gardens. Lily had been two floors above the replica home, having found the place where her two captors had tied up Maisie.

Jack had died on the way to hospital. Lily's half-brother was still in custody refusing to talk. Ewan had suggested she talk to Gabriel, but that prospect filled her with horror.

But she knew that it was a day that had to come. Just not yet.

She was taking medication for anxiety and was still suffering episodes of paranoia. Last week she'd fought to shake the notion that Ewan had been a part of it all and convinced herself that it had all been a ploy to get back with her. That was ridiculous.

Ridiculous.

But a more immediate fear had taken hold. Something that had been at the back of her mind since Jacqueline had told her about what her father had done. Those times when she'd been drugged and woken not knowing exactly what had happened to her. Like Lily had.

It was something she'd been denying, that she didn't want to confront. Today she would. It was another irrational fear, but she had to be sure.

Lily looked down at the pregnancy test stick in her hand and waited for the bars to appear.

THE END

Acknowledgements

A debt of gratitude to you, the reader, for choosing this story and accommodating my characters. I hope your imagined prison was as claustrophobic as the one I was glad to see them released from.

A huge thank you, as always, to my champion and wife, Anne-Marie, whose friends still worry about her living in the same house as me and also to my Mum and Dad, who gave me what all children need, the security of a loving home that I could take for granted until the day I left it.

And now to the unsung heroes at One More Chapter – Charlotte Ledger, my dynamic editor, who deftly identified the properties of the story that would give it extra dimension; Bethan Morgan, Assistant Editor, who guided the project through the fine edit process; Janette Currie, my copyeditor, for her astute notes; Melanie Price, Digital Marketing Manager; and Claire Fenby, Digital Marketing and Publicity Assistant.

And, as ever, I can't underestimate how grateful I am for the time spent by reviewers and bloggers who are such a vital cog in every author's career and convey their love for books by shouting about the ones they love. Thanks for your generosity online but, moreover, for giving up your valuable time to point readers towards a wealth of great writing. A special salute to Karen Cole, Jen Lucas, Nicki Richards, Claire Knight, Sarah Hardy, Liz Barnsley, Melissa Suslowicz Bartz, Donna Maguire, Zoe-lee O'Farrell, Nigel Adams, Suze-Clarke-Morris, Kaisha Jayneh, Amanda Oughton, The Book Cosy, Sean Talbot, Rachel Broughton, Alison Drew, Magdalena Johansson, Diane Hogg, Martha Cheeves, Joyce Juzwik, Amy Sullivan, Kelly Lacey, Norma and Kayleigh Farrelly, Rebecca Pugh, Chelsea Humphrey, Ellie Smith, Lorraine Rugman, Steve Robb, Emma Welton, Stephanie Rothwell, Cleo Bannister, Abby Fairbrother, Sheila Howes, Linda Strong, Maxine Groves, Joanne Robertson, Susan Hampson, Malina Skrobosinski, Shell Baker, Kaz Lewis, Tina Boyd, Fran Hagan, Mandie Griffiths, Jo Ford, Marilina Tzelepi and Scott Griffin. Special thanks also to Finn Cotton, Commissioning Editor at HQ, new editor Hannah Todd and fellow authors Noelle Holten, Mandy Baggot, Tom Bromley and Louise Mullins.

Please swing by my website for all the latest: http://richard-parker.com or find me on Instagram (bemykiller), Twitter (@Bookwalter) and Facebook (RJParkerUK).